GUARDED
Souls

AMANDA CAROL

This is a work of fiction. Names, characters, places, and incidents either are the product of the author's imagination or are used fictitiously. Any resemblance to actual persons, living or dead, events, or locales is entirely coincidental.

Guarded Souls
Copyright © 2021 by Amanda Carol

Cover Designer: Vixen Designs
Editing: Sandra Dee from One Love Editing
Interior Book Formatting: authorTree

For Katey - Hey, Assbutt! Family don't end with blood.

Quote

"THE NOIR HERO IS A KNIGHT IN BLOOD CAKED ARMOR. HE'S DIRTY AND HE DOES HIS BEST TO DENY THE FACT THAT HE'S A HERO THE WHOLE TIME."

- Frank Miller

You are not alone

If you, or someone you love, is a victim of domestic violence please call 1.800.799.SAFE (7233) or you can visit https://www.thehotline.org to chat live with someone who could help. Please know that you are not alone.

Author's Note

To be as authentic as possible, I received some assistance from a retired police officer, and friends who are related to an officer. Some information was embellished for story telling purposes only, however, other moments were based off my own personal research and the assistance of those asked.

Trigger Warning

This book has scenes of domestic violence, reader discretion is advised.

PROLOGUE

17 years old

I sat on my bed, staring at my reflection in the mirror. The bruise on my cheek was now turning yellow from where *he* hit me. If Nana hadn't come home early like she did that day, I'm pretty sure I'd be in a coma…or worse. When *he* got angry, he blacked out and held nothing back. You see abusive relationships portrayed on TV, and you never think it could happen to you. But then it does, and suddenly you're sitting on your bed wondering where it all went wrong. What did I do to make him so angry all the time? What could I have done differently? Would other people love me the same way he did? Was this what love was? He said he loved me, but was this what happened when you loved someone too much? Was I even worth it anymore?

When we first started dating, it was blissful. He was the nicest, sweetest guy who would cherish me as if I was the only girl in the world. Then before I knew it, a monster had taken over and had me pinned on the floor, choking the life out of me because I wanted to hang out with my friends. They always told me how intense he was with me, but I always blew it off because they never saw what I saw…at least in the beginning anyway. He beat me, called me names, and even threatened his own life if I ever left him. I had no escape; he made sure of that. Sometimes I even thought about letting him end it all for me. I'd be at peace then, and I would see my parents again.

A soft knock on my bedroom door pulled me from my thoughts, and I darted my eyes over at Nana, who had peeked her head in. "Is it okay if I come in?"

I nodded. I hadn't really spoken much since *he* was arrested. I kept myself holed up in my room, only coming out to shower and eat dinner. And by eating, I meant moving the food around my plate, wishing my mom and dad were still alive. Nana had been great though, taking care of me since I was five and giving me enough love as both as my parents combined. But sometimes I just wished they were here. To feel their arms around me and telling me it would be okay. It'd been so long that the memories I did have were starting to feel distant, like they never even happened.

Nana came over and sat on the bed beside me, holding a present in her lap. Her eyes connected with mine in the mirror. "How are you holding up?"

"I'm okay," I said, trying to sound positive.

One thing I remembered most about my dad was how optimistic he was. If I would get hurt during Little League soccer, he would always say, "You have to get up and try again, Breezy. Never show any kind of weakness, or your opponent will use that to their advantage." I think he took the coaching thing a little too seriously, but it was something that always stuck with me, especially after the car accident.

"You know you don't have to lie to me," Nana said. "I remember rushing into the emergency room after the accident that took your parents. You were scared, cold, and you had a bump on your head the size of a golf ball. When

2

I got the call, I prayed and prayed that you were safe, and when I finally got to you, do you know what you said to me?"

I shook my head.

"You looked up at me. Tears had welled up in your eyes, and that bottom lip was quivering, and you said, 'I'm okay, Nana. I'm okay. It's just bumps and bruises,' And I knew that was your father talking. It's what your grand-pappy told him growing up. You've been that way ever since."

"You never told me that," I admitted. I remembered that day because it was my fifth birthday. My parents took me ice skating at the rink at Rockefeller Center. Then we had dinner at McDonald's, and I only got to play for a little bit before it started snowing. It was the best birthday I ever had, and the last memory I would ever have of my parents was singing in the car on the way home.

"The officer that pulled you from the wreckage stayed right by your side too. You clung to him until I got there, and I prayed every night that you would be okay after such a tragedy."

Nana grabbed my hand and gave it a gentle squeeze. "You're a survivor, Aubrey. You always have been, and I know that the good Lord will guide you, as He has guided me to give you this."

She handed me the present, beautifully wrapped with a bow.

"You always wrap presents so nicely that I almost never want to open them because I don't want to ruin it," I said, gliding my fingers over the shiny paper.

Nana chuckled softly. "You never gave it a second thought when you were little."

I cracked a smile, the first one since the incident with

him. "Well, that was also when I believed in Santa and before I knew how to cherish the little things."

"Well, let's pretend this is a gift from Santa, then," she said, leaning her forehead against mine for a moment, then pulling away. I opened the present and gasped when I saw the box.

It was a brand-new camera. *He* had broken mine before he gave me the shiner. It was the only camera I had ever owned, and I loved it. I knew the ins and outs of it, and every setting was perfect because it had been my mother's. I never changed a thing. It was already perfect.

"I know how much you loved your mother's camera and how much it meant to you. It broke my heart to see you pick the pieces up off the floor," she explained as I started reading the box, getting teary-eyed. She didn't have much money, and I wouldn't get my trust fund money from my parents until I turned eighteen in a month.

"Nana, this is beautiful. Thank you!" I whispered, then turned to hug her.

"Do you like it? The clerk at the store said this was a popular camera for photographers."

"Do I like it? I love it!" I replied, wiping a tear from my cheek. "I can't wait to use it at college. But are you sure you can afford this?"

Nana smiled brightly; her eyes started to fill up with tears. "Don't you worry about me. You've worked so hard getting good grades, and that scholarship. I can afford to spoil my favorite granddaughter."

"I'm excited to go to River Falls University. I'm ready to feel more connected to my parents." I ran my fingers over the box. They were itching to tear it open and learn all the specs. I'd never been to River Falls, but I'd always wanted to go. My mom grew up there, and that was where my parents met and fell in love. When Grandpa Daniels got sick, they moved back to the suburbs so they could help Nana take care of him. Even though I was old enough to drive, Nana's old car wouldn't have been able to make the trip, and *he* would have asked why I was going up there. Even if he "allowed" me to go, he wouldn't have let me go alone.

"I'm sure going to miss having you around," Nana said, and the excitement that I was feeling turned to dread.

"I wish you could come with me," I answered. She was the only family I'd ever really known, and I'd lost most of my friends because of *him*. She was all I had.

"You will be just fine, my little bee. I'll always be a phone call away."

"I know, I'm just afraid that…*he* will show up again."

"Don't you worry your pretty little head about him. He's in jail, and you'll be long gone by the time he gets out."

I nodded but didn't say anything. He would be charged as an adult with attempted second degree murder in the state of New York. I would be there to testify that he was trying to kill me because his words were still loud and clear in my head. I still felt his hand around my throat, choking the life out of me.

"I'm going to fucking kill you."

She gave me a kiss on the cheek, then got up to leave. I never told him where I was going to college, and part of me was glad that I hadn't. I felt ashamed and guilty for allowing someone to drain the life out of me, for allowing that to happen for almost a year and never having the courage to stand up and say not anymore. If he wanted to, Ray Owens would find me again, and he would finish what he started.

PROLOGUE

Dean

*B*eing a cop, you had to keep your emotions in check to defuse any situation that came your way, and I was good at it. I never let on that my heart was racing as I stared down the barrel of a gun, or that sheer second of panic that coursed through my veins the second a blade was pulled out. And don't even get me started on rolling up to a car accident that involved a drunk driver and family. I was always calm in the moment of chaos, but today was different. Today, we were burying my partner. He was more than just my partner; he was my best friend.

Fuck.

I swallowed thickly, adjusting the dress blues around my neck, keeping my shit together just like I was trained. But damn was that hard to do when I heard the sobs from his mother coming from next to me. Normally, I would be sitting with the district members behind the family, but the Colemans were my family. Her son and I had been friends since the second grade, and our fathers even worked together in the same precinct before Wyatt's dad transferred to the city.

I felt a hand clap down on my shoulder and looked up to see my dad. He gave me a solemn look and took the seat next to me. My mom was leaning down and comforting Mrs. Coleman, and then she came to me. She gave me a hug, kissed my cheek, and sat down on the other side of my father. It didn't surprise me that they'd made the trip down from River Falls. Wyatt was like a second son to them.

The music stopped, and the priest came forward. Once he started talking, I tuned him out.

I tuned everything out.

If I had listened to a word he said, then I would have to face the reality of it all. That wasn't something I thought I'd ever be ready for though, so I made damn sure I didn't listen.

Instead, I thought about how Sergeant Price would be assigning me a new partner. Anger rose to the surface because I didn't want a new partner. The only person I ever trusted with my life was lying in a pine box less than twenty feet in front of me, killed in the line of duty. Wyatt would be replaced, and there wasn't a damn thing I could do about it. Just like there wasn't a damn thing I could do to save my brother, and fuck, did I try.

But I couldn't do it.

I couldn't save him.

It was supposed to be me.

I blinked back tears and let my mind go blank until it was time to leave the church and go to the gravesite to honor the fallen.

Clenching my jaw tightly, I was one of the six carrying Wyatt's casket up the grass to his final resting place. Sergeant Price turned to me as he held the American flag in his hands. I shifted my body to face him as he handed me one side of the flag. We shook it out gently and placed it over the casket.

"Present arms." I heard Serge say loud and clear.

I stood tall and saluted without even registering the movement. The command had been drilled in my brain for as long as I could remember. I was motionless throughout the 21-gun salute and the duration of "Taps" played on the trumpets by some of my comrades. My leg, still aching from the bullet hitting my knee, started to throb, but I ignored the pain. I was advised not to come, but I told the doc I wasn't going to sit this out. I could endure the pain—hell, I was trained to fight through it. But the pain of losing my best friend was worse than the bullet wound.

What the fuck am I supposed to do without my best friend?

I kept my hand strong and steady on my forehead as Serge brought his right arm up and pressed his fingers into the call button on his radio. My entire body stiffened, and I started to grind my molars together to keep my face emotionless. I knew what was coming next.

"Calling Deputy Coleman." Pause.

I hated the damn pause. *He's not going to answer.*

"This is the last call for Deputy Coleman." Pause.

Why was there a pause? *He's never coming back.*

"No response. Radio number 23 is out of service after nine years of police service."

The silence was almost deafening after another fucking long pause. If I waited any longer, my resolve would break, and I'd lose my shit up here. No one wanted to see that— no one should see that.

"Gone, but never forgotten."

He's really gone.

My brother is gone.

"Holden," I heard Serge speak softly in my ear. "Dean."

I looked over at him. He was frowning, but he gave me a look to let me know that it was time to let him go. I felt my bottom lip quiver, but I kept my shit together as I let my arm fall back down to my side. The rest of Wyatt's funeral was a blur after that, and afterward, my parents went over to the Colemans. I declined, not wanting to be around people anymore. I was maxed out for the day, and if I had one more person tell me that they were sorry for my loss, I would have started throwing punches. If anyone should be sorry, it was me.

Before I went home, I wanted to hit up the liquor store right by my apartment that I shared with Wyatt. I grabbed two bottles of bourbon off the shelf and shuffled up to the counter.

"I saw what happened on the news. Man, I'm sorry to hear about your partner. He was a great guy," the clerk, Mr. Robinson, said as he rang me up and then put the bottles into a brown bag.

I slapped a hundred-dollar bill on the counter. "Keep the change."

I picked up my bag and walked out.

Ignoring the searing pain in my knee, I hopped back in my truck and drove back to my place.

Once inside, I set the bag on the counter and went to my room, passing Wyatt's on the way. I stopped and stood in his doorway, flicking the light on. His bed was unmade, and his fishing gear was still out because he hadn't put it away from our trip over a month ago. His Eli Manning football jersey was draped over his desk chair, and of course, there was an open can of Coke right next to it.

Dread washed over me, and I knew that I would have to pack his shit up.

But that wouldn't be tonight.

I flicked the light off and shut the door behind me. I went back to my room and stripped off my suit, cursing at the fact that I ripped a stitch open. I put on a pair of gym shorts and replaced the old bandage with a fresh one on my knee. It wasn't bleeding that much, and one stitch wouldn't kill me. I would stop by the clinic tomorrow to get it fixed.

I limped my ass back out into the kitchen, grabbed a bottle, and went over to the couch. I opened the cap and took a hefty swig, ignoring the burn in my throat. I took another swig, and another, and another, until almost more than half the bottle was gone and I was good and numb. I didn't feel any more pain. I felt nothing, and feeling nothing was better than feeling guilty.

I looked up at the ceiling and lazily lifted the bottle in the air. "Cheers, brother."

ONE

3 Months Later

S *nap!*
        I zoomed the camera out.
Snap!
I turned the camera vertical.
Snap!
I glanced down at my watch. "Okay, one more, then we can stop. It's almost time to meet up with Sophia and Chloe."

"Oh, thank God. I'm starving," Cassie said.

Cassie was my college roommate and first friend at River Falls. We clicked instantly, and she introduced me to Chloe. They grew up here, so they showed me around town. I met Sophia in my English 101 class, and I invited her to brunch to meet Cassie and Chloe. Ever since then, we've become sisters. It was nice finally making new friends and being away from home in the New York suburbs. I had a hard time getting close to people at first because the fear of Ray was still very real, but I had told myself enough times that he wasn't coming back, and eventually, I started to believe it. I missed Nana, but we talked and saw each other when we could.

"Me too," I responded, turning my camera off and putting it away. I had gotten new equipment and wanted to test it out, and Cassie was my guinea pig. She didn't really have a choice now because we were still roommates. Instead of living in a tiny dorm, we rented an apartment together. I was able to use some of my trust fund money to get us some nice furniture, but the money that I didn't use I put in my savings account. One day, I would open my own studio, so every dime I made at the Bistro and from photography gigs, I put right into the "Aubrey's Studio" fund.

Cassie pulled her red hair up into a ponytail. "Do you mind if I invite Ford over later tonight?"

"No, I don't mind," I said, zipping up the last of the equipment. "I was actually going to develop some of these pictures after dinner."

"Oh! In color or black and white?" she asked, plopping down on the couch.

I thought about it for a moment.

"Both, I think. You have such gorgeous hair, so I love doing color when I develop your portraits. But I also love the elegance of black and white," I answered. "I took some beautiful ones of Sophia the other week."

"The ones with her in that off-the-shoulder black sweater that Chloe designed?" Cassie asked, and I nodded. "Those are stunning."

"I think those are my favorites of her if I'm being honest."

Cassie leaned forward, batting her eyelashes. "What are your favorites of me?"

I chuckled. "I think these might be, because the lighting hits your features flawlessly."

"I'm excited to see how they turn out," she said, and I couldn't have agreed more. I stuffed the roll of film in my purse and slipped my shoes on. Cassie got up from the couch and went to grab her things from her room.

When we left the apartment, she patted her pocket. "Shit! I forgot my phone. I'll be right back. Hold the elevator for me!"

I headed toward the elevator, checking in my purse to make sure I had my car keys. When I rounded the corner, I walked right into a hard chest that reeked of booze and stale nuts mixed with a touch of cologne.

"Oh, sorry," I whispered, but my apology died on the tip of my tongue when my eyes locked with dark green ones.

"Watch where you're going," he growled, and I refused to let the deep timbre of his voice make my panties dampen like the first time they did when this asshole spoke to me.

"I said I was sorry," I gritted back through my teeth at my neighbor.

His eyes roamed over my body, and again, I tried not to let it affect me, but a shiver ran down my spine at his heated, angry gaze. "Yeah, well, sorry gets you nowhere, kiddo. Don't get in my way again."

I blinked, and before I could come up with some snippy remark back, he stepped around me, knocking into my shoulder as he did, and stalked down the hallway. Cassie opened the door just as he walked by and jumped at the sound of him slamming his door.

"What was that all about?" she asked when she got over to me.

I shrugged. "Just our neighbor being a giant dick…again."

We stepped into the elevator together, and I hit the Ground Floor button.

He'd moved in about a month ago, and when I went to welcome him to the apartment complex and introduce myself, he damn near slammed the door in my face.

"I'm pretty sure he's a cop. I've seen him get out of a cruiser in uniform," I said nonchalantly as we walked across the parking lot to my car. Ford would pick her up from dinner, and I would head straight over to the Camera Shop. The owner trusted me with a key, and as long as I cleaned up after I was finished, I could use the darkroom anytime I wanted.

We got to my car, and Cassie narrowed her eyes at me, a smirk forming on her lips. "Oh, so you've noticed."

I rolled my eyes, opening my door and getting into the driver's seat. "I'm a photographer, Cass. Of course I notice things."

"Well, he is pretty easy on the eyes," she admitted, buckling herself into the passenger seat. "That man may be an asshole, but he is six foot two inches of pure sexy and boy does he have a fine ass."

Cassie laughed as she went to put her feet up on the dash. I smacked her legs down as I placed my purse on the floor.

"That was a very specific description," I said, starting the car and pulling out of my parking space. I must admit though, my new neighbor was hot—high cheekbones, chiseled jawline, the perfect nose, and cropped, dirty-blond hair—but his attitude was what made him ugly… but he is *so* not ugly. On the contrary, he's the first guy that has ever made me wet with just a look. Normally, I ran for the hills when a guy was a dick. But with him, it was different. I could just tell that he wasn't always that way. Still, I swore to myself that I would avoid assholes.

"Just because I don't have your keen eyesight, Aubrey, does not mean I'm blind." Cassie laughed again.

"Fine, I'll admit that he's sexy, but that's all." I huffed, and Cassie squealed.

"Finally, now I can start planning your wedding. Chloe will design the dress, I'll make the cake, and Sophia can organize the whole thing."

I balked at her. "Never going to happen."

"You didn't walk into a hallway filled with sexual tension."

"There was no sexual tension!"

"If you say so."

Out of the corner of my eye, I saw Cassie biting her lip to hold in her laughter. She was wrong—there had never been and never would be something there. And besides, I didn't even know his name.

TWO
Aubrey

Sophia arrived at the Bistro a few minutes after we did, and since it was a nice night out, we got a table outdoors. Laura—a girl I've waited tables with before—Came by and took our drink order while we waited for Chloe to order food. I glanced up and waved at her when I saw her arrive at the hostess podium.

"Hey, babes, sorry I'm late. Rhett asked me to fix the buttons on his white shirt. The chief is throwing a banquet dinner in his honor tomorrow night, and since I'll be at the boutique all day tomorrow doing inventory, I won't have the time to fix it before we go." Chloe sat down in the seat across from me. "Of course, that turned into an argument of why he needs to tell me these things sooner rather than last minute."

"I'm sorry," I told her, but she waved me off.

"It's totally fine. I got this super-long apology text when I got here, and I told him he can make it up to me when I get home." Chloe winked before she took a sip of her water. She and Rhett had the kind of relationship that most of us dreamed about having. They were high school sweethearts, and after over ten years together, they were still so very much in love.

"He was promoted to lieutenant, right?" Sophia asked just as Laura arrived with our drinks.

"Hi, Chloe!" Laura smiled brightly as she handed us

18

our glasses. "What can I get you to drink, and are you ladies ready to order?"

We all nodded and gave her our orders, and then she scurried off to get Chloe her drink.

"Yes, he was. I'm so proud of him. He's worked so hard these past few months, and Chief Warren is not an easy man to impress." Chloe beamed as Laura dropped off her glass of chardonnay.

"Oh yes, Ford has talked about him from time to time," Cassie said, taking a sip from her wineglass. Ford was her boyfriend, and he worked at the same firehouse as Rhett as an EMT. They met at one of the firehouse banquets. They hadn't been together long, but they seemed to be getting along well. I could tell he was really into Cassie, but I wasn't entirely sure if she felt the same. She told me that there was someone who she truly loved once, but he'd joined the Marines and ended things during the summer right before college. Of course, what did I really know about love?

"How are things going with you and the hottie EMT?" Sophia asked.

"Really well, actually. He's amazing."

"That's great! I'm so happy for you, Cass," Chloe responded. I smiled, truly happy for her. I didn't have a lot of experience in the relationship department, but I did know that love wasn't like what Ray and I had. I was taught the meaning of love through my nana and her stories of Grandpa Daniels and my parents. My friends were also showing me too. Maybe I envied them a little bit, because my experience with love was bitter, but I was happy for them.

Not long after that conversation, our food arrived, and we fell into an easy banter.

After dinner, Ford was waiting to take Cassie back home, and I said goodbye to the other girls. I got in my car and drove all the way over to the Camera Shop. I locked the door behind me like I always did and made my way back to the darkroom.

I loved being in here. When I first moved here, I was this scared, lonely girl, and coming to the shop helped me soothe my fears of being away from Nana. It was my favorite distraction, and I knew I was safe here. I never spoke of Ray at first, thinking that if I said his name, he would just reappear and beat me to death solely for leaving him. It wasn't until one night at a party when a guy had put his hands on my waist that I sort of freaked out and had a panic attack. The girls took me back to my dorm, and that's when I told them everything. It felt good getting it all out in the open like that. I didn't have to live with this fear alone anymore.

After a while, the fear went away altogether.

Once I was finished developing the film, I cleaned everything up but left a note telling Elaine I would be by in the morning to pick the photos up. I checked my phone and saw a message from Cassie.

Cassie: There is rocky road ice cream for you in the fridge xx

I smiled. They must have stopped on the way home. I locked the Camera Shop up and walked back to my car. I heard a noise around me, and I glanced around. My heart rate kicked up, and I stayed quiet, making sure not to make a sound. When a cat came around the corner, I jumped, clutching my chest and breathing heavily. *Stupid cat.* I started to calm down a little bit, but I still had the feeling I was being watched, so I hurried to my car and got in quickly. I didn't even bother with my seat belt until I was pulling out onto the road.

I pulled back into my parking space and practically jogged to the apartment lobby. Once inside, relief washed over me, and I almost started laughing at how jumpy I was tonight. Note to self; no more *True Crime* marathons with Cassie late at night.

I stepped inside the elevator, and just when it was about to close, I heard a male's voice yelling to hold the doors.

I pressed the Open-Door button, and a man I'd never seen before stepped in, wearing dark jeans and a black shirt. We had tenants coming and going at all hours, and it wasn't unusual to see new faces every now and again in the elevator.

"Thank you," he said breathlessly, giving me a small smile.

"You're welcome," I replied, "What floor?"

"Oh uh, seven." He went to press the button, but I had already pressed it.

"Do you live here?" I asked. "I've never seen you around before."

"No, I'm just here picking up my partner, Dean. He's in apartment 708."

Ahh, so that's his name.

"Oh, that's right next door to me."

"So, you've met him?" he asked, just as the elevator reached my floor.

"Unfortunately," I murmured, and he chuckled as we stepped off and headed down the hallway.

"We aren't exactly—" I paused, considering my next words. "—friendly."

"Would you believe me if I said we aren't exactly friendly either?"

It was my turn to chuckle. "Actually, I would."

"I'm Dylan, by the way. Detective Dylan McCormick." He held out his hand.

"Aubrey." I placed my hand in his and shaking it. My neighbor—whose name I just learned was Dean—walked around the corner wearing gym clothes. "Speak of the devil."

Dean looked at Dylan and me standing in the hallway by my door.

"I hit traffic on the way back here. Give me a few to get changed and we can roll out," Dean said as he shuffled past us.

I lifted a brow. "It's almost midnight and you hit traffic?"

Out of the corner of my eye, I saw Dylan try to hide his smile, but Dean shot us both a look.

"I don't owe either of you an explanation," Dean growled, then continued to walk to his apartment. "Stop flirting, McCormick."

Dylan looked at me sympathetically and bowed his head. "Good night, Aubrey."

"Good night." I gave him a small smile, then nodded my head down the hall. "And good luck."

Dylan chuckled and muttered a thank-you before following Dean.

I went inside and noticed Cassie's door was closed with a scrunchie on the handle, our version of a sock. I laughed silently and shook my head. "When the scrunchie is present, the night will be pleasant."

THREE

Dean

"You ready for this, man?" Dylan asked as he shut the door behind him.

I sat my gym bag on the floor and went into the kitchen to grab a bottle of water. I'd moved back to River Falls a month ago, and it wasn't by choice. *Captain Holden*—aka my father—said it was already done. My transfer papers were already signed by Sergeant Price and the captain at District 21.

Now here I was, back to living in this crappy town. Wyatt and I, we wanted out. We wanted to work in the Big Apple, because that's where we thought we'd see the most action. And damn did we see some crazy shit, but...

I shook my head. I was not going down that road.

I put my focus on the subject at hand.

My new sergeant, Aaron Miller, wanted Dylan and me to keep watch on a house that they believed was the source of the meth problem hitting the streets. Eyewitnesses had reported suspicious activity, and a few of our informants had told us there was someone making and distributing the drug, but they didn't know from where. We were told to follow up on a lead and look for strong enough evidence to get a search warrant. Truth be told, I was a little shocked that this town had crazy drug-trafficking problems, but it wasn't uncommon. Especially since we were near the Canadian border.

"I'm as ready as I'll ever be, although I don't understand why we have to. That's what beat cops are for," I said after almost guzzling down half the bottle. I offered one to Dylan, but he declined.

"According to Captain Holden, the precinct doesn't have the resources," Dylan answered.

I rolled my eyes. "Of course they don't."

I left him standing in my kitchen as I went into my room to change. I had showered at the gym, knowing that I probably wouldn't have time to shower here. Dylan usually showed up fifteen minutes early for shifts.

Even though I hated being back home, I had to admit that moving out of the apartment and the city was probably for the best. Living there was just a painful reminder of how bad I fucked up. Of course, a change of scenery still didn't wash away how dead I felt on the inside, especially being back home where Wyatt and I grew up. They prepare you for a lot in the academy, but no amount of training prepares you for... *Not going there.*

I sat down on my bed, rubbing my knee. It'd been three months, and it still ached, pretty much on any day that ended in *y*. Grabbing the ibuprofen bottle off my nightstand, I popped four pills in my mouth and swallowed, then got up to go to the bathroom. I was at the gym for hours, which was probably why my knee hurt so damn bad. I hadn't been able to walk right on it, but I guessed that's what happens when you blow off rehab.

I was a stubborn asshole. I knew it, my bosses knew it, and I was pretty sure the entire 21st knew it. I didn't care back in the city, and I didn't care now.

I quickly changed into some street clothes, then made my way back out into my kitchen where Dylan was staring down at his phone. He glanced up as soon as he heard me and put his phone back in his pocket.

"Sergeant Miller wants us to keep him updated. If we see anything, we are not to engage but to gather evidence and bring it to a judge so they can sign off on the warrant."

I nodded but didn't say anything as I emptied out my gym bag and filled it with water and a few sodas. I grabbed two thermoses from the cabinet and started a pot of coffee. This would be Dylan's first stakeout as a cop. Once he was out of the Marines, he'd joined the police academy. He passed with flying colors obviously, and because of his rank in the core and the fact that my grandfather and his served together, my father offered him a job as my partner. I still wasn't sure why he entrusted me to train the kid, but I stopped questioning my father's motives a long ass time ago. I would give him credit where it was due—Dylan had caught on to the job quickly, so that was a plus.

"So, uh. Your neighbor Aubrey seems nice," Dylan remarked. I turned around and lifted a brow, wondering who the fuck he was talking about.

"The girl next door. 707." He pointed in the direction of the apartment next door. "Blonde hair, blue eyes. You know, the one you were a dick to just fifteen minutes ago?"

Oh…her.

I must have made a face because Dylan nodded. "Yeah, her."

"I don't have her number if that's what you're insinuating, and I'm not giving her yours. If you want it, be a man about it and give it to her." I leaned up against the counter, crossing my arms over my chest. She had a smart mouth, and there would have been a time I would have loved to get to know all about what that mouth could do. But I had zero interest in getting to know her, or anyone else for that matter. I was damaged goods, and nothing was ever going to change that.

"She's not my type," Dylan said, sitting down on a stool at the tiny bar in my kitchen.

"You two seemed pretty cozy." As soon as those words left my mouth, I instantly regretted them. They made me seem jealous, which I wasn't. She was just a pretty girl who lived next door, nothing more. The last thing I wanted was to get wrapped up in someone who couldn't handle being with a cop.

Been there, done that.

"Nah. It was just small talk. She's cute, but I'm not into blondes."

I looked over at him, and he seemed lost in thought. I didn't care enough to continue this conversation, so I left it at that, and when the coffee was finished brewing, I filled both thermoses up and handed one to Dylan so he could fix it the way he liked it. Turns out, we had one thing in common: we liked our coffee black.

We left my apartment and headed for the unmarked police car in the parking lot.

I hated these damn cars. The small space made me feel trapped, and I would rather be in an SUV. When I questioned why we didn't have SUVs, I was told we didn't have the resources, but that's small-town life for you. Dylan handed me the keys because he drove to the station to pick up the car before coming to get me. I tossed my bag in the back, then got in the driver's seat. I needed to have full control, especially if I was feeling confined. Dylan learned that pretty quickly and surprisingly didn't mind riding shotgun all the time.

"I think Aubrey might be good for you. She—" Dylan started to say, but me slamming the car door shut cut him off. Since when did the Marine become a love guru?

"Look, let me make this very clear." I paused, turning in my seat. "I don't need relationship advice or you asking me how I'm doing all the time. I don't need nor want a relationship, and that includes being your best pal. I'm your partner—we're coworkers, that's it. I come in, do my job, and go home. And I swear, the next time you ask me if I'm okay, I'll start throwing punches. I'm fine."

Dylan's brows lifted as he held his hands up. Thankfully, he dropped the small talk, and we went to stake out the house. That put me in a shit mood, and all I wanted to do now was to shut it all out, but I had four hours to sit through. It was going to be a long fucking night.

FOUR
Aubrey

My alarm went off way too early, but I had to be up to get my gear packed and get ready for this family photo shoot I had in two hours. I jumped in the shower, got dressed, and dried my hair. The humidity was not my friend, and if I didn't dry my hair, then my wavy strands would frizz up, and I would look like a hot mess.

I walked out into the kitchen and started a pot of coffee. While I was waiting, I grabbed a yogurt from the fridge and was cutting a banana when Cassie emerged from her room.

"Good morning." She yawned, then sat down on the stool. "Oh, you're making coffee."

She reached for a banana and started to peel it open.

"Yeah, I need the pick-me-up if I want to have the energy for this shoot."

"So, you're making the good stuff?" Cassie winked as she took a bite of her fruit.

"You know it." I smiled, and just then, Ford came out of Cassie's room, dressed in his EMT uniform.

"Morning, Aubrey." He came over and wrapped his arms around Cassie. "Good morning, babe."

She flushed as he leaned in behind her and kissed her cheek.

"Would you like a cup of coffee before you leave?" I offered him, but he shook his head.

"No, thanks. I'm actually running a little late this morning…" He trailed off, and he didn't even need to continue. I'm just glad that I showered with my music on so I wouldn't *hear* why he would be running late this morning.

Cassie walked Ford to the door, and he kissed her goodbye. Once she sat back down, I lifted a brow. She had this weird vibe about her, one that I'd noticed before when guys would get too close.

"What's wrong with this one?" I asked, and her eyes widened.

"Nothing, actually."

"Really?"

"What? I'm being serious!" she all but shouted. "We get along really great, *and* he's pretty good in bed. He treats me well, and I like him."

"But…" I said, drawing out the word.

"There's no buts! Honest. I think I'll keep this one around awhile."

I smiled. "Good. I'm happy for you, Cass. You deserve it." I checked my watch. "Crap, I have to get going. See you later."

Cassie mumbled a goodbye as I put my coffee in a to-go cup, grabbed my things, and rushed out to my car. It was early but was hot as hell out already, and I was meeting the Sweet family at the park that had a beautiful lake, perfect for family portraits.

I glanced down at my gear shift and thanked the high heavens that I had a hair tie. I always styled my hair before a shoot because I wanted to look professional, but I usually ended up tossing my hair in a ponytail to keep my hair out of my face. I made a mental note to ask Chloe for some tips on professional-looking updos.

After the shoot, I decided to stop by Chloe's boutique to see if she needed any help with the inventory. Once I stepped inside, I sighed with sweet relief as the cold AC hit me in the face.

"Hey, Aubs!" Chloe said from behind the register. "What brings you here?"

"I have the rest of the day off, so I thought I could swing by and help you with inventory," I told her, coming over and leaning up against the cool counter. Summer was great and all, but I was a fall girl at heart.

Chloe beamed. "You're the best! Rhett's banquet dinner is happening in six hours, and if I don't get this done by five o'clock, I won't have enough time to get ready."

"Don't worry, Chlo, you could pull off a potato sack and still look hot," I chuckled as she shot me a look. "I promise I will help you get done in time if you let me have these."

I held up a pair of pretty purple, lacy, boy short underwear.

Chloe laughed. "Deal!"

Just then, the door chimed, and I turned to see Sophia walking in.

"Hi, Soph! How was class?" I asked as she came up to the counter. Sophia was taking summer classes so she could get her bachelor's degree in psychology quicker. The funny thing was, she didn't want to be a therapist or anything like that; she just loved learning everything she could. She was lucky because most universities didn't offer summer classes, but River Falls University did.

"It was rather boring, if I'm being honest. The professor was rambling on about stuff that I already knew, so I started reading the next chapter."

"How many chapters ahead are you now?" I asked, trying to hide my smile.

Sophia blushed. "About five."

Chloe and I busted out laughing.

"This is why I love you," Chloe said, picking up a bin of panties.

"What? I can't help if I get bored in class," Sophia whined playfully.

"Have you thought about online classes?" I asked her.

"I have, but I love being in the classroom."

Chloe paused and looked over at Sophia, her face serious. "Do you sniff books? I'm sure I can get Rhett to ask one of the EMTs if they've heard of anything like AA for book sniffers."

She leaned across the counter and gave Sophia's hand a squeeze.

"Chloe!" I all but shouted, trying not to laugh.

"I don't sniff books, Chlo." Sophia narrowed her brown eyes at Chloe, then laughed.

"I'm kidding, but I am a little worried about you. You seem stressed out to the max, and that's not healthy. I don't want you to burn yourself out," Chloe told her, her features full of concern.

I turned and faced Sophia. "I am too. Last night was the first time I've seen you in a week."

"I'm honestly okay. I work better under pressure, but I promise if I get too stressed, I'll take a break," Sophia reassured us. We fell into an easy banter as we counted everything in the store after that.

We finally finished at 5:00 p.m. on the dot, and Chloe promised to send us pictures of the event. Part of me was a little bummed I wasn't there to take them myself, but apparently, they had already hired a photographer. I gave Sophia a hug, and she went home to study.

Cassie had to work tonight at the Bistro, so I was on my own for dinner. I decided Chinese was the way to go, so I stopped there and then the liquor store for some wine. I browsed the wine section, but I knew damn well I was going end up choosing my favorite, white zinfandel, like I always did. I walked around to the other aisle and stopped dead in my tracks. Of all hours in the day, he had to be here at the exact time I was.

Dean looked a little annoyed—what else was new—as I quietly approached. Of course, my favorite wine just happened to be placed right in the exact spot he was standing.

"Excuse me," I said as politely as I could.

Nothing. He didn't even flinch. Okay, maybe he didn't hear me. So I cleared my throat and spoke a little louder. "Excuse m—"

"I heard you the first time," he said nonchalantly, bending over to pick up a bottle of whiskey on the shelf.

"Well, if you could just—"

"Nope. I haven't found what I'm looking for yet."

"If you could just let me squeeze—"

He paused and turned his head up toward me, and scowled.

You know what? Fine. I bent down and reached over his outstretched arm and grabbed the bottle of wine. My shoulder brushed up against him, and I caught a whiff of his cologne. If he wasn't such an ass, I would have thought he smelled amazing.

I caught a glimpse of the Gentleman Jack bottle he was looking at. I turned my head to look at him, and my breath hitched at how close we were. I could see a dusting of freckles on his nose, and his dark green eyes narrowed in on my face.

"I wouldn't recommend the Gentleman for you—it's way too classy," I whispered low enough so no one else but Dean would hear. "Why don't you try Fireball? It's cheap, and it's something you'll regret in the morning."

He leaned in closer, a smirk forming on his full lips. "It sounds like you know that from experience."

With our gazes locked, he pulled the bottle of Gentleman Jack off the shelf, then left.

I took a moment to gather my wits. Why did he have to be so good-looking? And why was my traitorous body aroused by that? I should probably talk to Sophia; she might be able to tell me why.

He was standing at the register when I finally walked over to check out. I tried to avoid looking directly at him, but I failed miserably, and our eyes connected once more.

"Have a good night, sir," the clerk told him.

With his eyes still on me, Dean said, "Oh, I will. Thank you."

Then he walked out of the store.

After I drove home, I waited in my car for a few moments, hoping that he was in his apartment and I could get to mine safely without being seen. I mean, what were the chances of us running into each other again today? I raced up to my apartment and thanked fate for allowing me to get inside without disruption.

I showered and put on my comfy clothes, put my food

on a plate, poured myself a glass of wine, and got settled on the couch. I turned on Netflix to binge-watch *Gossip Girl* and had only taken a few bites when my phone buzzed on the coffee table, so I leaned forward and picked it up.

Chloe: SOS! Grab your camera and meet us at the firehouse! The photographer is a no show.
Me: On my way-be there in twenty!

I put my takeout in the fridge and changed into black slacks and a yellow top. I quickly fixed my hair and makeup and grabbed my camera bag. I shoved a new SD card in the side pocket, grabbed an extra battery because I wasn't sure how much battery I had left after today's shoot, and was out the door, locking it up tight behind me.

FIVE
Aubrey

I pulled up to the firehouse and parked my car next to Chloe's. I sent her a quick text, letting her know I was there, and grabbed my camera bag from my back seat. I made my way to the front doors, and when I stepped inside, it was packed with firefighters and the police. All of a sudden, my stomach sank. If the police were here, that meant Dean might be here, and I was not ready for round two with him. I was also glad I didn't place any bets on my chances of seeing him again. My eyes scanned the room, looking for Chloe, but they landed on Rhett, who was talking to Nash Warren, the battalion chief. I'd met him before since Chloe invited us to the firehouse every Fourth of July for a big cookout and fireworks.

"Thank God you're here!" Chloe's voice came from my left, and I flinched as she wrapped her arms around my shoulders. "C'mon, let's go talk to Nash."

Chloe looked gorgeous as always. Her short black hair was slick straight, and her rose-gold, formfitting dress looked flawless against her sun-kissed skin. She was the only one out of all of us who could pull off a dark plum lip color and look like a goddess.

Chloe grabbed my hand and pulled me through the crowd, over to where Rhett was standing. I avoided looking around at the other attendees, because I didn't want to know if Dean was here or not. When Rhett saw us walking over, his shoulders sagged with relief.

He gave me a hug and kissed my cheek before whispering in my ear, "You're a lifesaver."

He pulled back and gestured to the man standing next to him. "Hey, Warren, you remember Aubrey Daniels, right? She's a good friend of mine and Chloe's."

Nash grinned politely and held out his hand. "Sure, yeah. I've seen you here a couple times."

I returned his smile as I shook his hand.

He was handsome in a rugged sort of way. He was tall, had broad shoulders, and he had the most gorgeous light sea-green eyes I'd ever seen that paired well with his salt-and-pepper hair. He wasn't that much older than us—I believe Rhett said mid-thirties—and I would have questioned how he became the battalion chief at such a young age, but I'd heard stories from Rhett at how good Nash was at his job. Apparently, he'd been with the same firehouse since he was in high school. I remember he was honored by the governor for his quick response times and how he commanded his battalion.

"Thank you for coming on such short notice," Nash said, his voice deep and rough.

"It's not a problem. I'm happy to do it. Just tell me what you need me to get some pictures of, and I'll make sure I get them. I'll also go around and snap some candid shots, if that's okay?"

He nodded. "Sure, that's fine. We just need a few shots from the ceremony and speeches. Other than that, you can do whatever. Do you work for the paper?"

I shook my head. "No, but I will sign the waiver that gives you full rights to the photos so you can submit them to the paper."

"Awesome. That would be great. Thank you."

"You're welcome. I should have them ready for you in a few days. I'll edit them up, print out some copies, and also give you the final disc. I'll bring the form over with me when I drop everything off."

"Sounds good to me. How much do we owe you?"

I thought about it for a moment. I'd been running my business for a while now, and I think the reason why I got a lot of business was because my prices were fair. I charged for gas money (depending on how far I had to drive), and I charged for printing costs, because that could add up if they wanted a lot of copies for family members. I made a lot of Christmas cards during the holidays, which was my busiest time of year. I never charged for my time if it was less than a thirty-minute shoot, although my friends thought I'm crazy for that. I loved what I did, and I loved seeing the satisfied faces of my clients. Typically, after the first half hour, I'd charge fifty dollars for every thirty minutes. I'd cut that in half if we only went an extra fifteen instead of a full thirty. Weddings were different though; that was the only time I'd charge for my time since I was there all day.

I'd never done a shoot for anything like this before though. These guys were first responders, and I knew they had a budget. I couldn't take away their money if it could be used elsewhere.

"This is on the house," I finally answered.

"No, seriously. Please let me reimburse you," Nash insisted, and out of the corner of my eye, I saw Chloe and Rhett exchange a look. Once my mind was made up, that was it, and there would be no more arguing.

"Seriously, Chief Warren, this one is on me. I'm happy to help out. Besides, you saved me from sitting at home on my couch eating Chinese takeout and binging *Gossip Girl* for the third time in a row."

Rhett clapped his hand down on Nash's shoulder. "Chief, this is one argument you are never going to win. Consider yourself lucky."

Nash eyed me for a moment, then gave me a warm smile, the kind that reached his eyes. "Thank you, Aubrey. I appreciate it."

I smiled. "Do you have a place that I can set my stuff and get my camera ready?"

"You can come sit with us at our table. We have an extra chair," Chloe interjected. We said goodbye to the men, and I followed Chloe through the maze of tables, when we finally got to one in the middle.

"Anything you want from the boutique is yours," she said as I set my bag in a chair and opened it. I didn't want to disturb this elaborate place setting. White tablecloths, white silverware, and the centerpieces were simple; it was just a mason jar filled with red, yellow, and orange gerbera daisies. The mason jar even had the firehouse emblem on it.

"Chlo, you're always giving us free stuff," I commented, removing the SD card that had the family photos on it. I placed it carefully in the tiny compartment in my bag and zipped it safely in place. "When are you ever going to let us pay you?"

She crossed her arms over her chest and pouted a little. "Never."

"Exactly."

I replaced the battery, put in a brand-new SD card, then got to work.

I WAS SATISFIED WITH ALL THE PICTURES, SO I decided to put my camera away and head out. Plus, I was running out of battery life. I got some amazing shots of Rhett receiving his medal and lieutenant bugles that I knew Chloe would want framed. I went around and took some great candid pictures of everyone in attendance. I saw Dean, but he lurked in the back, and the look on his face told me he didn't want his picture taken. That was perfectly fine by me. I did manage to get a picture of the police captain with Dylan—Detective McCormick—and Sergeant Miller. I ended up talking with them for a few minutes before I went and took a picture of Nash and his brother, Noah.

The police captain reminded me of Dean. They had the same nose, lips, and eye color. My suspicions were confirmed when he talked about his son and he called Dean by his name and gestured to where he was standing.

I pulled my phone out and saw that I had a text from an unknown number.

Unknown: Hey...

I didn't recognize the number, so I deleted the message and shoved my phone back in my pocket.

"You're leaving already?" Chloe asked just as I zipped up my camera.

"Yeah, I'm finished here. And I'm pretty beat," I told her. I wasn't exactly hungry because Chloe made me take a small break to eat. So, I would have leftover Chinese and wine tomorrow night.

Rhett approached the table and gave me a hug.

"Thanks for doing this, Aubrey," he said as his whiskey-brown eyes met mine. There was a sheen to it, and I was pretty sure the reason why Chloe was sober was because she was the designated driver.

I smiled. "Will you stop thanking me?"

He ran his hand down the back of his neck. "Sorry."

I chuckled. "Anyway, congrats on becoming lieutenant. Tell Chief Warren I'll be by the station in a few days."

"I will, thanks."

I gave him a pointed look, and he laughed.

"Need me to walk you out?" Chloe asked.

I shook my head. "No, I think I'll be okay. Enjoy the rest of your night, and text me later."

With one last hug, I made my way through the crowd —which was starting to get a tad rowdy because it was an open bar—and out to my car. Once outside, I took a deep breath. The hot summer air felt fresh in my lungs. It was a lot cooler out here than inside, and the breeze felt nice against my clammy skin.

I started walking in the dimly lit parking lot. It was a lot darker now than it was when I arrived. The feeling of being watching crept over my skin like a caress, and goose bumps rose on my arms. I picked up my pace, heart beating fast because I swore someone was following me, and I was too scared to turn around and see if I was correct or if I was just losing my mind.

The footsteps behind me told me I wasn't crazy.

So, I started to run, panic setting in as I weaved around parked cars. My only option was forward right now. I risked a peek behind me and saw a hooded figure jogging after me. The moment I turned back around, I smacked into something, or rather someone, as I felt hands wrap around my arms.

Everything happened so fast after that.

There was a commotion, and I was thrown headfirst into a parked car.

My ears started ringing, and my vision went black. I blinked, trying to stay alert as I heard voices and what sounded like a scuffle. My fight-or-flight instincts were trying to kick in, but I was too disoriented to do either. I blinked again, and when my vision started to come back, I saw two people running off, or was it one? I was pretty sure I heard two voices, but my ears were still ringing loudly. I tried to get up and ended up falling over again. An unsettling fear washed over me, and memories I had long since buried deep inside a locked box in my brain started to drift to the surface.

He's not here. It's not him. He's still in jail.

I needed to get up, to get back inside, but I still felt off-balance, and my head was throbbing. I touched my forehead, and when I pulled my hand away, it was covered in blood. Finally, my flight instinct kicked into high gear.

Or so I thought.

I reached up and placed my hands on the hood of a car and pulled myself up, willing my body to work with me. Once I was sort of steady on my feet, I stared at the building in front of me, trying to focus on it long enough to get my body moving in that direction. But something caught my attention, and the longer I stared at the bright moving lights, the more I tried to figure out what it was. Realization settled in, and I knew that it wasn't lights at all.

The building was on fire.

SIX
Dean

I didn't want to come to this damn banquet, but it was the captain's orders. The way he explained was that he wanted to "unify the departments."

We'd been working closely with the River Falls Fire Department—or RFFD for short—for a while now. Well, it started before I got here, but Dylan and I were the assigned detectives working the arsonist case. Over the past couple of months, a series of fires had been popping up all over town, away from the public. There hadn't been many, but it was enough to raise a red flag. The battalion chief suspected that it was arson, which was damn near impossible to solve. The only thing left at the scenes were gas cans with no prints, and you could get a gas can just about anywhere these days. Unless we found a receipt, we literally had nothing.

"How are you doing, son?" my father asked, clapping a hand down on my shoulder.

"I'm fine," I lied. I was far from fine. I'd been sipping on cheap beer all night, but I'd much rather be half-buried in a bottle of bourbon or even the Jack Daniels I had bought earlier to refill my liquor cabinet. I'd always hated coming to these sorts of things, and back when Wyatt was still alive, we'd always find an excuse to dip out early.

I brought the beer bottle to my lips to swallow the

emotion down. I fucking hated being around this many people for this long. It was always a constant reminder that he was gone. I wished they had something stronger than this piss water because then I'd be able to tolerate this banquet. Once I started seeing people leave though, I was gone. But the only person I saw leaving was my neighbor, who apparently was the photographer hired to take pictures. We managed to avoid each other, and that was fine by me.

"Sure. You know, Wyatt was like a son to me and—"

"I said I'm fine, Pop." My clipped tone caused my father to stop talking. "I don't want to talk about it."

My father clenched his jaw, and I knew he switched from being my father to being my captain, all with a look.

"Don't make me order you to talk to the district psychiatrist. I know you did the mandatory sessions in the city, but they don't know you like I do. Believe me, I will bench you if you don't start getting your shit together, Dean. I know that Wyatt's death is still taking its toll on you. Hell, your mother and I are still trying to cope with his loss. I brought you home because I thought it could help you. Don't think I don't know about the frequent visits to the bar and liquor stores. Your old captain and sergeant knew it too, and if it weren't for me bringing you back home, you wouldn't have a badge."

As much as it pissed me off being home, I understood why my father did it.

I was sinking and sinking fast.

Sometimes, I thought it was a good thing. I didn't think I deserved a second chance.

He pinched the bridge of his nose. "Dean, I can only help you if you want to be helped."

Before I could respond, someone shouted, "Fire," and all hell broke loose. The battalion chief led the firefights outside, while the police officers were making sure to get everyone else to safety. Chairs and tables were scraping across the floor as the guests of the first responders started panicking. A few glasses fell to the floor and broke when someone knocked into a table nearby. My father and I exchanged a glance and then started to follow everyone outside. He suddenly stopped, and I caught myself right before I ran into him.

"What happened to her?" he asked, "Is she alright?"

I glanced at the man in front of us holding a woman in his arms.

"I'm not sure. After she screamed that there was a fire, she passed out," the newly promoted lieutenant—Rhett, I thought his name was—said as he lifted my neighbor in his arms. She had blood running down her face, and it looked like her hands were scraped up. There was a woman standing next to them, close to tears. I'd seen her with Aubrey earlier; I didn't need to use my detective skills to figure out that they were friends.

"Baby, we have to get her to Kenna and Ford." The woman's voice was shaky and laced with concern.

"Yes, go!" my dad commanded, and Rhett turned abruptly, heading for the direction of the ambulance.

My dad spun around to face me. "I'm going to talk to the battalion chief. You grab McCormick and talk to the girl. She's a witness to this, and hopefully she saw something."

I nodded. As much as she annoyed me, I still had a job to do.

I walked outside, looking around for my partner, but something caught my attention.

A car alarm seemed to be going off in the back lot. I pulled my small flashlight out from my pocket and made my way over there, examining the ground and the cars, looking for evidence of what may have gone down out here.

There were a few bloody handprints on several of the cars, I guessed from where she stumbled and caught herself. I grabbed my phone and took a few photos. I went up further, toward the car where the alarm was still going off, and pointed my flashlight down at the front bumper.

"Oh yeah, she's definitely going to feel that," I murmured out loud. I took more crime scene photos, and when I knelt to get a closer look, some of her blonde hair was stuck inside the grille. I walked over to the driver side door, and saw a slim jim stuck in the window. Someone was trying to break in. Upon further investigation, I saw that they had succeeded because the door was unlocked. Opening it, I shined my flashlight around and didn't see anything out of the ordinary. The car was clean, so I popped the hood so I could turn off the alarm.

I had just shut the door when I heard footsteps quickly approaching and spun around, ready to grab my gun, but it was only Dylan.

"They got the fire out quickly. Chief Warren, Sergeant Miller, and your dad are all over there talking. They found a melted gas can but nothing more. Your dad sent me to find you, said there may be a witness?"

"Yeah. I'm not sure how helpful she's going be though," I told him, then pointed my flashlight down at the grille again.

"Ouch."

"Here, hold this light for me, will you?" I handed

Dylan the flashlight and popped the hood. "Shine it there."

He pointed it at the fuse box, and within a few moments, I turned the alarm off. Thank God too, because it was starting to give me a damn headache.

"Where's the witness?" Dylan asked, just as the hood slammed down. The ambulance roared to life and pulled out of the garage. Great, more alarms.

"Probably in there." I nodded toward the moving rig.

"Looks like we're headed to the hospital."

I huffed. "Looks like."

We made our way back to find Sergeant Miller to let him know we were headed to the hospital and informed him of what we found outside.

"Keep me posted," Serge said, then excused himself.

We walked back out to our cars, when a male's voice called out my name.

"Hey, Detective Holden!"

I turned and saw Rhett jogging toward me with a small bag in his hands.

"I'm glad I caught you before you left. Would you mind giving this to Chloe, my girlfriend?" he asked, handing me the sparkly little purse thing. "She left with Aubrey and forgot her purse with her phone in it."

"Sure," I replied, although I wanted to tell him that I wasn't his errand boy.

"Thanks, man. I appreciate it," he said and then stopped himself before he turned to leave. "Oh, and tell her to call me."

"Okay. Anything else?"

He shook his head. "Nah, I'm good, thanks."

I gave him a curt nod and then continued to my

truck. I tossed the big piece of glitter on a chain onto the passenger seat as I climbed in. Dylan was taking his own car and said he'd meet me there. At least I'd have a few minutes to myself before I had to interact with the population again.

SEVEN
Dean

When I got to the hospital, I sat in my truck for a few moments. I knew we wouldn't be able to see her right away, so a couple of minutes wouldn't hurt. I glanced down at the brown bag sitting on the floor in the passenger seat.

Gentleman Jack.

I didn't know what possessed me to grab that bottle instead of the black-label one I was looking at.

That's a lie, Holden.

I knew why. A blonde-haired, blue-eyed, snarky woman got under my skin for a moment, and I fucking let her. I didn't even like Gentleman Jack, but I chose it anyway just to be a dick. There was something about her that when she opened her mouth, she didn't give a shit what I'd been through; she would give it right back to me. She gave what she took, and if I wasn't careful, she could take all of me.

Shaking my head to get rid of those thoughts, I grabbed the chain of sparkle and made my way inside.

Walking into the emergency room started giving me flashbacks of *that* night. Except, the last time I was in one, I was being rolled in on a gurney. When the hallway split, I went one way, and Wyatt went the other in a body bag. It was a memory I tried to keep guarded away. Every time I was reminded of that night, guilt consumed me, and I

48

ended up drowning myself in alcohol. Of course, now I had a job to focus on, so I locked it all back up again and found Dylan waiting for me at the nurses' station.

"She's awake, but the doctor is checking her out now," he informed me. "He said he'd be out in a few minutes to give us an update."

"Okay," I answered, stepping off to the side and sitting down in a chair. Dylan sat down in the one beside me, and we waited. After about twenty minutes, a doctor was headed in our direction, so we both stood up.

About damn time.

"The patient is fine and is okay to go home. She has a small laceration on her forehead that the nurses cleaned and bandaged up. She also has a minor concussion, but I see no cause for concern," he explained to us. I felt an odd sense of relief wash over me for a split second. The feeling was gone the moment that it came. I ignored it and followed Dylan into her room.

"I know this cream we can put on it so it doesn't scar," Aubrey's friend Chloe said, being the doting friend. Aubrey gave her a small smile but didn't respond. Instead, her eyes met mine, then flicked over to Dylan.

"I take it you're here for my statement?" she asked, her voice raspy.

"Yeah, but if you're not feeling up to it, we can get it another time," Dylan told her.

Her blue eyes danced between us, and she sucked in a deep breath.

"No, I'm fine. We can talk." She paused, looking down at her hands folded in her lap.

Just as I was about to ask my first question, another woman came rushing into the room.

"Aubrey, are you okay?" she asked, giving Aubrey a

gentle hug. "Cassie texted me and said you were headed to the hospital."

"I guess we can give them a few more minutes," I said. My tone was sarcastic, maybe even a little annoyed.

The brown-haired woman turned to us, her face flushed. "Oh, I'm sorry. I didn't mean to interrupt."

"It's okay, Soph. This is Detective McCormick and his partner, Detective Holden," Aubrey answered, gesturing to us. I wondered how she knew my last name, but I did see her talking with my dad earlier, so it wouldn't surprise me if he told her.

"C'mon, Sophia, let's let them talk," Chloe said, reaching for her other friend. I handed the sparkly purse thing to her, and she thanked me before turning back to Aubrey. "We'll just be outside."

Aubrey nodded, and we waited for her friends to leave. She hugged her arms and ran her hands up and down them, and I noticed there was a slight bruise starting to form. It looked as if she was grabbed.

"How'd you get those bruises?" I asked, just to make sure I was right.

"What?" Aubrey stopped moving and glanced at her arms. "Oh."

"Why don't you start from the beginning," Dylan said, taking out his phone. "Do you mind if I record this?"

She shook her head. Once Dylan hit the Record button, she started talking.

"Well, I was walking toward my car when I thought I heard someone following me." Her voice started trembling, so she took in another deep breath and continued.

"Um, so, I started walking faster, you know. But that's when I heard the footsteps for sure. I was running after that."

"Was there anyone behind you?" I asked, and her eyes connected with mine.

They slowly filled with tears, and she quickly wiped them away as she nodded.

Dylan handed her a tissue. "Were you able to get a look at the guy?"

Aubrey wiped her eyes. "No. It all just happened so fast, you know. At first I was running, then I smacked into something...or someone...and I was thrown into a car."

"Why didn't you run toward the building full of cops?" I asked. "Or scream for help?"

"Dean," Dylan started to say, but both Aubrey and I ignored him.

"Don't you think I would have if I knew I could get there safely?" She glared at me. "I was already halfway across the parking lot when I looked to see someone following me, and by the time I turned around, it was too late."

"Why didn't you call out for help then?"

"Would you have heard me with the party going on inside?"

"Someone would have—" I started to say, but Dylan stepped in front of me. I have no idea where this anger was coming from. I wasn't even mad at her. Annoyed, hell yes, but not angry.

"Whoa, okay. Let's just all relax," he said, trying to ease the tension in the room. I pinched the bridge of my nose, trying to calm my temper. Deep down, I knew she was right.

Dylan cleared his throat and turned back to Aubrey. "Alright, so Aubrey, are you saying that you saw two people?"

"I hit my head pretty hard, but it would make sense

how someone got in front of me so fast, unless they were already there. And I'm pretty sure I saw two figures running away, but like I said, I hit my head pretty hard, so I'm not one hundred percent sure. I'm sorry, I can't really give you any more than that."

"That's okay. You just focus on feeling better," Dylan told her, hitting the Stop button on the recorder and slipping his phone back in his pocket.

"Thank you, Detectives," she murmured.

We walked back out to the waiting room and told her friends they could go back inside.

"Arsonists don't run in teams," Dylan whispered.

"I know."

"So, one of them had to be our guy."

"And the other was at the wrong place at the wrong time?" I asked, lifting a brow. "Someone tried breaking into that car. I guess they got spooked by Aubrey and whoever was chasing her."

"It's a possibility, but don't you think we should cross-reference everyone in attendance, including looking at Aubrey's statement."

"Yeah, we can look it over tomorrow," I said, wanting to be done with all this shit tonight. Although, somehow, a part of me knew that wasn't going to happen.

EIGHT
Aubrey

I took a deep breath after the detectives left the room. I was thankful for Dylan being here because Dean and I would have been at each other's throats. Him angrily berating me with questions irritated me, but somehow, I knew it wasn't me he was angry with. I didn't have time to dwell on that though because the girls came back in the room, promptly followed by the doctor. He gave strict instructions not to drive home tonight, so Sophia told him she would be taking me home. She was the only one of us with a car anyway because Chloe rode with me in the ambulance.

I felt alright minus the headache, so I would have been okay to drive home, but Sophia wouldn't allow that. She was the type to never break any rules, which I guessed was a good thing because she kept the rest of us on the right path. We'd all been trying, to no avail, to help her live a little, but she said she was content staying in and reading her books.

I got off the bed, and the girls walked with me out of the room. They offered me a wheelchair, but I politely declined. When we went past the nurses' station, I was surprised to see the detectives were still here, given how well that interview went. I thought for sure they would be long gone by now. When I said "they," I really meant Dean.

"Thank you so much again for coming," I told the girls when we stepped outside the emergency room.

"Are you kidding? I never would have let you go alone," Chloe responded, looping her arm through one of mine as Sophia did the same to my other.

"I called the Bistro and spoke to Cassie while you were talking to the detectives. She said she couldn't leave work until closing. She was going to come here, but they released you, so she's waiting for you at home," Sophia told me.

My heart swelled. I loved these girls with every fiber of my being. We always took care of each other.

I stopped suddenly, eyes going wide.

"Please tell me my camera is okay."

Chloe, whose face was full of concern, let out a chuckle. "Yes, girl. Your camera is safe and sound at the firehouse. Rhett found it with your purse in the parking lot unscathed."

A sigh of relief escaped my lungs. I had another camera, the one Nana had given me, that I could have used, but the one I was using tonight was the digital one I used for my business. The other was for taking film photos.

"Aubrey!" I heard my name being called, and we all turned to see Dylan running toward us. "You forgot your phone."

I grabbed it from him, thankful it wasn't broken because it had been in my back pocket. I took it out when I got to the hospital and set it on the table. "Thank you."

"No problem."

"Alright, let's get you home," Chloe said, gently pulling me around.

"You mean, take me to get my car," I responded.

Sophia clicked her tongue. "The doctor gave us orders not to let you drive home."

"The both of you live all the way across town."

"So?" Chloe and Sophia said in unison.

"Detective Holden can take you home."

Dylan's words halted me in my tracks, and out of the corner of my eye, Dean stopped walking too.

"Come again?" I heard his gruff voice say.

Dylan looked a tad nervous but then continued on. "You guys live in the same apartment complex. You're going there now anyway. It makes the most sense."

Sophia and Chloe were looking back and forth between the three of us, and I swore I could smell smoke coming from their ears from the gears turning in their heads. I knew I would be questioned later about this exchange. Cassie was the only one who knew who Dean was, so this whole thing was news to them.

Dean looked like he wanted to punch Dylan. He glanced over at me, and I hoped he would say no. I could only handle him in small doses, and I'd already had mine for the day. I didn't need to be stuck in a car with him.

"Fine, whatever," he finally said, and my shoulders sagged.

On the way over to his truck, Chloe leaned in close and whispered in my ear. "You've been holding out on us. He's hot."

I rolled my eyes. "He's an ass."

"He's an ass that is attracted to you."

I scoffed. "Absolutely not. Never going to happen."

"Hey, Soph, when you walked into her hospital room, you got smacked in the face with sexual tension, right?" Chloe asked Sophia, who grinned.

"Oh yes, it was like this thick fog of tension. I could hardly breathe."

Chloe looked back at me. "See?"

"You guys suck, and I hate you," I said as we finally reached the passenger-side door of his truck. Chloe opened the door while Sophia helped me slide into the seat. I said goodbye and promised to text them later. I buckled myself in and glanced down at my phone. I had texts and a missed call from Cassie, and another text from the same unknown number, so I opened it.

Unknown: Why are you ignoring me?

I think this person has the wrong number. I texted it back saying just that and blocked it. I didn't want to take the conversation any further than that. I scrolled through the texts from Cassie, all asking if I was okay and out of the hospital yet. I sent her a quick text letting her know that I was fine and that I'd be home soon. I looked at the time, and I knew that the one person I wanted to talk to would be asleep, but I ended up calling her anyway.

*Hi, you've reached Nana Daniels and little bee. We can't come to the phone right now, so leave a message and we will call you back! *Beep**

"Hi, Nana, it's me. I miss you! Call me!" I tried to sound cheerful in the message. I was alright, and I didn't want to worry her, but I just needed to hear her voice. I hadn't heard from her in over a week. Then I remembered that she told me she was going down to the Florida Keys because a friend of hers owned a house in Islamorada. I would try her cell phone tomorrow. It wasn't uncommon to go weeks at a time without talking, so even if she didn't call me back, I'd hear from her eventually. When I left for college, she retired early and started traveling. I loved getting postcards from her from all the places that she had been.

Dean turned the AC on, and I let out a moan involuntarily. I felt overheated and sticky, so the cold air felt amazing. I closed my eyes and leaned my head back on the seat. This wasn't so bad. If he continued to keep his mouth shut, I could tolerate the ride home. After a few minutes, I found myself studying him.

He had the perfect profile, and if I liked him, I'd ask if he'd let me take his picture. His sharp, intense features would look amazing in black and white. He reminded me of a noir hero—perfectly flawed. I hated to admit that he was good-looking, but he was. His eyes had a sadness behind them. I knew the look well because my eyes had told a similar story. Where there is sadness, there is pain behind it, and Dean was drowning in it.

"You know, if you took a picture it would last longer." His husky voice brought me to my senses.

"I'd love to," I quipped back. "Then I'd have something to remind myself that you can keep your mouth shut."

He glanced over at me, lifting a brow, and I could swear that his lips tipped up ever so slightly before he turned back to look at the road. It was blissful silence after that.

We finally arrived back to the apartment complex, and as we were walking together, I felt like I was being watched again. It was the same feeling I got earlier and when I was

57

in the Camera Shop parking lot. Goose bumps covered my skin, and my heart started beating faster. I stopped and started to scan the parking lot, even though I didn't think that I would actually see anything.

"What are you doing?" Dean asked.

"I—" I started to say that I felt like I was being watched but decided against it. "Uh, nothing. Never mind."

He held the door open, and I stepped inside, muttering a thanks to him. We got onto the elevator together, and the air got thick. Of course, my mind went straight to Chloe's comment, and my gaze connected with Dean's in our reflections. Was he feeling it too? Or was it just me? No, it was just me. This stupid concussion was making me imagine things.

He held my gaze for a moment longer before I broke it. It was taking forever to get to the seventh floor, and when the door finally opened, I breathed a sigh of relief. He got out first, and I followed behind him. I made it to my door first, and my mouth started moving, and words were coming out before I could stop them.

"Dean," I said, and he turned to me. "Thank you for bringing me home."

He stared at me for a moment. "You're welcome."

He faced his door again, but there was one thing I needed to say, and I'd blame it on the concussion in the morning. "Hey, Dean."

His jaw clenched as he looked at me again with raised eyebrows.

"You won't hurt forever."

I left it at that and walked inside, shutting my apartment door behind me. Cassie got up from the couch and came over to hug me. I told her that I was okay and I'd join her after I changed my clothes and washed my face. Once I was finished, I went back out to the living room. She opened her blanket, and I sat down on the opposite end of the sofa. She covered us back up, and we picked up where she was on *Gossip Girl*.

NINE

Dean

$\mathcal{I}$ stood there dumbfounded, staring down the hallway at her door. How in the hell did she even know? I mean, she and Dylan seemed to be the best of pals, so maybe he'd told her about Wyatt. I would've questioned how Dylan even knew, but I knew my father, and so Dylan had probably been debriefed. I'd had more than one person call me out on my attitude, but no one had ever called me out for *that*. She saw right through me, and that…stirred something deep inside of me.

Wyatt would have kicked my ass knowing how much of a dick I'd been to this woman.

But he wasn't here, and I was still a dick.

I unlocked my door, then slammed it shut with my foot. I changed out of my suit, then went into the kitchen to grab a whiskey glass from the cabinet. It was empty. I happened to glance down and saw all my dishes sitting in the sink, waiting for me to put them in the dishwasher.

You need to pull yourself together, Holden.

Whatever. That wasn't going to happen tonight.

I grabbed the Gentleman Jack and took a hefty swig from the bottle. The liquid was smooth going down my throat, and moments later, I started to get this warm feeling creeping up through my veins. That was the sign I was looking for, because in about thirty minutes, I'd start feeling nothing, and that was the plan. I sat down on my couch and turned the TV on. Some fishing channel was on, and I sagged back on the couch, not able to take my eyes off the screen.

"YOU THINK IT'S TRUE? THE STORY THAT PRICE KEEPS *telling us?" Wyatt asked as we pulled up to my parents' lake house.*

I glanced over at him. "You talking about the car crash that killed the two parents but left that little girl alive unscathed?"

"Yeah, that would be the one."

I shrugged, getting out of his truck, and reached in the back to grab my fishing gear. "I think so. I mean, he tells it just about every time we roll up on a crash site. Especially ones involving kids."

"I guess we all have that one case that really sticks with us," Wyatt said, grabbing his gear before we started walking up to the house.

I opened the front door, set my duffle bag down, and carefully leaned my fishing pole against the wall.

"Yeah, I'm sure that crash last night will be that case for Stover. He was white as a ghost when we pulled up." I grabbed two beers from the case and put the rest in the fridge. I handed one to Wyatt as he sat down in a kitchen chair. I popped the cap off and took a swig before continuing. "I feel bad for the man. He just lost his partner less than two months ago, and then he rolls up on a wreck like that."

I let out a low whistle. We'd all seen our fair share of accidents, but last night had to have been the worst I'd seen in a while: drunk driver kills a family of six, and the driver walks

*away. I read the report, and I'd have hated to be the first one
on the scene.*

*"Didn't he just get back on the job too?" Wyatt asked,
taking a sip of his beer.*

I nodded. "I think so."

*There was a moment of silence before Wyatt spoke up
again.*

*"If anything ever happens to me —" he started to say, but
I shook my head, cutting him off.*

"Don't go down that road, Coleman."

*"I know, I know. It's all a part of the job though—being
prepared. So, Dean, if anything ever happens to me, just do
me a solid and don't shut people out."*

I scoffed. "I don't shut people out."

*Wyatt chuckled. "You're so full of shit. I know you better
than you know yourself. The first thing you do is shut people
out, and the only time you get to talking is if you're drunk or I
force it out of you."*

"You got me there."

*"Yeah, so, like I said, if something ever happens to me,
don't shut people out. You won't hurt forever, man."*

*I downed the rest of my beer and stepped forward, clap-
ping a hand down on his shoulder. "Fine. But nothing is
going to happen to you. I got your six, brother. Always have,
and always will. Now, let's fill the cooler with some brew and
go catch tonight's dinner."*

A SOFT KNOCK ON MY DOOR PULLED ME FROM MY
thoughts, and I almost knocked the whiskey bottle on the
floor but ended up catching it at the last moment. I shuf-

fled over and opened the door, and lo and behold, it was Dylan.

"What do you want, McCormick?" I asked, lifting a brow.

"Just wanted to come by and check on my partner," he said, pushing his way inside.

"Make yourself at home," I mumbled, shutting the door.

Dylan saw the whiskey bottle sitting on the coffee table and lifted it up. "Nice, Gentleman Jack. Got a glass?"

"You like Gentleman Jack?" I asked, not really sure why I was surprised.

"Did you think I liked fruity drinks?" Dylan quirked a brow, his lips tipping up. "Don't answer that."

I held my hands up, then walked back into my kitchen and cleaned two glasses.

"Why are you here?" I asked, pouring the amber liquid into a tumbler and handing him one.

He held up a case file. "I wanted to go over the arsonist file."

"And this couldn't have waited until office hours?"

"Nah." He sat down on my couch and opened up the folder.

I sat down next to him and took one look at the file. The first page was Aubrey's statement of the events, and that brought up what she'd said to me earlier. I set that moment to the side for now and looked at the paper underneath her statement.

"What's this?"

"Oh, that's a list of everyone who was in attendance at the banquet tonight," Dylan answered. "I stopped back at the firehouse and talked to the battalion chief, Nash

Warren. He's a good guy, by the way. Anyway, like I said, he gave us a list of the firefighters who were there."

"Nice work, McCormick." I was a tad impressed by his initiative. "But again, couldn't this have waited until the morning?"

"I had nothing better to do, and it looks like you didn't either."

"Don't you have a girlfriend you can go nag or something?"

"Not yet," Dylan said, then took a sip from his tumbler.

"Well, there's a girl next door for you," I said.

"I told you, she's cute but not my type."

"What is your type? Actually, you know what, don't answer that. I really don't care," I gruffed out, taking a swig from my tumbler. Then I remembered the shit he pulled earlier. He was right when he said it didn't make sense for her friends to bring her home when I was headed back here anyway. It was the only reason why I agreed to it.

Sure it was.

Whatever. I was an asshole, but I was an asshole with common sense.

"Oh, and by the way, if you ever pull a stunt like that again, I will have you mopping the floors and cleaning the shitters," I warned.

Dylan gave me a half-hearted grin. "Yes, sir."

TEN

Aubrey

$\mathcal{A}$ constant buzzing sound pulled me from sleep, and I threw my arm out toward the coffee table, smacking it against the hard surface until I found my phone. I noticed that I had a few text messages and a missed call from Sophia. I opened our group chat and wasn't surprised at what I read.

Cassie: Aww, look at our sleeping beauty

Cassie: *Picture of me sleeping*

Chloe: She's adorable! And who says she's not photogenic?

Sophia: She does… which clearly is a lie.

Chloe: I wish I looked that good sleeping, sometimes I scare myself when I wake up.

Sophia: That's simply not true, Chlo!

Chloe: Thanks babes, feel free to stop by the boutique and pick out anything you want!

Cassie: I think you're always beautiful. *kissing emoji*

Chloe: *blushing emoji* shucks. You can come too!

Chloe: Anyway, enough about me, how's our girl?

Cassie: She's doing well, and, as always, is in good spirits.

Sophia: That's a good sign. Please remind her to schedule an appointment with her Dr

Chloe: Leave it to Soph to get all mom like. *eye roll emoji* *laughing emoji*

Cassie: *laughing emoji*

Sophia: What?! I can't help it.

Cassie: We know, it's one of the many reasons why we love you. *heart emoji*

Sophia: Love you guys too! I've got to get to class, but Aubrey, you better call me later! *heart emoji*

I smiled to myself as I sat up on the couch, the smell of coffee filling my nose, and turned around just in time to see Cassie walking back over with two mugs in her hands.

"Good morning, sunshine," she said, handing me a mug, then sitting down on the opposite end of the couch. She tucked her legs in beside mine and pulled the blanket down. "How are you feeling?"

I took a small sip of coffee, pondering her question. I wiggled my toes and took an inventory of my body. "I feel fine other than a slight headache. Nothing that some aspirin and a hot shower can't fix."

I wasn't lying; I did feel much better. I no longer felt dizzy, which I guess was a good sign.

"I should be good for my shift tonight," I said, checking the time on my watch. "Oh crap, I should start getting ready."

I started to get up, but Cassie stopped me. "Sit your ass back down, missy. It's been handled. Claudia and I are covering for you. She will work until four because she has to pick her daughter up by five, and I will be working from four to six to cover the rest of your shift, then popping over to the bar to finish mine. Jared will be fine by himself for two hours."

I sunk back down on the couch as she explained the plan, and I wasn't sure if I should have felt guilty for making her work longer than she had to or grateful that she thought to do that.

"You didn't have to do that," I told her, but my heart warmed when she smiled at me.

"I know I didn't have to, but you're my best friend, and you had a bad night. Besides, I know for a fact you would have done the same for me," Cassie replied. She had me there—if our roles were reversed and it was her that got thrown headfirst into a bumper, I totally would have taken her shifts. I couldn't mix a good drink to save my life, but Cassie could. In fact, Cassie was amazing at anything in the kitchen. I've told her she should open her own restaurant, but she said she didn't want her favorite hobby to become a job. Of course, I would argue with her that if it was something you loved, it wouldn't really feel like a job. It's how I felt about photography.

"What do you say I whip us up some french toast with fresh strawberries?" she asked, smiling gleefully.

I placed my hand on my heart. "You spoil me, Cassie Newton."

"I know." She shrugged playfully.

Before either of us could say anything else, there was a soft knock at my door.

"Oh, that's probably Ford. I texted him and asked if he wanted to stop by before his shift." Cassie got up from the couch and answered the door. Ford walked in, pressing a kiss on her cheek, then looked over at me.

He waved. "Hey, Aubrey, how are you feeling?"

I gave him a small smile. "Hi, Ford. I'm feeling better today, just a small headache, but other than that I'm good."

"Good."

I slowly got up and walked over to the kitchen table and sat down in a chair.

"I'm making french toast. Would you like some?" Cassie asked, walking into the kitchen.

Ford smiled, and that was the first time I noticed he had a slight dimple in his cheek. "I would love some."

Oh no. He said the *L* word. Even though he didn't tell her he loved her, she didn't like that word. It was the word that made her run for the hills. To my surprise though, she smiled back at him, and it was one of her genuine smiles, not one she plastered on when she was ready to dump someone.

"Great, have a seat," she said, and he took a seat next to me at the table.

We were all talking and having a good time when my phone buzzed. I picked it up, and it was a message from an unknown number. *Weird.* At least it wasn't the same number from last night. I opened the text, and I felt all the blood drain from my face.

Unknown: Why did you block me?

I dropped my phone down as I stood up, staring at it as if it would come to life any second.

"What, Aubrey? What is it?" Cassie asked, voice laced with concern. It seemed irrational to think this was Ray. But I couldn't help but let my mind wander there. He would send me messages similar to this if he thought I was ignoring him.

He's still in jail. He's still in jail. He's still in jail.

Panic started to set in, and I started having doubts. What if he wasn't in jail? No, he would be on parole, and he wouldn't be allowed to leave the county. He didn't even know where I was. Maybe this was just a prank, although I didn't think any of my friends would do this. Soak all my bras and panties in water and put them in the freezer, sure, but not this.

"Aubrey." Ford placed his hand on my arm, and I jumped away, momentarily stuck in another time.

"COME HERE, BITCH." RAY GRABBED MY ARM SO forcefully it almost came out of its socket. He knocked me onto the ground and got on top of me. "What did I say about talking to that guy?"

Smack.

My face stung where is his hand had just connected to my cheek. Tears welled up in my eyes as I stared up at him, wondering why he was doing this. That guy was just my lab partner, and I was supposed to be working with him on a project.

He pulled his hand back again, and I covered my hands over my head and curled up into the fetal position.

"I'm sorry, please, Ray, I'm sorry!" I cried out, hoping that he would calm down. "Please, I didn't mean to. I won't do it again, I'm sorry."

Painfully long minutes passed by until I felt his body lie gently on mine. His hot breath that smelled of marijuana and cigarettes danced across my neck as if it were waiting to puncture my skin if I moved the wrong way.

"Bree, baby. I didn't mean it. I'm sorry, baby, I didn't mean to hit you. I'll get you some flowers. You like flowers, right? I promise I won't do it again." He pressed gentle kisses on my cheek, and I had to swallow the bile that was rising in

my throat. Ray was filled with rage and empty promises; I knew better than to hold him to any of it.

I PULLED MYSELF TOGETHER BEFORE I GOT TRAPPED in a long-lost memory.

"I'm sorry," I said, then excused myself from the kitchen. I went to my room and shut the door behind me, taking in calming breaths. I started pacing. My body felt hot, my throat felt dry, and it was like I wanted to crawl out of my own skin. I tried shaking my hands to rid myself of the anxious energy. I hadn't had any of those memories surface in a long time. I guessed the trauma from last night triggered it, along with the texts from a number I didn't recognize. It was possible someone I didn't know had my number; I did leave business cards anywhere I could so I could get my name out there.

Yeah, that's all it is.

Once I came to that conclusion, I started to relax a little. If Ray had been released, Nana would have called me. Nana's house phone number was the only one they had on file because we agreed that after I left for college, I'd put it all behind me. After a few more deep breaths, I emerged from my room and walked back out into the kitchen, only to find it empty. I started to wonder where they went, but as I went to grab my phone, Cassie walked back inside, and she was white as a ghost.

ELEVEN
Aubrey

Setting my panic to the side, I rushed over to Cassie. She was in a trance as I guided her over to the couch. I'd never seen her like this before, and it honestly scared me. I sat her down, then took the seat next to her. Her eyes were cast forward, as if she was lost in thought.

"Cass?" I waved my hand in front of her face. "What happened?"

"I didn't even know he was back," she whispered, ignoring my question.

"Who was back?" I asked, trying to get more information out of her. "Who are you talking about?"

"It's been what? Ten years?" her eyes flicked to mine. I wiped a tear from her cheek with my sleeve as she continued. "We haven't spoken in so long. I—I didn't even know he was back."

"Cassie, who are you talking about?"

"D-Dylan. He's back."

I blinked. Dylan was the guy she told me she once loved. She never opened up and told me exactly what happened with them.

"Where did you see him?"

"In the lobby after I came back inside from walking Ford out. He walked right out of the elevator." She paused, eyes going wide. "Oh God, and he even lives here? How have I not seen him before?"

I shrugged, not sure what to say to that. Instead, I asked, "You were neighbors, right?"

"Yes. His parents, the McCormicks, and my parents are best friends."

I did a double take. "I'm sorry, did you just say McCormick?"

"Yes." Cassie looked at me. "Why?"

I sighed, kicking myself in the ass for not making the connection sooner. "I've met him. He's a detective with RFPD. He doesn't live here, but his partner—our neighbor Dean—does."

"You what!" Cassie shrieked, jumping up from the couch. "You knew he was here and didn't tell me?"

"I didn't know that Dylan was your Dylan!" I said, and she opened her mouth but closed it. I'd never even seen a picture of him before, that's how much their situation hurt her.

"I never did tell you his last name, did I?" Cassie sagged her shoulders.

"No, you kept that a secret." When it came to Dylan, she was very tight-lipped about him. I never held that against her, and neither did the other girls. It was her story, and when the time was right, she would tell it.

She frowned. "I just...never thought I'd see him again."

"How come?" I asked.

Cassie was silent for a moment, her features telling me she was contemplating telling me, but then she shook her head. "You know what? It doesn't matter. I'm with Ford, and I'm happy now."

I lifted a brow, confused about the sudden change in

her tone. Before I could respond any further, she jumped up off the couch and announced she was going to take a shower. I started cleaning up the mess in the kitchen, it seemed like we weren't getting our french toast after all. Worrying about Cassie helped calm my erratic nerves; it put my focus on someone else instead of me. Plus, Dylan was here, and Ray wasn't, so I really didn't have anything to worry about anyway.

I got a shower after Cassie, careful not to mess with the bandage by my hairline. That was a reminder that I needed to call my doctor today to follow up. Once I was dressed, Cassie dropped me off at the firehouse before she went to work so I could grab my camera, purse, and my car. She was oddly quiet the whole time, which wasn't like her, but I guessed it was from seeing Dylan.

"Hey, there she is!" Rhett said as he saw me walking up toward the garage.

I felt all the blood rush to my face as I took in the gorgeous sight in front of me. All the firemen at the house were shirtless as they washed the trucks, water glistening down their biceps and six-pack abs. My finger was ready to start snapping photos, to capture this moment on film.

It truly was a sight to behold.

I smiled at Rhett. "Here I am."

"How are you feeling?"

"Great now that I'm witnessing this." I gestured to the guys behind Rhett.

He laughed. "You've been hanging around Chloe too long."

"She's a terrible influence," I joked.

"Don't I know it." He smiled. "Anyway, you here for your stuff?"

I nodded. "Yeah."

"Nash has it in his office. Walk through those doors, hang a right, and it's the office straight back. You can't miss it," Rhett explained. I thanked him, and with one last look at the sexy men, I went inside. I took a right and went straight back to Nash's office where he was sitting down at his desk, filling out paperwork.

I knocked softly, and his head jerked up. "Hi, Chief, I'm sorry to interrupt."

He waved his hands. "You weren't interrupting. Come on in. I take it you're here for your things?"

I nodded as he got up from his chair and went over to a file cabinet.

"How are you feeling?" Nash unlocked the bottom drawer, and I felt relieved when he pulled out my camera bag. He handed it to me.

"Thank you so much. And I'm doing okay, just a small headache."

Nash smiled, but it didn't reach his eyes. "Well, I'm glad you're feeling better." I gave him a small smile as he continued. "It's the least I could do. Rhett made sure nothing was broken or stolen. Then I locked it up in here."

I thanked him again, and before I turned to leave, I stopped. "Do you by any chance know whose car I was thrown into last night?" I just started running last night, and it was dark, so I didn't have a clue where I ended up... or rather whose car I ended up being thrown into.

He made a face. "About that..."

I gave him a confused look as he scrubbed a hand down the back of his neck.

That's odd. Why does he seem a little nervous about that?

"How upset are they?" I asked. "Is the damage that bad?"

I started to wonder how much I would need to pull from my savings.

"The damage isn't bad, but I don't think the owner has seen the damage yet."

"How could they not have seen the damage yet. I—" I was smacked in the face when it finally hit me. I turned abruptly and left the office, storming outside toward my car, with Nash hot on my heels. As soon as I got close enough, I realized that I was right. The car I was thrown into was mine.

How ironic.

"How fucked-up is this?" I started laughing like a crazy person. Of all the things that could have happened, this was the one I least expected. I guessed fate had a sense of humor last night and thought it would have been funny that I would hit my head on my own car. Nash stood there awkwardly, rubbing the back of his neck again. Probably contemplating calling Ford over here to take me back to the hospital.

I calmed down. "I'm sorry. It's just..." I trailed off, not knowing what to say.

"It's okay." He came over and inspected the damage. "It's just cosmetic damage that will probably only cost about three hundred bucks. But a buddy of mine owns a shop—I could make a call, explain what happened. He'd fix it for free."

I was relieved. "That would be amazing, thank you. But I wouldn't let him do it for free."

"I figured. How about I give him a call and tell him to call you? You two can discuss payment options."

I smiled. "Sure, that sounds great. Do you need my number?"

"No, I can get it from Rhett. Oh, and if Bill gives you

a hard time, tell me, and I'll kick his ass for trying to hustle a woman."

I chuckled. "Noted."

I thanked Nash again and left. I really appreciated what he was doing for me. The guys at the firehouse were a family, and they took care of their own. I was family by association with Rhett, since I was best friends with Chloe. It was the same with Sophia and Cassie as well.

I stopped at Starbucks drive-thru to grab a coffee before I went back home and started editing the banquet photos. Rhett knew how much my camera meant to me, so I knew he wouldn't lie about it being okay. It gave me comfort to know that all my pictures were fine. I was waiting in line when my phone rang, and I answered it without looking at the caller ID.

"Hello, this is Aubrey," I said cheerfully, in case it was a client. There was silence on the other end of the line. "Hello?"

The phone beeped in my ear, letting me know that whoever it was hung up; I guessed it was a bad signal. I shrugged it off because it was my turn to pay. I handed cash to the clerk as she handed me my iced coffee, because who wants to drink hot coffee on a hot day? I thanked her and told her to keep the change as I drove off.

My phone rang again. "Hello, this is Aubrey!"

Silence again. I glanced down at my phone and saw it was an unknown number, but before I could bring the phone back up to my ear, they hung up again. My mood shifted from happy to nervous in an instant.

What if it was the same number that sent the text this morning?

My body started to overheat again, and I was thankful that I was pulling into my apartment complex because I felt another panic attack coming on. I parked and sat in my car, with the AC on blast, taking in deep, calming breaths. I didn't know why I was letting an unknown number get the best of me. I'd gotten plenty of calls from numbers I didn't recognize, but this one seemed off...and persistent. I pulled up the number, and my heart rate kicked up into high gear. It was the same number.

You're safe. You're okay. He's still in jail. He can't get to you.

I repeated those words until I was calm enough to walk inside. I locked the dead bolt and shut all the blinds. It seemed silly to do so because I was on the seventh floor of a twelve-story building. Unless someone scaled the walls or used a drone, the chances of someone watching me through my windows were slim. I knew I was being paranoid, but it would ease my anxiety, and I was looking to escape.

Even though I had put Ray's abuse behind me, it didn't mean I wasn't still afraid from time to time. I picked up my phone, and dialed Nana's cell but it went straight to voicemail. She must have forgotten to charge it. She hates it, and the only reason she has one was to keep in contact with me. This wouldn't be the first time she's forgotten to charge the damn thing. Or it's possible she left it home. She's done that too.

Everything is fine. You're just being paranoid.

There was one thing that I knew I could get lost in and forget the world entirely. So, I grabbed my laptop and set myself up on the couch. I popped the SD card in the correct slot on my computer, placed my phone in Do Not Disturb mode, and dove straight into editing.

TWELVE
Dean

*A*fter a long-ass day of going over everyone in attendance at the firehouse banquet a few nights ago, Dylan and I were ready to update Sergeant Miller on our progress. We were able to clear everyone, although Aubrey had a sealed file that we couldn't get into because she was a minor when it was filed.

"This is impressive work, gentlemen," Sergeant Miller said as he looked over the paperwork. "Have you gotten in touch with the precinct to look at that sealed file?"

"Yes, sir," I said. "I went through the proper networks; we should hear back soon."

He nodded, handing the file back to me. "Good. Keep me updated."

"Will do," I replied, then went back to my office that I shared with Dylan to lock the file in the cabinet.

Dylan and I started to pack up to head out when there was a knock that pulled my attention to the doorway where my father stood.

"Hi, Captain," Dylan said, standing up straighter. It was something that he always did when my father came around. I guessed it was a military thing, because he always seemed to do it whenever someone of a higher rank came to talk to him.

"You two going to Monroe's tonight?" he asked, and both Dylan and I shook our heads. "Well, you should.

One of the firefighters was injured during a house fire today. He's in stable condition, but they're raising money tonight for his family."

"Was it arson?" I asked, although I doubted it.

My father shook his head. "No. The cause of the fire is still under investigation, but Chief Warren suspects it was because of the electrical wiring in the house. Thankfully, no one was home when the fire started."

"That's good to hear," Dylan commented, and I agreed.

"Yes, it is. Hopefully, I'll see you two there."

My father didn't even wait for a reply, not that he needed one. It came out like a suggestion, but I knew he meant it as a command.

"Well, I was going to ask what you were getting into tonight, but I think I have a pretty good idea," Dylan said as he locked his desk up. I think it was safe to say that Dylan had caught on to my father's persuasiveness.

"I'm only going for one drink and to put money in the boot," I answered, locking up my desk. "Then I'm getting the hell out of there."

I didn't mind helping a fellow first responder; we did it all the time back in the city. I just didn't feel like having to make small talk with anyone, and I knew going to Monroe's, there would be a lot of it.

"Honestly, same."

I eyed Dylan for a moment. He had been acting strange since he left my place the other day. Not that I knew the kid well, but he didn't seem like his usual talkative self, which was fine by me as I preferred the silence. He wasn't bringing it up, and I wasn't going to ask him about it, so I left it at that. We walked outside, and Dylan veered off to the left to head toward his car. He said he needed to get home and take care of his dog, Moose. It was still too early, so I decided to head home first to shower and change before going to Monroe's.

As I passed Aubrey's apartment, I remembered the sealed file. My instinct was telling me that what was in that file wasn't going to help us with the arsonist case. It was going to be yet another dead end, but still, we needed to rule her out. Not that I even thought that she would be setting fires; she was too nice for that. I honestly didn't think that woman had a mean bone in her curvy little body. Snarky, yes, but mean? Hell no.

I showered quickly, and once I was dressed, I left my apartment and headed over to Monroe's. I parked my truck in the back and walked inside. The place wasn't too crowded, but from the looks of the set on stage, it would be soon. I walked over to where Chief Warren was with his brother, Noah, and a few other firefighters.

"Thanks for coming, Detective," he said, holding his hand out.

I slapped my hand in his. "No problem. How's your guy?"

"He's got some third-degree burns and smoke inhalation, but the doctors are saying he's going to make a full recovery."

"That's good to hear." I reached into my back pocket and pulled out a fifty-dollar bill. "Where's the boot?"

He set out a rubber boot on the bar top, and I put the money inside. "I appreciate it, man. Thanks. Oh, first round is on me."

I gave him a half-hearted smile, said thanks, and made my way over to a quieter spot at the bar. I sat down and flagged Manny over.

"Well, look who it is," Manny tossed a towel on his

shoulder. "I'm *so* glad you decided to grace me with your presence again."

"Yeah, it's good to see you too, Manny," I replied as he stood right in front of me.

"You know, I'm a little disappointed you haven't been in here since you moved back. I thought we were friends."

Wow. Actually, I wasn't even a little bit surprised. This was what happened in River Falls; people knew when you were leaving, and they also knew when you were back.

"I'm sorry—"

"Save it, Holden," Manny said with a tone that made me feel guilty, but when I glanced up at him, he had a grin on his face. "You can make it up to me by serving your goodies for my calendar."

"What?"

"Babe, will you stop trying to get other men to pose nude for you? I'm right here, you know," I heard a male's voice say to my right. I looked over and saw one of the firefighters lean over and meet Manny halfway for a kiss over the bar top.

"Ollie, straight men like to have calendars of swimsuit models with their breasts and vajayjays out. Me, I like my men with huge guns and long fire hos—"

"Shh!" Ollie—or Oliver Abbott; I recognized him from the background checks—cut him off with his fingers pressed on Manny's lips. "We can finish this conversation later."

Manny pouted. "Alright, but as long as I can have your fire hose—"

I cleared my throat...loudly.

They turned to look at me, and from the looks on their faces, it was almost as if they had forgotten I was here.

81

"That better be a promise," Manny pointed two fingers at his eyes, then aimed them at Oliver.

"Have you ever doubted me?" Oliver winked before turning around to go stand over by the other firefighters.

"He's so dreamy," Manny cooed.

"I'm happy for you, Man," I said to him. I meant that too. I remembered back when we were kids, Wyatt and I always used to stick up for him. We hated bullies, and they knew not to mess with us. It didn't matter to us who Manny liked, and we made sure it didn't matter to the other kids too.

"Thanks, Dean. What can I get you?"

"I'll just take a beer."

"Bottle or tap?"

"Whatever you got on draft is fine. I won't be here long."

Manny opened his mouth to say something but then closed it. He knew better than to bring up Wyatt right now. He grabbed a glass, walked over to the beer tap, and filled it up, then set it down on a napkin in front of me.

"You should stay to watch the band," he said, wiping down the counter.

"Since when does Monroe's have open mic night?" I asked, taking a swig of beer.

Manny huffed. "Since I need to keep this bar afloat. This bar has been in my family for generations, and they have been slowly losing business because the university kids are going to the nightclubs. Ollie and I talked about doing theme nights to bring in new customers."

I knew that the bar had been in Manny's family, but I didn't think they'd lost business. This was a college town, so kids would go anywhere for a cheap drink. Not that Monroe's had cheap drinks, but it was one of many stops they did as they barhopped. There were only really four places to go to drink around here. There was the bar at the Bistro, but that was high-end shit, Monroe's, the nightclub down on Sixth Street, and then a speakeasy-type bar that you needed a reservation to get into. Monroe's was more of a western-style bar, which only attracted the older generation and the first responders.

"One of my girlfriends suggested an open mic night actually," he told me just as the bell dinged on the door, and I glanced up to see Aubrey walking in with her friends. "Ah, there she is now. Excuse me."

I watched as he walked over to her and gave her a hug and kiss on the cheek. He did the same for her other friends. I recognized Chloe and Sophia, but I was drawing a blank on the redhead. I knew that was her roommate though. The door opened again, and Dylan walked in. I noticed he and the redhead exchange a tense glance, but I looked away and focused my attention back on my beer. I was going to nurse this until my father arrived, and then I would dip out.

I felt someone take the seat next to me.

"How long do we have to stay?" Dylan asked, and I could hear a strain in his voice. He flagged Manny down for a beer.

I shrugged. "Long enough to say hi to the captain. Whenever he decides to show his face."

"Hopefully he shows up soon."

"Not soon enough."

We both sat in silence, watching the bar fill with more police and firefighters. My ears kept zoning in on a woman's laughter, and every time I glanced over at the source, it was Aubrey, smiling and laughing with her friends. The last time I saw her was when she was in the hospital. It wasn't like I was trying to avoid her; I was just busy. I let my eyes linger on her for a moment. Her honey-blonde hair fell in soft waves past her shoulders, and her blue eyes sparkled in the dimly lit space. Her smile...it was radiant, enough to make any man fall to their knees. I knew that if Wyatt were here, he'd already have us over there talking with those women. He'd leave Aubrey alone, knowing damn well I was a goner for a blonde-haired, blue-eyed girl.

What the fuck am I thinking?

You don't deserve her.

Shaking those thoughts from my head, I took a long drag of my beer. I was thankful to be rid of thoughts of Aubrey when Manny got up on a small platform in the front end of the bar.

"Ladies and gents, let's give a warm River Falls welcome to Crimson Rhythm!" Manny shouted into the mic, and applause erupted in the bar. The band got onstage, and they started playing a song that was a mix of blues, rock, and a hint of jazz.

Dylan leaned over to me. "They're pretty good," he said as he watched them play. I started to get lost in the music, but something else caught my attention.

Aubrey.

I let myself really look at her, and I found that I couldn't take my eyes off her. The way she moved around, taking pictures of the band, like it was second nature to her. Every now and then, she would bob her head along with the music. She was in her own little world, and part of me wanted to be in it; to get to know her in ways I didn't deserve. But the bigger part of me needed to keep her away. I was damaged goods. I'd always be damaged goods. I hated that she was digging her way under my skin, and she didn't even know it. Hell, I didn't even realize it until now.

You didn't want to realize it, Holden.

I finally saw my father, and he waved to me. That was my cue to get the hell out of dodge. I slapped a twenty on the counter and got up to leave, saying goodbye to Dylan.

On my way out, my gaze locked with Aubrey's when the band changed things up to a cover of "Tennessee Whiskey." Her eyes saw right through me once again, piercing me in the chest as if they would melt away all the coldness inside me, but I didn't deserve her warmth.

I wasn't worthy of her.

THIRTEEN
Aubrey

The crowd cheered and applauded, but I barely heard it because I was too wrapped up in Dean's intense stare as he left. His face was void of any emotion, but his eyes told me a different story. They were full of regret with just enough wonder to make me curious. But I wasn't curious enough to chase after him. I didn't chase men, not since Ray. Those fears of being taken advantage of and abused were enough for me to keep my guard up. I'd gone out on dates, but nothing ever ended up being serious enough for me to let my guard down and let someone in.

Shaking my head, I turned back and walked over to my table. Cassie was on her way to being absolutely plastered because Dylan was here. She purposely sat in a chair that had her back facing the bar. One glance at Dylan and I could tell he was just as tense as she was.

"Here, Aubs, you have to try this!" Cassie shouted over the band that started to play again. She held up a shot glass with orange and red liquid in it. "It's called Manny's Surprise."

I took the shot glass from her and threw it back, surprised that it didn't burn my throat.

"Wow!" I said, setting the glass down on the table.

"I know, right! No burn!" Cassie leaned over the table

and brought her hand up to her cheek like she was going to whisper something. "That's the surprise!"

"I think she should probably have a shot of water." Sophia laughed before she took a sip of her red wine.

"Nonsense, she will be fine," Chloe shouted, downing a shot, then holding her hands out to Cassie. "Dance with me, Cass!"

Cassie cheered and took Chloe's hands as she led them to the dance floor that was starting to fill up with a few people. Those girls knew how to party, and all eyes would be on them. They were always the center of attention at social gatherings. Me, I loved capturing the pure moments of happiness. I would be out there with them taking pictures if I didn't start getting a little light-headed. The doctor said that would be normal for a few days, along with some mild headaches for the next two weeks or so.

Sophia scooted into the chair beside me and leaned in close. "How are you feeling?"

"I'm okay. A little light-headed, but it's feeling better now."

"Good."

We couldn't really converse long because the music was loud, and that caused the people in the room to get louder. Some of the guys from the firehouse joined Chloe and Cassie on the dance floor. One of them was Rhett, and another was Ford. The latter I didn't even see walk in. I stole a glance at Dylan, who was watching them with hurt in his eyes. From the look he was giving them, I could tell that he didn't know that Cassie was with Ford. Before I could think better of it, I picked my camera up and took a picture of the moment in front of me.

Now that I was no longer feeling light-headed, I wanted to grab more pictures. I took a sip of water, then excused myself from Sophia, who was content sitting at the table guarding our purses and drinks. I snapped some more photos of the band and the crowd and got almost all the firefighters. I made my way over to the captain, who was chatting with Dylan.

"Hey, gentlemen, mind if I grab a picture?" I asked, and they both smiled politely and posed.

"May I see it?" Captain Holden asked.

"Sure!" I showed him the photo, and he smiled brightly.

"Wow, you take lovely pictures."

I beamed. "Thank you. I take a lot of pride in my work."

"As you should." Just then, the captain's name was being called by Nash. "If you two will excuse me."

I waited until he was out of earshot before I looked up at Dylan.

"How are you?" I asked, although I knew he wasn't doing quite well right now.

He shrugged. "I'm good."

I lifted a brow and looked behind him at the dance floor, then back at him. I could tell by the way he turned his head, then back around again that he knew I knew he was lying.

"She'll come around," I reassured him.

"I doubt it."

"I don't."

He looked at me, his blue eyes lighting up with hope, but before I could answer, my phone vibrated in my back pocket. I pulled it out, and when I read the text, my entire body went ice-cold.

Unknown: You look pretty tonight.

As my eyes scanned the crowd, looking for anyone suspicious who could be on their phone and finding no one, my phone started ringing in my hand. It was an unknown number calling me. For the past few days, I had gotten no new calls or texts, and I was just starting to not be so jumpy every time my phone rang or I got a text. I thought they'd finally stopped, but apparently, I was mistaken. My finger tapped the Answer button, just as I handed my camera over to Dylan and plugged my ear with my other hand.

"Listen, I don't know who the fuck you think you are," I said threateningly, making my way through the crowd to go outside, "but you need to stop fucking calling me. And while you're at it, stop with the texts too."

"Oh, I'm sorry, Miss Daniels," a man on the other end of the line said. "My assistant just gave me a message from Nash Warren over at the firehouse."

I flushed, embarrassed at my outburst.

"Oh my God!" I slapped a hand over my face. "I'm so sorry. It's Bill, right?"

"Yes, ma'am."

"I thought you were...never mind. Again, I'm so sorry."

"Don't worry about it. It happens all the time." He chuckled into the receiver, and I leaned my body against the brick building. "I have an opening this coming Tuesday at three if you'd like to bring your car in then."

I sighed. "Yes, that would be great. Thank you so much!"

"It's not a problem, Miss Daniels. I'll see you then."

"Okay, bye!"

I hung up the phone just as Dylan walked outside with my camera.

"Everything okay?" Concern laced his tone as he handed me my camera back.

I debated on telling him what was going on but thought better of it. Instead, I asked, "What would you recommend to a friend if they were getting weird calls and texts?"

Dylan lifted a brow. "Weird as in…?"

"Like calling and breathing into a phone and hanging up. Sending cryptic messages…kind of weird."

Dylan scrubbed a hand down the back of his neck as he thought about it.

"I would tell them that they should probably get a new number and maybe file a police report if they felt threatened."

I chewed on my bottom lip. I didn't want to file a police report. It wasn't like the messages were threatening —I'd seen and been through threatening. These didn't scream that I was in immediate danger; they were hang-up calls and a few texts. I'm only letting my paranoia get the best of me.

"Why do you ask?" Dylan asked, pulling me from my thoughts.

I shook my head. "No reason. I was just watching this cop show on Netflix, and that thought just crossed my mind."

"Oh," he replied, although it didn't look like he believed me.

Cassie rushed out of the door, followed closely by Sophia.

"Aubrey! My other best friend! There you are." She stumbled over to me, but then she spotted Dylan. "Oh. Hi."

Dylan rubbed the back of his neck. "Hey, Cassie."

"I'm mad at you," she said, and my eyes flicked to Sophia. We weren't sure what to do. Cassie had always been really calm and collected and a very happy drunk. Only a few times had I seen her go from happy drunk to sad drunk.

Dylan frowned. "I know."

"Cassie, we should get you home," I stepped up to her, but she slipped around me and right up to Dylan.

"You. Broke. My. Heart. Dylan McCormick." She poked his chest with each word, and I could hear the sad tremble in her voice. Dylan didn't say a word, but his face said it all. Cassie was on the verge of tears, and that looked like it broke Dylan. His emotions were that of heartache and regret. Those two clearly had unresolved issues that were going to implode one day if they didn't sit and talk things out.

The door burst open again, and out walked Ford.

"There you are, babe. I've been looking for you."

"I'm right here. I've always been here," she answered, but I knew it wasn't directed at Ford.

Ford wrapped his arms around Cassie and told us he would take her home and make sure she was okay. From the way it looked tonight, things would not be okay…not for a while.

Sophia and I looked at each other, both of us shocked at Cassie's emotional outburst. I stole a glance at Dylan, his jaw clenched tight as he watched Ford help Cassie into his car.

"Oh no," Sophia said. "Cassie's purse is still inside."

I sighed. "Crap. Looks like I'll be calling it an early night."

"I'll call Cassie and let them know." Sophia pulled her phone out and stepped away. I would have suggested calling Ford, but I knew Cassie always carried her phone around in her back pocket when we were out.

I turned to Dylan. "Hey, would you mind walking me to Cassie's car?"

I was still a little shaken by the text, so I didn't want to walk alone.

His sentence isn't up. Everything is fine.

"Sure, let me pay my tab. I'll meet you at your table."

We walked back inside, and I said my goodbyes to Chloe and Rhett. I gave some cash to Sophia so she could put it in the boot for the firefighter who was injured. She was going to hang out a little longer since she didn't have class the next day. Just as I stuck my wallet back into my purse, Dylan walked over.

"Ready?"

I smiled at him. "Yeah."

We walked to Cassie's car, and I started to get that feeling like I was being watched again. I turned around, scanning the parking lot but didn't see anything out of the ordinary. I'd never felt so grateful to not be alone. When we finally made it to her car, I put my purse and Cassie's inside and turned around to face Dylan.

"Thank you," I said, and he gave me a warm smile.

"Anytime," he replied. "Drive safe."

He started to turn away, but I reached out and grabbed his arm. "Don't give up on her."

Dylan sighed. "I wasn't going to."

I let go of his arm as he walked away, and I got in Cassie's car and immediately locked the door. I quickly pulled out of the parking lot and drove back to the apartment complex.

FOURTEEN
Aubrey

I woke up the next morning feeling tired. I tossed and turned all night and maybe only got a few hours of actual sleep. But the sun was shining through my curtains, so it was time for me to get up and start the day. I wanted to finish up the edits from the banquet and drop them off at the firehouse before heading into work tonight. I reached for my phone on the nightstand and cursed when I saw it was dead. I must have forgotten to plug it in after Ford and I got Cassie into bed. He would have stayed, but he had an early shift and didn't have his gear with him.

I got up, plugged my phone in, and laid my work uniform out on my bed. Cassie's door was still closed, so I was sure she must still be sleeping. I checked on her a few times since I couldn't sleep, and she was okay. I left her a bottled water and some Advil for when she woke up so she didn't have to get out of bed because I had a feeling she would be hurting a little bit today.

I put on a pot of coffee, and while that was brewing, I quickly took a shower so I could get back to editing pictures from the banquet. I enjoyed editing, and I was really loving how these pictures were turning out. Once I was finished with my shower, I grabbed my laptop and a cup of coffee and sat down at the kitchen table.

I opened my laptop, and the picture of when Rhett

was getting his bugles popped up, and a wave of excitement washed through me. This was one of my favorites, and of course the one of him and Chloe was a favorite too. They were a stunning couple.

I finished editing those, and the last picture I had left was the one with Captain Holden and Dylan. They were both handsome men, but someone in the back caught my eye, so I zoomed in. It was Dean, sitting down at a table. I had captured his side profile on camera. I switched the filter to black and white and played around with the lighting. I sat back in the chair, mesmerized at how striking he looked. Nothing beat looking at the real thing, though I would never admit that out loud.

Once I was satisfied, I saved the photos onto a disc and finished getting ready for my shift, even though I had plenty of time to kill. I needed to go to the Camera Shop and print out some photos so I could drop them off at the firehouse. Maybe then if I had enough time, I could stop by the park and take some nature photos on film to develop later. I'd been a little on edge lately, so being in my happy place would help ease some of the tension I'd been having. I turned my phone on, and it immediately started pinging with missed texts.

Unknown: I saw him walk you to your car.

Unknown: Is he your boyfriend?

Unknown: Are you two fucking?

Unknown: Answer me!!

Unknown: You're nothing but a whore.

Unknown: I don't know why anyone would want to fuck you.

Unknown: You can't ignore me forever.

Unknown: You're so fucking easy, slut.

I dropped my phone on the floor like it was burning my hands and covered my mouth. The coffee I had drunk earlier was threatening to come up, and my body started shaking uncontrollably. My skin felt clammy. It was like the world was turning on its axis and I was freefalling. These were exactly the type of texts Ray would send after he would see me talking to a random guy, even if that random guy was someone he knew.

There is no way he's out.

I dropped down to my knees on the floor next to my phone and dialed my nana's number. I needed to know if she got any messages from the lawyers or county jail if Ray had been released. He was currently serving fifteen years in jail, there's just no way he could have found me.

Hi, you've reached Nana Daniels and little bee. We can't come to the phone right now, so leave a message and we will call you back!

Damn it. I wished her trip wasn't open ended. I hung up and decided to try her cell phone again, hoping she at least had it charged now.

I placed my hand on my forehead, taking in deep breaths as I waited for the call to connect. "Please pick up, please pick up."

This is Dianna. Sorry I missed your call. Please leave a message and I'll call you back!

. . .

My stomach churned as my call went straight to her voicemail…again.

This is okay. I'll be okay. He didn't find me. He's still in jail.

I repeated those words to myself as I sat back against my bed. After few minutes, I had finally calmed down enough to pick up my phone and call Sophia. I didn't want to disturb Cassie, and I knew Chloe was already at her boutique working. I wasn't sure why I hadn't told any of my friends sooner about the calls and texts, but I think it was because I was afraid that if I admitted it out loud, then it would be real. I didn't want to believe that someone could be stalking me, and that I feared it was Ray. I didn't think it was possible, at least not this soon anyway. I still had time. We never had one of those fancy answering machines that you can call to check your messages if you were out of town. So if, by chance, Ray wasn't in jail, I wouldn't know unless I went back home.

"Hi, Aubrey," Sophia said on the other end of the call. Hearing her voice made my resolve crack, and I started crying on the phone. "Are you okay? What's wrong?" I couldn't get the words out to answer her. After I stayed silent for a moment, she asked, "Are you still at home?"

"Yes." My voice broke on a sob.

"Don't go anywhere, I'm on my way."

She hung up, and I sat down on my bedroom floor crying. I was scared because I had been through something like this before. The weird calls and texts—it reminded me of Ray, and all those feelings that I had long since buried deep in my soul came rushing to the surface. It felt crazy that after all these years, it would still affect me just as much as it did back then. I guessed those fears never really went away but lay dormant until something triggered me into living in constant fear again. The text messages were almost exactly like the ones Ray would send, and they were different from any other messages that I would get for my business.

I curled up, hugging my knees until Sophia came rushing into my room. We all had keys to each other's places that we only used in emergency situations, and this would be considered an emergency. Sophia came over and sat down next to me, pulling me into her arms.

"What's going on, Aubs? I haven't seen you this worked up before," Sophia said. I was just about to tell her when Cassie's bedroom door opened.

"Soph, what are you doing—" Her question was cut off when she looked at me. "What's going on? Aubrey, are you okay?"

I shook my head as she came over and sat down in front of me. I pulled myself together and told them everything that had been going on. I showed them the texts, to which both had the same disgusted reaction that I did.

"First things first," Sophia said. "You are not a whore, so clearly this person doesn't know you very well."

Cassie nodded in agreement. "Yes, and second, you are totally fuckable."

I chuckled softly. Cassie had this natural way of making me laugh, even when I didn't want to.

"Thanks," I replied.

"What are you going to do?" Sophia tucked a lock of her brown hair behind her ear.

"I'm going to take Dylan's advice and change my number, so hopefully it will all stop."

At the mention of Dylan's name, I saw Cassie flinch, but she didn't say anything.

"You should really file a police report too," Sophia suggested.

"I agree with Soph. I don't think this is something you should take lightly," Cassie chimed in.

I sighed. I didn't want to go through all that trouble, but I knew they were right. It wouldn't be smart of me to not file a report. "Okay. Would you guys mind coming with me?"

"Absolutely not," they said in unison.

"We wouldn't let you do this alone," Cassie said. "Let me change and brush my teeth, and we can all go together."

I smiled at her before she walked out of my room. Sophia and I went into my kitchen while we waited for Cassie. One thing I loved most about my friends was that I was never alone. Not anymore.

FIFTEEN
Dean

I pinched the bridge of my nose, feeling a tension headache coming on. We weren't getting anywhere with the arsonist case, but Dylan and I kept going over everything. There was another fire across town that seemed to be related to the other arson fires. Again, we had nothing to go off, and this was the only case we were assigned to right now. We were able to gather enough evidence from the meth house for a search warrant and made the proper arrests. That was an open and shut case, but this arsonist case was proving to be damn near impossible to solve. Opening my desk drawer, I pulled out some ibuprofen, popping them in my mouth and taking a sip of water to wash it down.

"Did that file come back yet?" Dylan asked.

"No, not yet. I expect it might take a while," I leaned back in my chair.

Just then, Noah walked into our office. "Hey, McCormick. Some woman is here to see you. Says her name is Aubrey."

"Okay." He stole a glance over at me before getting up out of his chair and following Noah out to the front of the precinct. What could Aubrey want to see him for? He said he wasn't really into her, but I guessed these things changed. Although, I hadn't really cared for what he had to say.

He's better for her anyway.

I heard his voice in the hallway, then saw him usher her inside the office. He shut the door behind them and pulled up a chair for her to sit in. She looked nervous, and her eyes were a little red and puffy as if she'd been crying. She glanced over at me, chewing on her bottom lip. Of course, my eyes zoned in on her lips, and it was the first time I really noticed how full they were.

"What's going on?" Dylan asked, sitting down on the edge of his desk and crossing his arms over his chest.

Aubrey fidgeted, her fingers playing with the hem of her purse. "Uhm, well. I've been getting these strange calls and texts." She paused to glance up at Dylan. "You knew that."

Dylan nodded. "I had a feeling."

He knew about this? When did this conversation even occur, and how come this message wasn't relayed to me, his superior officer?

"Anyway, the first text I received was the night of the banquet. After the second one, I blocked the number. Then I got one the next day, from a different number, asking me why I blocked them. I ignored that, and after I picked up my car from the firehouse, I kept getting weird phone calls, although no one answered on the other line. I leave my number at places around town for my photography business, so I was used to getting calls from a number I didn't recognize, but after what happened last night..." She trailed off, and I found myself leaning forward in my seat, unconsciously getting closer to her.

"What happened last night?" My voice was low and husky.

She turned her head toward me, almost shocked that I

was still in the room. I couldn't blame her for that though —I was always running away from her.

"When I was taking pictures of the band at Monroe's, I got a text saying that I looked pretty."

I felt my blood start to boil. I was there. Some creep was in the bar last night, and I didn't even know it. Yeah, Aubrey was my annoying next-door neighbor, but she didn't deserve a creep watching her every move.

"Is that what brought up the question of what should you do?" Dylan asked, pulling her attention away from me and onto him.

She nodded. "I'm sorry, I didn't want to bring it up in case I was slowly losing my mind, but this morning I…" She trailed off again, opening her purse and pulling out her phone. She tapped a few buttons, then handed the phone to Dylan. His jaw clenched, and he looked pissed as he read what was on the screen. I got up from my chair to take the phone from his outstretched hand. My eyes scanned the messages, and I could see why he was pissed.

"Some asshole sent this to you?" I asked her.

She nodded, her eyes starting to fill with tears. Dylan handed her a tissue, and she wiped her tears away.

"I called my friend Sophia, and she came right over. That's when they told me I should take your advice and get a new number. We went to the phone store, then we came straight here to file a report." She sniffed, and then she sat up straight. "What do I need to do?"

"First off, you did the right thing by coming to us. I'll take your statement, and we will get this filed," Dylan told her as I reread the texts.

"Do you mind if we keep this?" I asked.

Aubrey shook her head. "No. I don't think I want that back. I already have everything I need on my new phone."

"Okay," I responded, putting the phone in an evidence bag. This person is probably using a burner phone, but it wouldn't hurt to have our technician take a look. "Is there anyone who would want to hurt you?"

She contemplated my question for a moment before answering. "One, but he's currently serving fifteen years in jail. I'm sorry, I can't think of anyone else."

"Can you give us a name so we can follow up?"

"R-Ray Owens." It seemed like she hadn't said that name out loud in a while. I wrote the name down and reassured her I would check in to make sure that he was still in jail.

Aubrey finished giving Dylan her statement, then escorted her out. When he came back into the office, he sat down in his desk chair and scrubbed a hand down his face. He seemed a little more tense now than he did before he left.

"Those were some fucked-up messages," he said. "Do you think it would have anything to do with her sealed file?"

I pondered his question for a moment. "It's possible. We won't know until we read it. I think it might have something to do with whoever this Ray guy is." I got the impression that there was more to her story than she was letting on, but she didn't want to talk about it. All the more reason to get that file—it might clue us in, or it might not. I knew she didn't have anything to do with the arsonist, but we had to have proof.

"I wish there was more we could do."

Me too.

"We will send her phone to the technicians to see if they can trace anything and hope we get that sealed file sooner rather than later. And we will make a call to check on the whereabouts of Ray," I responded. "So why didn't you tell me about what happened?"

Dylan turned to me. "We've just been working on this case all morning, the thought didn't even cross my mind. I'm sorry, I should have mentioned it."

"When something like this happens and you knew or suspected something, you gotta let me know. I'm not your best friend that you tell all your secrets to, but I am your partner. Those are the things I need to hear about," I said to him. "Especially if it can help solve the case."

We needed all the pieces to the puzzle in order to put together what was happening. I needed a partner I could count on. Wyatt and I had been the best team, and I didn't want to make any more mistakes. *Although, I still manage to fuck shit up.*

"I'm sorry, it won't happen again," Dylan replied.

"You're damn right it won't."

Dylan and I had looked up Ray and saw that he was let out on the Monday through Friday work release program. We called his corrections officer, and we were told that Ray was showing up at work on time, and then he was at home. They had informed us that he had excellent behavior and qualified for the program because of it. He had been cleared by all personnel and was able to stay with a cousin within a mile of his workplace. Although, something about that didn't sit right with me. Attempted second degree murder was a serious charge. Plus, if you laid a finger on a woman in violence, you'd always be a scumbag in my eyes.

AFTER WORK, I RELUCTANTLY AGREED TO MEET MY parents for dinner at the Bistro. My dad had been begging me for weeks now, but then he got my mom involved, and there was no backing down from her. I didn't want to go, but I was hoping that my agreeing to dinner would get them off my back for a while. I walked inside and saw them sitting at a table by the window. I informed the hostess that I saw my party and went over to them.

"Hi, Mom," I said, sitting down in the chair across from her. "Dad."

"Hello, Dean." My mom smiled at me, but it didn't reach her eyes. I loved my mom, but being around her didn't make me feel better about losing Wyatt. It was the complete opposite. She always made me feel like I wasn't allowed to grieve because of the job I'd chosen. She was always looking at me like it was the last time she would ever see me. I chose to be a cop to help people and to be a hero like my father, who I always looked up to. I knew that joining the academy would come with a price, but I didn't know that I would have to cash in so soon.

"How's the arsonist case coming along?" my dad asked, and my mom balked at him.

"No, John. We promised no work talk. We are here to have a nice dinner with our son, who I haven't seen in months."

"Yes, ma'am." My dad leaned over to kiss her cheek. I looked down at the menu, even though I already knew I wanted a burger.

"Hi, my name is Aubrey, and I'll be your server for this evening," I heard a familiar voice say. I glanced up at our waitress and saw my neighbor.

"Oh, Miss Daniels! How lovely to see you again. I

didn't know you worked here," my dad said, almost too cheerfully. "Honey, this is Aubrey Daniels. She took pictures of the firehouse banquet, the one I was telling you about."

I rolled my eyes.

"Yes, yes, I remember. It's nice to finally put a face to the name." My mom looked up at Aubrey, then turned to look at me. "Have you met my son, Dean?"

Her blue eyes flicked to me. "Uhm. Yes, I have. We're neighbors, actually."

Both my parents turned to me.

"Oh really?" my dad lifted a brow. "He never told me that."

"It never came up in conversation," I answered nonchalantly.

"Uh-huh." The tone of my dad's voice sounded like he didn't believe a word of that. Sure, there were plenty of times I could have told him she was my neighbor, but I didn't because I honestly didn't care.

"Are you from River Falls, Aubrey?" my mom asked.

"No, I moved up here for college. I'm from the suburbs a little outside of New York City," Aubrey answered, looking a little flushed.

"And your parents?"

A wave of sadness crossed Aubrey's features, but she quickly recovered herself. Something I probably wouldn't have even noticed if I hadn't been looking at her. "My mom was from River Falls, and she met my dad at the university."

"So, they still live here?" my mom pried, and I could tell by the look on Aubrey's face that this wasn't a topic she talked about often.

"Uhm, no. They…they passed away when I five."

Both of my parents gasped, and I'd be lying if that didn't make my heart skip a beat. She'd lost her parents and was almost killed by some dickhead. You'd never know that she had a dark past if you spoke with her and that she was still standing. That would break most people, but she's not like most people.

No wonder she can see right through your bullshit.

"I am so sorry for your loss," my dad kept his voice soft. I prayed that he didn't bring up Wyatt, and I was thankful when he said that they should order now. I gave her my order after my parents, and when she walked away, the table was silent for a few moments.

"She's lovely," my mom finally said. "I really like her."

"You just met her," I replied, taking a drink of my water.

"I don't need long to decide if I like someone or not."

"What's that supposed to mean?" I asked, feeling a little pissed off, and hoping Aubrey would be back soon with my whiskey neat.

My dad cleared his throat just as my mom said, "It means that you're all alone here, surrounded by people that care about you, and all you've been doing is pushing people away."

I wanted to tell her that wasn't true, but she was right.

"Wyatt wouldn't want that for you."

My body stiffened, and anger bubbled up in my chest. I knew coming here was a mistake. I knew she would make me feel guilty for just wanting to be alone. For wanting to deal with Wyatt's death on my own.

"I'm not doing this," I growled, getting up from the table. I almost bumped into Aubrey on my way out but managed to avoid knocking my whiskey out of her hand.

My father could have it for all I cared. I stormed out of the restaurant and got into my truck. Since I moved back home, I started to feel like I was finally able to dig myself out of the six-foot hole that I was stuck in. But now the hole was getting deeper, and I didn't care if I got buried alive.

SIXTEEN
Aubrey

*A*fter changing my number and filing the police report, I was thankful that the calls and texts had stopped. It had only been a few days, but it was a nice reprieve from the anxiety I was facing daily. I was still a little jumpy, but I felt as if the weight had been lifted off my shoulders. I never made it anywhere that I had planned to go the other day, so now I had to make up for it. Especially the firehouse, and since it was my day off, I was going to take full advantage of it.

I had spoken to Nash over the phone, and he was very understanding of the issue and said that there was no rush. Of course, I felt bad for the delay, so on my break, I went over to the Camera Shop and printed off some extra prints with the firehouse crest to make it look more professional. I was proud of those, and I hoped he liked them. I had told the Sweet family my turnaround time for edits was two weeks, so I still had plenty of time to get them their photos.

I grabbed my camera bag, the CD with the pictures, and the manilla folder which held the prints. "Bye, Cass, I'll be back later!"

Cassie peeked her head out from the bathroom. "Do you want me to come with you?"

"No, I think I'll be okay. Go have fun on your day date with Ford," I told her. They rarely ever had the same days off, so when they did, they liked to get out and spend the whole day together. She'd been acting strange since the night at the bar, and I could understand why. If I was in her shoes and my first love came home with unresolved issues between us right as I was starting to fall for another guy, I'd be acting strange too. Cassie was stubborn; I just hoped she made the right choices on how she handled this. Dylan clearly still loved her, and I thought part of her still loved him too, but she'd have to figure that out for herself.

"Okay, love you! Be safe and call me if anything happens!" I heard Cassie shout before closing the bathroom door. She and the girls had been a tad overprotective which, don't get me wrong, I loved them for, but it was starting to get a little…much.

When I got off the elevator, I waved to the lobby attendant, who was on the phone, and walked outside to my car. Every time I saw the damage, I winced. Luckily, my car ran fine; it was just cosmetic damage. I was ready to have it fixed though, because I already remembered the attack—I didn't need a constant physical reminder. Sliding into the driver's seat, I made sure the door was locked before closing my eyes. I needed to take a few calming breaths before driving off to the firehouse.

The drive there was quick, and I was able to park closer to the building this time. Grabbing everything I needed, I exited my car and hit the Lock button. Listening to it beep a few times was reassurance that it was locked. It made me feel better. I waved to Rhett and Oliver as I walked by. They were eating breakfast, so I didn't want to disturb them. I knew from Chloe that sometimes they could get called even while they were eating. Emergencies didn't wait until it was convenient for everyone.

I knocked on Nash's door, "Hi, Chief Warren."

"Hi, Aubrey, please come on in," he answered from behind his desk.

"I come bearing gifts," I said excitedly, handing the folder and CD to him.

He smiled and opened the folder with the pictures. "Wow."

"Do you like them?"

"Yeah, these are amazing," He flipped through the portraits. "They even have our crest on them."

"Yeah, I thought it would give them a more professional look."

"Oh, this one is great!"

I leaned over the desk and smiled at the picture of Nash giving Rhett his lieutenant bugles.

"That's a personal favorite of mine," I told him proudly. "The CD has all of those plus all of the candid shots I took. All edited, of course. Oh, and the waiver to give you the rights to all of the photos is in the folder. I already signed it, so they are officially yours."

"This is so great. Thank you, Aubrey." Nash stood and shook my hand. "Are you sure I can't reimburse you?"

I shook my head. "No, I was happy to do it. If you ever need me for anything else, just let me know. You never have to pay me, and if you feel you need to, just buy everyone a pizza and save me a slice."

He laughed. "Okay, you've got yourself a deal."

"Good. Anyway, I'm going to head out. Be safe out there." I waved, turning to leave.

"You too, Aubrey." Nash's tone was serious. When I told him the shortened version of what was going on over the phone, I heard him curse under his breath. The men at the firehouse and precinct had been taking what happened to me very seriously. So seriously, in fact, that I wasn't surprised to see Rhett and Oliver come over to me to walk me back out to my car.

"You guys didn't have to do this," I said as we made our way across the parking lot.

"You know Chloe would have my balls," Rhett joked.

Oliver laughed. "I'm sure you'd like that."

"You're probably right."

I cringed. "On that note, how's that firefighter that got injured? Christopher, right?"

"Yeah," Rhett answered. "He's doing well. I don't think he will be back to the firehouse though, but only time will tell."

"Well, at least he's doing better. How much were you able to raise for his family?"

"Close to a thousand dollars." It was Oliver who answered. "Manny is having another fundraiser next weekend for him since the open mic night really took off. I know Chris's family was really grateful for the money, but Manny wants to be able to do more."

"Manny is amazing." I smiled and looked up at Oliver.

He beamed. "He really is."

We finally reached my car, and even though I didn't need them to walk with me, I appreciated their company. Oliver picked me up and gave me a huge hug and then kissed my cheek before setting me down.

"See ya later, Aubs," Oliver stepped aside so Rhett could squeeze in and give me a hug. His wasn't as big as Oliver's, more like a big-brother-type hug. He'd been like that for all of us girls since we first met him.

"Be careful out there, Aubrey." Rhett let me go but kept his hand on my shoulder. "You see anything out of the ordinary, you call 9-1-1 and stay on the line. Describe—"

"Describe everything I see and hear, even if I think it's not important," I finished for him, and he smiled.

"Good, you remembered."

"Of course she remembers. She's one of us now," Oliver said, playfully twisting one of the curls in my hair.

I swatted him away, "Okay, you boys go and get back to work."

Getting back into my car, I waved to them as I set off to the park to take some pictures. The darkroom at the Camera Shop had been calling my name since the last time I was there, and I was excited to get back to my happy place.

THE SUN WAS STARTING TO SET WHEN I WALKED inside the Camera Shop.

"Hey, Aubrey!" I heard someone call my name, and I looked over to see Elaine, the owner, waving at me. She was helping a customer check out.

"Hi, Elaine!" I said. "I'm just going to use the darkroom."

"That's alright, dear. I'm just about to lock up for the evening, so I will be locking you in here."

"That's fine, I have my key."

"Good. Have a good night."

"Thanks, Mrs. Foster! I appreciate it!" I smiled at her before walking down the long hallway to the darkroom. I shut myself inside and got started. I missed being here. It felt like I hadn't been here in so long. My life had been interrupted by some jackass that wanted to scare me. I mean, it worked. But with my new number, I felt like I could go back to living again. I dipped the photo paper in one solution, then into the next, and kept repeating the process. This was my safe space, the only place in the entire world where it was me and my photographs and everything was right in the world.

The lights went out, and I fumbled around, careful to set the tongs on the table and not in the solution. I took off my gloves and started to feel my way to the door. I didn't want to use my flashlight on my phone because the exposure would ruin my photos. I needed to check the breaker to make sure I didn't actually blow a fuse. Sometimes that would happen since the wiring in this place was so old. This wouldn't be the first time the fuse blew on me.

Once I was safely outside the darkroom, I grabbed my phone and turned the flashlight on. I walked down the hallway, and when I got closer to the front, I saw a hooded figure standing in front of the door, illuminated only by the streetlights outside. I stopped dead in my tracks. My heart started pounding against my rib cage when they started banging on the glass door. It wasn't until I saw the huge crack that my fight-or-flight instincts kicked into overdrive.

I spun, sprinting as fast as I could back to the darkroom, the glass door shattering behind me setting off the alarm. I ran inside the darkroom, slamming the door shut behind me and locking it. Panicked, I looked around for anything to barricade myself inside. Using the light from my phone, I found a chair and placed it against the handle. As soon as I got the table pressed up against the door, whoever was outside started pounding on the door.

My hands were trembling as I fumbled around trying to dial 9-1-1. I knew the light would ruin my pictures, but at this point, I didn't care. I could retake them. *If I get out of here alive.*

I flinched, praying that they wouldn't break it down from how hard they were beating on the door.

"9-1-1, what's your emergency?"

"H-hi, my name is Aubrey, and someone is trying to break in," I said frantically. My breathing was labored as I backed up as far away as I could. My back hit the back corner of the room, and I sunk down to the ground.

"Where are you, Aubrey?" the operator asked calmly but firmly.

Bang. Bang. Bang. Bang. Bang.

The banging got louder, and I screamed, holding the phone up to my ear with one hand and using the other to cover my other ear.

"I'm at the Camera Shop. 1923 Mapleview Road." My voice trembled with unshed tears, my body trying to get as small as it could to get away from the threat.

Bang. Bang. Bang. Bang. Bang.

"Please hurry!" I hollered into the phone, squeezing my eyes shut.

"I've dispatched a squad car. Someone will be there soon. Try and stay calm."

Bang. Bang. Bang. Bang. Bang.

I jumped with every bang of their hand on the door, trying not to drown myself in a sea of locked memories of when Ray beat on my bedroom the night he went to jail. I dropped my phone on the ground and locked my body up. I was frozen in fear, unable to move a muscle. The banging stopped, and all that was left was the alarms and the sounds of my heavy breathing.

SEVENTEEN
Dean

*D*ylan and I were driving through town in our unmarked squad car when a call came through the scanner.

"Calling all units, we have 10-31 in progress at 1923 Mapleview Road."

Dylan turned up the police scanner. "That's a couple miles north from here."

"110. I am closest to the location; I can check it out," I heard Noah's voice come through.

"10-4, 110. Please be advised that there is a woman named Aubrey hiding somewhere in the building. I've dispatched EMS to the scene."

"10-4, dispatch. I'm en route."

"Wait, did they just say Aubrey?" Dylan asked, eyes going wide and looking at me.

I didn't think twice; I turned the siren on and sped my way through town, while Dylan let dispatch know we were headed that way also.

"Where am I going?" I asked, my eyes focused on the road in front of me.

"Turn left at the light. We're going to the Camera Shop," Dylan answered, holding on to the handle by the door. I knew exactly where I was going from here. I came up to a red light and slowed down, making sure to carefully enter the intersection. It was late, so not many cars were on the road. I was thankful for that. We came up on the scene, and I jumped out of the vehicle before I barely had the car in park.

We were running toward the front entrance when I saw glass scattered everywhere. The alarm was still going off as I entered the building. I didn't get very far inside when I saw Noah carrying Aubrey down the hallway. I wasn't even sure why I did what I did, but I was the one who took her from Noah while he and Dylan went to search the perimeter.

She was awake, so I sat her down carefully in the passenger's seat of the patrol car. Her face was pale as I wiped her hair away from her wet cheeks.

I don't like seeing you like this.

She was catatonic, so I got up and went to the driver's side, asking where the damn ambulance was. ETA was two minutes. Once confirmed, I started to go back over, but Dylan had taken my place down in front of her.

"Are you okay?" His voice was calm, and I started kicking myself in the ass for not asking if she was okay. I mean, anyone with eyes could see that this woman was far from okay.

A sob broke free from her, and she fell forward onto Dylan's shoulder, clinging to him for dear life. His eyes shot up to me, and he politely wrapped his arms around her. He whispered that everything was okay now and rubbed her back gently. An emotion stirred deep inside me, one that I barely recognized because it was rare that I ever felt jealous.

"There's no one around back or in the store. The suspect broke in, then must have fled out the back door when they heard us coming," Noah told us as he came back around. Aubrey leaned back in the seat, but Dylan stayed down at her level.

"They wouldn't stop banging," Aubrey whispered, and all attention was focused back on her. She blinked a few times, shaking her head and taking in a deep breath, almost as if she was grounding herself. "I-I mean, they just kept banging on the door, but they did stop. I can't tell you how much time passed from when they stopped banging on the door to when you showed up."

"Did you get a good look at whoever did this?" Noah asked. I saw her head swivel toward him, and she shook her head.

"No, I'm sorry. The lights went out, and I could hardly see anything," she replied. Noah and I exchanged a glance, and an understanding passed between us. He was going to check the power, while we waited out here with Aubrey. I heard sirens in the distance and knew that the ambulance was getting close. They turned off the siren as they pulled up. A petite blonde jumped out and rushed to the back of the rig, while another came around the corner and came straight to Aubrey. I recognized him, but I couldn't place his name. Dylan jumped out of the way, while the EMT started checking on Aubrey. Just as we stepped aside to give them some space, Noah approached us.

"I didn't want to say anything in front of her, but you guys need to see this."

We followed Noah back into the shop and came up to a room, way back in the building. He shined his flashlight on the door, and written in red were the words "You're a fucking nobody, cunt. No one wants a filthy whore."

My jaw clenched at how close we had gotten to this pervert but couldn't catch him.

What if he had gotten to her?

No. I rid myself of those thoughts. She was safe now, and we would catch this son of a bitch.

"Holy fuck," Dylan whispered.

Noah nodded. "Yeah, those were my exact words when I rolled up. She had that door barricaded, man. It took me a few minutes to get her to come out, and as soon as she opened the door, her legs gave out. She was petrified."

"Did she see this?" I asked, pointing to the door.

He shook his head. "No. I figured it would be best if she didn't."

Smart thinking. She was already shaken to her core; seeing this would definitely make it worse.

"Also, I checked the breaker. Turns out the wires were cut," Noah informed us. This asshole was doing everything he could to scare her, and it worked. That pissed me off even more. All of a sudden, an uneasy feeling settled deep in my gut. I knew that the correction officer said that Ray was doing what he was supposed to, but what if he was playing the system? I needed to know for sure. I made a mental note to give them a call and ask them to send someone out to verify his whereabouts. I knew men like him, I've put many away myself. If he held any type of grudge, he would find ways to work the system.

When we walked outside, Aubrey was sitting on the rig getting checked out by the EMTs. The petite blonde walked over to us.

"Hey, Kenna," Noah said flirtatiously, and she flushed. Great, this was Noah's current conquest.

"Hey," she replied, then looked to us. "All her vitals are normal, and she's refusing any more treatment, so she's free to go. Although I did recommend that she didn't drive home alone."

"We can follow her home." The words flew out of my mouth before I could stop them.

Kenna nodded. "Okay."

She walked back to the rig and packed everything up.

Aubrey walked over to us. "My things are inside; I'll be right back."

"I'll get them," Noah answered, "Where are they?"

"Back in the darkroom. In the cabinet."

He nodded and went to grab her things. He was going to stay back and clean everything up until the shop owner came down.

"Is your roommate home?" Dylan asked her.

"Yeah, although she wasn't supposed to be. Ford got called into work because an EMT called out. So, she's home and will be waiting for me in the lobby when I arrive," she answered. Dylan looked a little hurt by that, but he quickly composed himself.

She's also your neighbor. You'll be home in a matter of hours.

I wouldn't be able to keep her safe.

I couldn't even keep my best friend safe.

Noah arrived with her things and made sure she made it to her car safely. He checked in and around her car to make sure it was safe and then gave the all clear. I pulled out of the parking lot right after she did and followed her all the way back to our apartment building. Dylan and I waited until she walked into the building and saw that she was with her redheaded friend, Cassie. Our shift was over in an hour, so we drove back to the precinct to file a report on what happened tonight. I called and left a message to the correction officer for him to call me. I was hoping that I was wrong, but if I wasn't, then I believed that Ray was Aubrey's stalker. Now, all I had to do was prove it.

EIGHTEEN
Aubrey

assie was sound asleep next to me in my bed, but all I could do was lie there. I couldn't sleep. The shadows danced around my room, and I jumped at every little sound. All I could think about was the attack. A nerve-wracking feeling latched itself onto the pit of my stomach, and I knew it wasn't just your run-of-the-mill robbery attempt. It was an attempt to get to *me*. They wanted me, and they'd found me in the one place where I always felt safe. Now nothing felt safe anymore.

I hadn't heard from Dean or Dylan about Ray, so was I to assume that no news was good news? I wracked my brain and couldn't come up with anyone else who would want to hurt me, let alone scare me. I wasn't sure which was more terrifying; having Ray be my stalker, or someone I didn't know. I shuddered at the thought. I rolled over and I could still hear the banging on the door as if it was still happening.

"Knock, knock," Ray knocked on my door. I had just finished putting cover-up over the bruise that was forming on my right cheek. I'd made the mistake of not texting him back as soon as I was finished with my study group with my friend Jane. My nana had picked me up, and we went to the ice

cream parlor to celebrate the straight A's on my report card. I guess I just lost track of time, and when I finally texted him, he was so angry that I didn't text him right away.

Ray came over, holding a bouquet of yellow roses and moving my hair away from my bruised cheek. He leaned in to kiss it gently. "I'm so sorry for hurting you, Bree baby. I just need you to keep your word when you say you're going to text me. This is what happens when you don't keep your word."

He reached up, running his cold fingers down my cheek, emphasizing the slap mark. I recoiled, and I saw his eyes go from brown to black in an instant. I was terrified he was going to hit me again as he grabbed my face and turned me to face him.

"Don't you ever pull away from me again," he spat, dropping the yellow roses to the floor. "You. Are. Mine."

His other hand started gliding up my leg and stopping just at the apex of my thighs. He thrust his hand forward, grabbing the hard junction of my inseam. The momentum caused me to yelp out in pain. "This pussy is mine. You belong to me."

Disgust filtered through my veins. I felt trapped, practically dead inside.

He jolted me, squeezing harder when I didn't reply. "Say it, Bree!"

He shook me once more before I reluctantly said the words he so desperately needed to hear. "I-I be-belong to you."

The words tasted like venom on my tongue, and just when I thought the moment was about to get worse, he smiled. What made his smile so eerie was how perfect it was. He reminded me of Ted Bundy. Nana and I had watched a documentary on him once, and he reminded me of Ray. Charming and disarming; a deadly combination.

"That's my girl." He let me go and reached down to pick

up the bouquet of yellow roses. He smiled as he handed them to me. "I got your favorite flowers, Bree. To say I'm sorry."

I FELT DIRTY AND DISGUSTING AS I SHOOK AWAY THE memory of Ray. I was in desperate need of a long, hot shower. Even though it was warm out, a cold chill seeped in and settled on my bones. I was hoping a steaming shower could help put a little warmth back to me and rid me of the toxicity that was Ray.

I kept having to remind myself over and over that he was still in jail, and he couldn't get to me anymore. If he was getting out early, Nana would have called and told me. Of course she would have to be home to get the message. She was the only one from back home who knew where I was. We both took that precaution when I moved up to River Falls. We just wanted to be safe rather than sorry. No one knew Ray like I did, and I knew he was capable of terrible things.

I washed my hair, letting the hot water cascade down my back. My body was starting to warm up when I heard the bathroom door open. I held my breath and pressed my back into the tiles, then slid down the wall to curl up in a tight ball. I tried to call out to Cassie, but it was like my voice was broken. The only thing coming out was air, and the next thing I knew, I felt like I was suffocating.

A shadow formed just behind the shower curtain, and it was then I was finally able to find my voice.

"Cassie!" I screamed so loud, my own ears started ringing. "Cassie! Help me!"

The shower curtain flew open. A wide-eyed Cassie was staring at me, and I just broke. Tears started falling down my cheeks, getting washed away by the running water. I couldn't get air into my lungs, they felt so tight. Like someone had their arms wrapped around me, squeezing the life out of me. Then the water stopped running.

"Aubrey, I'm here." Cassie's voice started to break through the panic, although I couldn't calm down. "It's okay, you're safe. No one else is here but me."

She wrapped her arms around me, then there was a bang, and I heard the front door burst open. I jumped and practically leapt out of Cassie's arms, making myself as small as possible in the tub. Cassie stood up and spun around, grabbing the towel rack off the wall and holding it up like a baseball bat. I noticed her body relax as she lowered the metal bar.

"What happened?" came a voice I recognized. Dean was standing in the doorway of my bathroom. I could see his legs through Cassie's. *I must have screamed louder than I thought.*

"She's okay. She just had a panic attack," Cassie answered him. "Can you grab Aubrey's bathrobe that's hanging on the back of her chair in her room? It's the bedroom straight back."

I didn't hear what he said, but I saw him move in the direction of my room. Cassie turned, grabbing the towel that was now on the floor, and came over to me. "C'mon, let's get you out and dry."

I nodded and unclasped my hands from around my knees and stood on shaky legs. We heard a throat clear just as Cassie wrapped the towel around me.

"Here." Dean's husky voice came through the doorway. He held my blue fuzzy bathrobe in his outstretched hand, and his head was turned slightly.

I guess he can be a gentleman.

"Thanks. We'll be out in a bit," Cassie replied, taking it from him. I was able to dry myself off and put my warm bathrobe on. My body was still shaking, and I wasn't sure if it was because I was freezing or the fact that I just had a full-blown panic attack.

I followed Cassie out into the kitchen, and my eyes widened at my front door that was busted in. Out of the corner of my eye, I saw Dean's head turn to the door.

"Don't worry, I texted my partner to make sure that gets fixed within the hour. He's working with the apartment facilities manager," he said reassuringly. I wasn't sure why, but I trusted him. Cassie led me over to the table and then went to make some hot tea.

My gaze met Dean's. "Thank you."

He gave me a curt nod. "You good?"

"I'm fine," I lied. Everyone in this apartment knew that was a lie, but telling the truth meant showing a side of me that I hated for people to see. I wasn't embarrassed; I just didn't like showing my weaknesses.

The muscles in Dean's jaw clenched. "I'm going back to my apartment, but if you need anything…" He paused to get his wallet out of his back pocket. He pulled out a business card and handed it to Cassie. "Give me a call, or just come over."

"We will, thanks," Cassie responded, and Dean turned to leave.

The second the door shut awkwardly behind him, I went back on high alert. With him here, I felt safe. And that was such an odd feeling to have from a man who didn't seem to like me.

NINETEEN
Aubrey

"*D*o you want to talk about it?" Cassie asked, coming over and sitting down next to me at the table.

I sighed. "I just got spooked, you know? Last night was terrifying. Not the scariest thing that's ever happened, but it's the scariest that's happened in over ten years."

Cassie nodded. "You were thinking about Ray, weren't you?"

"Yeah. He used to do things like that. The calling and texting and sometimes even snuck up on me. I mean, I know he's not getting out of jail anytime soon. But lately…" I trailed off.

The courts only had one number on file to call if Ray was being released, and that was my old house number. I'd seen the look in his eyes when he looked at me from the back of the cop car. They promised retribution, and Ray was the type to hold a grudge and keep a promise.

"Do you really think that they would call?" Cassie asked, concern lacing her features. She knew that I was supposed to be notified of his release if it were to happen earlier than expected.

"They're supposed to," I answered. "But Nana hasn't been home. I've been trying to reach her on her cell, but you know how she is. She told me that her friend said that she could stay as long as she'd like. Plus, it's not like we've had to worry, you know? It's been what? Ten years since he went to jail."

"Well, maybe keep trying to reach her. Or if you're that worried, take a trip back home?" Cassie suggested.

"That's not a bad idea. I will when my car is fixed… Wait, what day is it?"

"Tuesday."

"Crap. I have to take it to Bill's AutoBody today at…" I glanced over at the clock on the wall. "In thirty minutes."

I started to panic again because one, I didn't want to go alone, and two, I hated being late.

"Aubrey, calm down," Cassie reached across the table and placed her hands on mine. "Just get dressed. I'll ride over with you, and I'll call Chloe or Sophia to see if one of them would be able to give us a ride back."

My shoulders sagged with relief. "Thank you."

Cassie gave me a reassuring smile as I got up to go change. I left my bedroom door open, and as I was getting dressed, I heard Cassie on the phone with one of our friends. If there was one thing I had learned from everything that happened with Ray, it was I didn't have to be alone in my fear, no matter what it was.

Once I was finished getting ready, I met Cassie out in the kitchen.

"Chloe will meet us at the shop and bring us back here. Sophia will be coming over after her class. We're having a girls' night in," Cassie said, and my eyes started filling up with tears. She came over and wrapped her arms around me, enveloping me in a hug. "You know we show up for each other."

I sniffed. "I know."

She pulled away, resting her hands on my shoulders. "Good. Now let's get going."

I pulled myself together as we grabbed our purses and headed out. We started walking down the hallway, but I stopped, spun around on my heel, and headed for Dean's door. Lifting my hand, I gently knocked on the wood.

I heard movement, and then the door opened, and my gaze locked with forest-green eyes. "Everything okay?" Dean peeked his head out and glanced down the hallway, seemingly looking for a threat that wasn't there.

I nodded. "Yeah. I just wanted to let you know that Cassie and I are heading out to take my car to the shop. I almost forgot I had the appointment. We will be back soon."

I wasn't sure why I felt like explaining myself, but he did burst through my door when he heard me screaming.

He lifted a brow. "Okay. McCormick is at the hardware store getting you a new lock. When he gets back, we will get your door fixed."

"Okay. Thank you, although you don't have to."

"Technically I do, since I'm the one that broke it." His tone gave nothing away, but his eyes said something different. He ran a hand down the back of his neck, almost like he wanted to say more, but held back.

I sucked in a breath. "Well, I'll see you later."

Before I could walk away, Dean shut the door.

At least he didn't slam it in my face this time.

Just when I thought we were starting to get along, he went and did something to fuck it all up again. I turned back to Cassie, and we headed for the elevator.

THE TRIP TO BILL'S AUTOBODY AND BACK WAS smooth. We had stopped at the grocery store to pick up junk food and had gotten a text from Sophia saying that she was already at our apartment complex. I managed to have moments where I had all but forgotten what happened, but those moments were few and far between.

We parked, and we each grabbed a bag full of delicious goodies. The big bag of Swedish Fish had my name all over it. They were my all-time favorite candy, but that didn't include KitKat's, which I also had a bag full of the fun-size ones.

"Did you guys buy out the whole candy aisle?" Sophia asked, taking the bag that Chloe had handed to her.

"Yes. We got you Reese's Pieces and Cookie Dough Bites. Which I'm not even sure why you like those. It's not actual cookie dough," Chloe responded, closing her trunk.

"Real cookie dough is— "

"Harmful, yes, we know. But that doesn't stop me from living my best life."

Cassie and I exchanged amused glances as we followed behind Sophia and Chloe. I was beginning to relax as we entered the lobby of the apartment complex. A part of me was excited; we hadn't had an actual girl's night in forever. Where we hung out all night, watched movies, gossiped, and drank wine. Tonight, we agreed on binge-watching *Friends*. It was my comfort show. It was the show that makes everything better.

The elevator dinged, and the doors opened to the seventh floor. We had just rounded the corner when I saw Dylan closing my apartment door. Cassie faltered and fell a few steps back as I approached Dylan.

"Hey, I just finished fixing the door. It's as good as new, but you needed new keys." He handed me two keys, one for me and one for Cassie. "The facilities manager also has a key, but he's supposed to."

I smiled. "Thank you."

Dylan returned my smile. "No worries. I'm just glad you're safe." His blue eyes shifted behind me, and I knew he was looking at Cassie. "Anyway, a delivery guy stopped by and dropped some flowers off for you. I set them inside on your kitchen table. If you need anything, don't hesitate to call. You've got my number."

"Okay, thanks again." I wondered who the flowers could be from, but then I thought they were probably from Elaine. She usually sent me a bouquet of gerbera daisies if she knew I was having a bad day. Although, I should probably check in on her since it was her shop that was broken into last night.

Dylan nodded, then picked up the trash on the floor and walked next door to Dean's apartment. The girls and I exchanged glances as we walked into my apartment. We set everything down on my counter, and I was putting the ice cream away when I heard Chloe speak.

"Oh, these are beautiful. I wonder who they're from?" I heard her say. I had just closed the freezer door when I saw them. A large bouquet of yellow roses sitting on my kitchen table. If I was holding anything, it would have fallen to the floor. The smile faded from Chloe's lips.

"W-What does the card say?" I whispered. Although I knew what would be on that card, I needed to hear it.

"Are you su—?"

"Tell me, Chloe," I commanded, cutting her off, voice shaky with emotion.

Sophia and Cassie were standing on either side of Chloe, reading the card over her shoulder. I knew from the frightened look on their faces when Chloe spoke that I was right.

"I-I'm sorry I scared you, Bree. I h-hope you still like yellow roses."

I closed my eyes as I felt all the blood drain from my face. My worst fear had finally come to fruition.

Ray had found me.

TWENTY
Dean

Standing around in my kitchen with my dad, Dylan, and Sergeant Miller, we were meeting here to discuss what I found out about Ray. Since the attack last night—and my breaking down her door— we thought it would be best to meet here. Hearing her scream through these walls scared the hell out of me, and I was breaking down her door without even realizing I had run out of my apartment. I should have knocked and waited for an answer.

I broke protocol for a woman I'm not even dating.

My dad should have given me an earful, but for some reason, he let this slide. I was pretty sure it was because he had a soft spot for her.

"Alright, what do you know?" Sergeant Miller asked.

I crossed my arms over my chest. "The corrections officer called me back and said that Ray is missing. His cousin was taking his ankle monitor to work and clocking Ray in. He said he hasn't seen Ray in over a week."

"And you suspect Ray is Ms. Daniels stalker?"

I was just about to respond when there was pounding on my door.

I walked over, and the second I opened my door, Aubrey stormed past me and went straight over to Dylan. She was holding a bouquet of yellow roses in her hands.

Her friends stepped just inside the door but didn't move any further.

Did he give her those?

"Who gave these to you?" she yelled, shaking the flowers. "Who dropped these off?"

She was a pistol, ready and willing to bring anyone down to their knees. Even I was man enough to admit that seeing this little spitfire commanding the room full of cops was sexy as hell.

Dylan ran a hand down the back of his neck. "I'm not sure. It was some delivery guy."

"What did he look like? Was he five foot eleven, dirty-blond hair, brown eyes. Did he have a scar on his left eyebrow?" Her voice was trembling as she made a perfect description of Ray.

"Ms. Daniels, there's something we need to tell you," My father spoke up. "It's about Ray Owens."

Aubrey took a step back. Her face was pale, and she was visibly shaking. I took a step toward her and caught the bouquet of flowers just as they slipped out of her hands.

She looked at me, but her eyes were glazed over. "He found me. He's going to kill me."

What the fuck?

Her voice was barely above a whisper that I wasn't sure if anyone else in the room heard her. I wasn't even sure she knew she said that out loud. She blinked and ran out of my apartment. I set the flowers on my counter, not sure what to do with them, but I had a feeling that throwing them away right now would've been a mistake.

"Aubrey?" her friend Cassie called after her, and then they all ran out of my apartment.

"What the fuck was that all about?" I said out loud.

"Why don't we all go and find out? The girl was spooked," my dad said, and we followed him next door. We heard female voices coming from Aubrey's room.

"She's not picking up!" Aubrey's panicked voice rang through the hallway. She placed the phone up to her ear again and was pacing the floor.

"What's going on?" Sergeant Miller asked.

"She can't get ahold of her grandmother," Sophia told him. My eyes were trained on her. Everything about her demeanor was telling me that she was almost in some sort of denial, like she needed her grandmother to confirm what we already knew.

"Damn it," Aubrey cursed. "Voicemail again."

She stood frozen in the middle of the floor, as if she was lost in thought. Her blue eyes zoomed in on her closet, and she rushed over, digging through it until she pulled out a duffle bag.

"Will somebody please explain what's going on?" I commanded, and Aubrey narrowed her eyes on me.

"What's going on is none of your damn business."

I jerked back. Usually, this was the other way around. The way she would meet me tit for tat was becoming a bit of foreplay for me.

"Aubrey!" Sophia said loudly. "They're just here to help."

Aubrey paused from packing her bag, and she glanced at everyone in the room.

"Are you sure those flowers were from Ray?" I asked, and everyone turned to me. This is all the proof we needed to confirm that Ray was her stalker.

Aubrey and I stared at each other, and out of the corner of my eye, I saw her friends looking between us. I didn't care because this asshole scared the hell out of her.

"Tell him, Aubs," Chloe spoke up.

Aubrey was silent for a moment, chewing on her lower lip. It was like she didn't want to say the words out loud, because if she did, it would be real. I knew how that went, and part of me hated having to force it out of her. The cop in me had to get it out of her because we needed to find the SOB. The other part of me—that was starting to become annoyingly loud—was that not only did I need to keep her safe, I wanted to.

You might not be able to keep her safe. You couldn't keep Wyatt safe.

"Absolutely," she finally said.

"We need to put you in protective custody Ms. Daniels," My father spoke this time.

Aubrey shook her head forcibly. "Not until I go back home. I need to get back home. My grandmother isn't answering her phone, and I've been trying to reach her for over a week now."

"Is this normal for her?" Sergeant Miller asked.

"Yes...and no. We've gone weeks without speaking before since she travels, but if Ray is out of jail, then she could be in danger. She's got a phone book with a list of her friends names and contact information. If she's not there, then I can at least grab that and call her friend she's staying with in Islamorada to warn her not to come home. Not until it was safe." Aubrey zipped up her duffle bag and turned to Cassie. "Cassie, would you mind if I borrowed your car?"

Cassie nodded. "Yes, but you're not going alone."

"No," Dylan interjected. Both Cassie and Aubrey turned and stared daggers at him. "What I mean is, why can't we just have a patrolling officer do a wellness check, and grab the phone book?"

"You can do what you want. I'm going regardless," Aubrey spat at him. The look she gave Dylan meant that she was going whether any of us liked it or not.

Is she really going to go alone?

"Dean will take you," my dad said, and both Aubrey and I turned to look at him.

I lifted a brow. "What?"

"There's no need—" Aubrey started to say, but my dad cut her off by raising a finger.

"No, Dean will take you. You'll be safer that way, especially if Ray Owens is dangerous. In the meantime, Detective McCormick will stay behind and make sure nothing happens while you're away. Ms.—" My dad paused, looking at Cassie.

"Cassie Newton."

"Ms. Newton, do you have a place you can stay until Ms. Daniels gets back?"

"Yes, sir. I can stay at my boyfriend's place," she answered. Dylan looked like he would have rather her stay at his place, but that was none of my business.

"Good. Sergeant Miller, I need you to pull everything you can on Ray Owens. He's a wanted man now."

My dad turned and left the room, so I followed.

"Pop, I have to stay here. What if he shows his face?" I asked, and that sounded lame even to my own ears. I knew keeping Aubrey safe was a priority now, considering she was the target of his obsession. But I didn't want to get close to her. I couldn't let myself get close to her. *If I let myself get close to her, I could lose her.*

"Then he will have the entire River Falls police department hunting him down," he said.

He had me there. "I'm still waiting on that sealed file."

Okay, so I was reaching at this point.

"I'm willing to bet that what's in that sealed file has everything to do with Ray Owens. C'mon, son, don't tell me you're losing your touch."

"I'm not, but do you really think me taking her back to her house is the smartest move? Why can't Dylan take her?"

My dad scoffed. "Dylan is still on probation. It's not his job."

"And it's mine?" I asked, temper starting to flare. I knew deep in the back of my mind that he was right. I was the only one that could go with her and the only one trained to do so. Dylan and I were the only detectives at the precinct in River Falls, and since he was on probation, that meant that I was the one who had to go. Sergeant Miller would be the one he would report to while I was gone.

"It became yours when you kicked in her door. Your job now is to keep her safe, and that's an order," my dad commanded and walked away before I could even respond. How the fuck could I keep her safe when I couldn't even protect a trained officer?

TWENTY-ONE
Aubrey

I was waiting for Dean in my apartment while he packed his bag. I didn't think either of us wanted to be stuck in the same car for hours, but he nor I really had a choice in the matter. I knew going alone would have been stupid, but the need to see my nana—or to even hear her voice—to make sure she was safe...

He was taking forever to pack and I was close to stealing Cassie's keys and getting out of there.

"I could have taken you," Chloe offered. "I don't like you going alone."

"I won't be alone," I told her, pacing the floor. What was taking him so damn long?

"You don't even know Detective Holden all that well," Sophia chimed in. "What if he's a dirty cop?"

I shot her a look. "Dean may be many things, but a dirty cop isn't one of them."

Sophia was about to argue, but Cassie spoke up. "No. I believe Aubrey. Detective Holden isn't a dirty cop; otherwise, Dylan would have let me know. We may be on the outs, but it's against Dylan's very nature to not speak up if something is wrong."

"I still could have taken you," Chloe said again, almost pouting.

"And close the boutique down for a day or possibly more? No, I won't let you do that. You just opened earlier this year, and I know you're swamped on backorders," I said, sitting down in a kitchen chair.

Sophia opened her mouth to say something, but I cut her off. "No, I will not let you skip class either. It's the middle of August, and you have finals coming up soon. You will not skip class for nothing."

"It's not nothing," Sophia said. "What if something happened?"

I pondered her question for a moment as there was a knock on my door. I stood up, grabbing my bag.

"I will cross that bridge if I come to it. But right now, I need to get home. If Nana hasn't gotten back yet, then I will call her friend in Islamorada. It's safer for everyone involved if I do this with a cop rather than with friends. I just…I need to know *for sure*," I said my piece, then left the girls in the apartment. My only chance at survival was to stay with someone who Ray felt threatened by, and he would be threatened by Dean Holden.

THE WAY TO MY NANA'S HOUSE WAS ONLY A FEW hours, but this drive was taking forever. We took Dean's truck, which I hated to admit was nice and cozy. We sat mostly in silence, the music the only noise between us. Turns out, we both liked classic rock. Who would have thought we'd have the same music taste, but here we were.

The longer I sat in his truck, the more I thought about Nana. What if something happened to her?

What if Ray has already gotten to her?

No, I couldn't let myself think about that. Nana was fine—at least that was what I would tell myself until we got back to my house. A shiver worked its way through my body, leaving nothing behind but dread.

I tugged my hoodie tighter. It wasn't unusual to start having cooler nights in August, but it wasn't like it was freezing. I heard on the news to expect below-average temperatures this year. Dean was only wearing a button-down flannel with the sleeves rolled up. I guessed his muscles kept him warm, or his hatred for the world—it was anyone's best guess. He leaned forward and pressed a button on the console. Heat blasted through the vents, and after a few moments, my butt started to feel warm.

"Thanks," I muttered, and Dean nodded. Once my body stopped quivering, I laid my head against the window and closed my eyes, letting the heat wash over me. I didn't fall asleep though, even though my mind and body were exhausted. I kept my eyes closed, trying to keep my mind blank, when suddenly, I heard Dean humming along softly to "Whipping Post" by the Allman Brothers Band. I wasn't even sure if he was aware that I was awake or that he was even doing it. Before I knew it, I had fallen fast asleep.

"We're here," Dean said. I jolted awake, unsure of my surroundings at first. I took one look at my nana's house and instantly knew something was wrong. I felt it in my bones.

I opened the door and jumped down. Her rose bushes looked like they haven't been trimmed in a while, and there were a few packages sitting on the porch. Sometimes she would mail souvenirs back to her house so it would save room in her suitcase. *She just hasn't gotten home yet.*

When I got to the front door, Dean stepped in front of me.

"Let me go in first," he commanded, holding out his

hand to stop me from walking any further. I shot him a look. "It's my job, Aubrey."

I wanted to roll my eyes, but I didn't. I gave him the key, and he unlocked the door. As soon as it opened, a horrid smell hit my nostrils, and I took a step back, gagging. My stomach started to churn at the rancid smell.

Dean pulled out his gun and flashlight and turned to me. "Wait here."

He held up his gun and entered the house. It wasn't until a few moments passed that I gathered my wits and went in after him. Pulling my hoodie up over my nose, I crossed the threshold into the house. The thin layer of fabric wasn't doing much to mask the smell as I made my way past the living. Then something on the kitchen counter caught my attention. What was our old video camera doing out? We haven't used that thing in years. My feet kept moving toward it. Once I got closer, I realized that it was plugged into the wall, and a note was by it telling me to press play.

With shaky hands, I picked it up and turned it on. I gasped at the sight on the tiny screen. Nana was sitting on the couch, just feet away from where I was standing right now.

"C'mon, Dianna… give us a smile. Show Bree your pretty smile before I bash your head in." I heard Ray's voice from behind camera.

"Go to hell, Ray." Nana spat at him. I flinched at the sound of his hand smacking her across the face. *Oh God!*

"Tell me where she is!" He hollered, setting the video camera down at an angle I could see them both in. He punched her so hard she fell off the couch. "Tell me where she is or so help me Dianna I will kill you!"

Nana pushed herself up and looked at Ray dead in the eyes. "Then you'll have to kill me."

"No, Nana, No!" I heard a voice similar to mine say. Or maybe it was me because Dean came running down the hallway. It was too late. Ray was beating her to death right in front of my eyes. He grabbed my Little League baseball bat and kept whacking her; over and over again until I couldn't hear her scream out anymore. He started pulling her lifeless body out of the frame and I waited and waited for someone to pop up on the screen and yell, "gotcha!"

Dean tried to pry the video camera out of my hands, but I turned away. The camera shook then Ray's face was on the screen, covered in bloody splatter. He held up my River Falls graduation photo, then walked over to the refrigerator, standing in front of my nana's calendar. Where it said, "surprise lunch with Aubrey in River Falls."

Ray laughed. "Well, I thought I'd have to look much harder after this. Seems like I didn't have to look that hard at all, Bree. I'm coming for you, baby. 'Til death do us part."

Then the camera turned off.

"Aubrey," Dean's voice was soft as I felt him approach me. I didn't believe this.

"She's not dead," I sniffed, setting the camera down on the counter. "Nana!"

It's not true. She's fine.

I started walking down to her bedroom, the rancid smell getting stronger the closer I got.

"Aubrey, stop! You don't need to see this." Dean's commanding voice echoed on the walls, but I didn't stop. I couldn't stop. That's when he gently grabbed my shoulders from behind. He stepped in front of me, so he was blocking my view of my nana's room with his body. I needed to get to her—I needed to see her. I tried pushing past him, but it was no use. He spun me around and started leading me back outside.

"What are you doing? Let. Me. Go," I hissed, digging my heels into the carpet and trying to push him off. He was a lot stronger than I anticipated, but his grip on me wasn't tight at all. When we got outside, he let go, and I whirled around, ready to give him a piece of my mind, but the look on his face made the words disappear on my tongue.

It was then… *I knew*. I knew she was gone.

My throat burned. "No."

Denial. Denial. Denial.

He shook his head. "Aubrey, I'm so sorry."

"No." I took a step back, then another. Tears welled up in my eyes, causing Dean to look like a giant blur. My stomach churned violently, and I ended up heaving right into the rose bushes. I couldn't stop, even when there was nothing left to come up. My whole world was gone. Nana was gone. The only blood family I had left was dead.

I felt a hand on the small of my back, and I stood up straight, wiping my mouth with my sleeve. Dean kept his hand on my back as he handed me a bottle of water. I mumbled a thanks and took a tiny sip. But the second it hit my stomach, I felt like puking again but managed to keep it down.

"You need to remember her as she was and not like that," he said, rubbing my back. "I'll call this in, and when they show up, we can leave."

All I could do was nod as Dean led me to the truck and opened the passenger-side door. I got in, and he shut it behind me. I kept my mind blank as I stared forward, wishing this was all just a sick fucking joke. But it wasn't. The only person standing in Ray's way was Nana, and he'd killed her. All to get to me.

I was a danger to everyone. No one would be safe around me, not even Dean.

Lights started flashing as cops and an ambulance showed up. I was lost in thought when the door opened, and Dean jumped inside.

"My old sergeant set us up in a hotel for the night," he told me as he put the truck in reverse and pulled out of the driveway. I said nothing. I felt nothing. Another part of my soul was ripped away, and it was all because of me.

You're a survivor, little bee.

Hearing my nana's voice in my head caused a tear to slip free. I quickly wiped it away and stared out the window.

I'd made myself a vow the night Ray was arrested: I would never cower away again. And I'd be damned if I let myself break it now.

You're a survivor, little bee.

Damn right I was.

TWENTY-TWO
Dean

*I*t started raining as soon as we pulled into the hotel parking lot. Aubrey had been silent since we left her house, and I couldn't say that I blamed her. She just witnessed her grandmother being murdered. Hell, I barely talked now, and I'd lost Wyatt over three months ago. I knew what she was going through. I knew exactly how she was feeling because I was still living it. As much as I would've liked to stop and grab a small pint for tonight, I had to keep my wits about me. Things had just escalated from obsession to murder, and the sooner we caught him, the better.

Aubrey didn't move when I put my truck in park and turned the engine off. I got out, scanning the parking lot as I walked over to the passenger-side door. She didn't even flinch when I opened it.

"You ready?" I asked, trying to keep my voice low. When she didn't answer, I pressed further. "Aubrey? Are you ready to get inside?"

I placed my hand gently on her arm, and she snapped out of it. Aubrey nodded as she unbuckled her seat belt, and I helped her out of my truck. I grabbed both of our bags from the back seat and walked inside. I made sure to keep a lookout as we made our way to the front lobby. I checked us in and got our room keys. I led her up to the third floor to our room. As much as I didn't particularly like sharing my space these days, desperate times called for desperate measures. I was thankful we were able to get two doubles, not that I had any intentions of falling asleep. The alcohol was good for two things: numbing the pain and keeping the nightmares at bay.

I set her duffle bag on the bed closest to the window, and I set mine on the one closest to the door. If anyone were to break in, they would have to go through me. The chances of that happening were slim, though, because all evidence was pointing to Ray still being in River Falls. I wasn't a medic, but I thought Aubrey's grandmother had been dead for about two weeks, give or take. It was a good thing we packed because now I needed to stay in town a few extra days. I had to go back to her house to check out the crime scene. I had given the video camera to the cops who arrived on scene as evidence.

Aubrey walked over to her duffle bag. "I'm going to take a shower."

I nodded and pulled out my phone. I waited until the bathroom door was closed before calling Sergeant Miller.

"Miller," he answered on the second ring.

"Hey, Serge," I said quietly. "I have bad news."

"Hang on. I'm putting you on speaker. I'm at the precinct with McCormick and the captain." I waited for a moment. "Okay, go ahead."

I scrubbed a hand down my face. "Aubrey's grand-mother was dead when we arrived. Looked like she had been for about two weeks. Ray video tapped the whole murder. It was... it was brutal. She was beaten to death."

"And Ms. Daniels? How is she?" It was my dad who spoke.

"She's doing about as well as anyone is in this situa-tion," I told him. Admittedly, she was handling it a helluva lot better than I did…and still was. "What about things up there? Any sign of Ray?"

"Nothing. We're waiting for his information to come over. Since we have his mug shot, we'll put out an APB," Sergeant Miller said. "In the meantime, I want you and McCormick on this case. This is your top priority now. Tomorrow, I want you back at that house to look for more evidence. The videotape is proof enough, but I want to make sure Ray Owens never sees the light of day after this."

"I'll be down in the morning to help you," Dylan spoke up.

"When you're finished there, I want you to take Ms. Daniels to an undisclosed location. Detective McCormick will have all the details in a sealed envelope. Her safety is *your* top priority, Dean. Only the four of us will know where she will be. No one else can know, not even her friends."

Great. My dad tasked *me* to protect her. Did he not remember what happened the last time I was tasked to keep lookout? Wyatt was killed. And now he wanted me to protect her?

"Do you copy?" my dad asked harshly, and I pulled myself together.

"Yes, sir," I gruffed out. "I don't think we'll need that sealed file anymore."

"No, we don't. But it's already on its way to you," Dylan answered me.

"Okay, well it wouldn't hurt to look it over. Maybe it can give us a better insight into who we're dealing with."

"I agree. Keep us posted," Sergeant Miller said.

"Will do." I hung up after that. Aubrey was still in the

shower, so I sat down on my bed and started scrolling on my laptop.

I WAS ABLE TO FIND OUT WHO THE PATROLMEN WAS who was bringing over that file and managed to convince him to bring us some food. I was starving, and I focused better with food in my system. Especially if I was going to pull an all-nighter without booze. Aubrey had come out of the bathroom and climbed into her bed. She had the TV on, but I didn't think she was watching it. There was a knock on the door, and Aubrey sat straight up in the bed.

"It's okay," I said to her when her frightened eyes met mine. "I'm expecting someone."

She relaxed slightly as I walked past her to the door. I peeked through the peephole and saw it was an officer. I opened the door and thanked him and then locked the door back up. When she saw me pass by her again, she settled back down into her bed. I set the food down on the table and sat down in the chair. I opened the bag and pulled out a burger and fries. I made sure to ask for an extra burger and fries for Aubrey.

"Are you hungry?" I asked, offering her the bag.

She shook her head, so I closed the bag to keep it warm. I opened the burger packet and took a bite. Burger King wasn't the best burger I'd ever eaten , but it would get the job done for now. I picked the folder up and opened it, glancing over what was written down in it. Whoever wrote it needed one of those dotted letter books that taught children how to write. My eyes scanned over her name.

Aubrey Rose Daniels. *A beautiful name for a beautiful woman.*

"What's that?" Aubrey's soft voice pulled my attention to her.

Confused, I lifted a brow, and she motioned to the file in my hands.

I cleared my throat before I answered her. "It's a work file."

Her brows furrowed, and she got out of bed. My body stiffened when I took in her long legs and formfitting long-sleeved shirt. Those leggings did not help keep anything to the imagination. She grabbed the file from my hands and looked it over. Her bottom lip quivered, and her eyes watered as she read what was on the paper.

Her blue eyes locked with mine, and a tear slipped free. "Am I a suspect?"

I blinked at her. Why would she think she was a suspect? She was never even on my radar...as a suspect anyway. She's a victim. Another tear fell down her rosy cheek, and I had to hold myself back from wiping it away.

"Why would you think that?" I asked, voice low and husky even to my own ears.

"Because you have this."

I looked at her, and damn did a part of me want to wrap my arms around her. The more time I spent with her, the more my walls started to crack. I needed to plaster that shit up now. I could hear Wyatt now.

You'd be an idiot to let this one go.

Well, sorry pal. I had to let her go. I would be poison to her, never allowing her to blossom.

"No," I finally said. "We found out you had a sealed file as we were looking into the guests at the firehouse banquet. It was routine to check the backgrounds. We requested it before we knew about Ray."

"So, if I'm not a suspect, why did you still need my file?"

I sighed. "I guess technically we don't since we already know what's in it. I was just reading over it to make sure we get every last detail of who this guy is."

Aubrey straightened her shoulders, forcefully handing the file back to me. "You could have just asked, but since you didn't, I guess you'll be up all night, then." Then she stormed back over to her bed and lay down with her back to me.

Her and that damn smart mouth. It shouldn't turn me on the way that it does, but I just can't help to want to kiss her every time she spits fire at me.

TWENTY-THREE
Aubrey

J was living in a nightmare. I felt like I was stuck in limbo between panic and calm. My mind was my version of a panic room. Thoughts were racing through my head as I lay there staring at the wall. I knew that I needed to prepare myself for the questions Dean would be asking me. I knew that I needed to face this and talk about the one person who I kept picturing was lurking around every corner. It felt like if I spoke of *him*, he would hear me and come running.

I hated him. I hated Ray with every fiber of my being. I wasn't ready to talk about it, but the longer I lay here, the more my anger and guilt festered. It was my fault that Nana was killed. I'd led a killer straight to her doorstep. I'd invited him into our home. I'd loved him, and that thought made my stomach churn again. I sighed, rolling over and pushing the hair out of my face, swallowing down the bile that was rising in my throat. I stared up at the ceiling, giving myself a mental pep talk and taking in deep, calming breaths.

You can do this. Don't let the guilt hold you back.

I sat up and turned to face Dean, but he was fast asleep in the chair. I glanced down at my watch and noticed that I had been lying there for two hours. I had barely heard a peep out of him, but then again, I was lost in my own mind. I got up out of bed and went into the bathroom to splash cold water on my face. Wiping the water off with a towel, I looked at my reflection. The woman standing in front of me was not the same woman who left River Falls only a few short hours ago. She reminded me of a lost, scared seventeen-year-old girl, and the only thing she was missing was a bruise on her cheek and a black eye.

Walking out of the bathroom, I headed for the minifridge, hoping there would be a bottled water. Those were usually complimentary, right? When I opened the door, I breathed a sigh of relief. I wasn't hungry, nor was I that thirsty, but I knew my body needed something. I took a sip, the water feeling great on the back of my throat. Out of the corner of my eye, I saw Dean twitch in the chair.

I faced him, watching his fingers curl into fists as his body went stiff in the chair. His head jerked, and he mumbled what sounded like a "No, please."

He groaned in his sleep as his body twitched harder, his head jerked to the side. "Wyatt, no!"

I sat the water bottle down and slowly approached Dean.

"Dean, wake up," I said softly, gently touching his arm. Suddenly, he started thrashing his body, but his arms remained closed in on his chest.

"Don't go. Wyatt!" he shouted.

Dean was having a nightmare. I placed my hands on his biceps and gently shook him. "Dean, wake up! It's just a dream."

I used all the strength I had—which wasn't much since I hadn't eaten in hours—to hold him down. His fingers wrapped around my forearms, and his eyes burst open. Still gripping my arms, he sat up, and I shrunk down to the floor to my knees. We were eye level now; the only sound was Dean's heavy breathing.

Tension built between us as we stared at each other.

"Are you okay?" I asked, breaking the silence. Dean stared at me for a moment longer before his body relaxed. He let me go to cover his face with his hands. Curiosity got the best of me, and the second the words left my mouth, I instantly regretted them. "Who's Wyatt?"

He lifted his head, confusion written on his face. "What?"

"You said a name in your sleep."

Dean narrowed his eyes and got up from the chair. He went over to the minifridge, opened it, and cursed. He slammed it shut and pinched the bridge of his nose.

"What are you looking for?" I asked, thinking maybe I could help him find whatever he was looking for. "There was only one bottle of water—I only took a sip out of it. You can have it if you want."

"I don't want it," he growled. Grabbing his wallet and keys, he walked toward the door. "I'll be back."

Then he left. I sat on the floor, wondering what the hell just happened. What was I supposed to do? The only person who I thought I could count on to keep me safe had just left. Fear crept in and settled over my skin, seeping into my bones. I found myself moving closer to the corner of the room. I didn't want to cower away in fear, but I couldn't help it. I never thought that I would be hiding in shadows until the sun came up ever again.

TWENTY-FOUR
Dean

I made it less than halfway down the hall before I realized what I had done. I didn't know what scared me the most. The nightmare I was having about the night that Wyatt died, or the fact that when I woke up, I felt grounded by the person I least expected. Her touch calmed me, and I momentarily forgot what I was even dreaming about. So why the fuck did I storm out? Well, she'd asked about Wyatt, and that topic was off-limits to everyone. That included pretty blondes with blue eyes and a fierce attitude.

I stopped walking, rubbing my forehead to get my head level. I was a dick for leaving her alone, and if she could keep her shit together about what was going on, I could do the same for her. Honestly, I was surprised at her strength. Most people in her situation would be…well, they wouldn't be handling this the way she was. I'd read over that file. I saw what Ray did to her, and that angered me. How anyone could lay hands on another person like that…especially someone as kind as Aubrey?

I wasn't any better if I didn't turn the fuck around and go back in that room.

I couldn't leave her alone.

I turned around and walked back down the hallway. I put my room key in the slot and waited for the light to turn green. I went inside and glanced around. She wasn't sitting on her bed, and the bathroom door was open. I walked further into the room, and there she was, huddled in the corner. Her arms were locked over her knees, and her head was down.

Fuck, I was such a bastard.

I went over and knelt in front of her, careful not to touch her. She was already frightened, and the last thing I wanted to do was add to that.

"I'm sorry," I whispered.

Aubrey lifted her head. Her cheeks were wet, and her body was trembling. I was overwhelmed with guilt, more so than ever.

"Fuck, Aubrey, I shouldn't have left. I'm so sorry."

She wiped her eyes and looked away from me.

Please don't look away.

I wasn't even sure why I did it—maybe it was more for me than her—but I reached out and gently placed my hand over hers. Her skin was smooth against mine, and the air stilled around us. Her eyes met mine, and I didn't want to pull my hand away. But I needed to. I was surprised when she didn't jerk her hand away from me.

"If y-you promise not to leave again, I-I promise I'll talk to you about Ray. I-I'll tell you everything you want to know about him," she murmured. My heart skipped a beat at the tremor in her voice. I hated that. My job was to make her feel safe, and I totally fucked that up. She was willing to talk about Ray just as long as I didn't leave.

I definitely don't deserve her.

I made sure I made eye contact with her when I said my next words. "I promise I won't leave again. And you don't have to talk to me about Ray. Not until you're ready."

"I'm never going to be ready to talk about him. But I

have to. It's m-my fault Nana is dead." Her eyes swelled up with tears, and she moved her hands to cover her face. Her body shook as she cried, and I wasn't sure what to do. So, I did the only thing I could think of. I shifted my body to sit down against the wall next to her and pulled her into my arms.

It wasn't the first time I'd had to comfort a grieving victim, but it was different with Aubrey. It'd always been different with her. I knew she was dangerous to my heart from the moment I'd met her. She was pure, and I didn't want my demons to latch themselves onto her. I'd been fighting this strong attraction for months, trying to keep her out. Tonight would be the only exception to the made-up rule of "Aubrey is off-limits." She felt guilty for someone else's crime, and damn wasn't that a slap in the face.

"Listen to me," I told her, holding her a little tighter than I probably should have. But I realized that having her in my arms was something a part of me wanted to get used to. "Your grandmother's death is not your fault. You don't want to put that blame on yourself. Trust me."

I almost wanted to laugh at the irony of that statement.

Her soft cries stopped after a while, and I figured she had fallen asleep. I was about to scoop her up to put her into bed, but she sat up, and I got a whiff of her shampoo. She smelled like roses and peaches.

"Ray won't give up, especially if he has his sights set on something. He already killed my grandmother, and he almost killed me. I betrayed him by turning him in. He will retaliate, Dean. It's not a matter of if—it's when," she told me. Our bodies were still close, and I felt her breath caress my cheek.

"I won't let that happen," I promised her. She tucked her bottom lip under her teeth, and my eyes narrowed in on her lips. I hated making promises. More importantly, I hated making promises that I knew I might not be able to keep. Don't get me wrong, I was good at my job. But in this profession, you had to be careful with promises. You couldn't just hand them out like candy and not expect at least one of them to be stale. I hoped I didn't break that promise to her.

Aubrey nodded, then got up and walked over to her bed. I instantly felt cold the second she walked away.

"Call me, okay?" the brunette we met at the bar last night said as Wyatt walked her to the door.

"I will, I promise." Wyatt leaned in for a kiss, and I raised my brows. She waved goodbye, and after Wyatt shut the door, he spun around to me. "Damn."

I laughed. "Do you actually ever keep your promises?"

Wyatt plopped down on the chair in the living room. "Only to women I want to call back."

I shook my head but chuckled again.

"I actually meant it that time. I like her." Wyatt grinned. "I mean, she's sexy as hell. After we fucked, we talked. And it wasn't that dumb small-talk shit."

"Did she ask you what your hopes and dreams were?"

Wyatt flipped me off. "For your information, Deano, that's exactly what it was. But it was different with her. It felt natural, like I had known her my whole life."

"Don't tell me you're becoming a big sap now?" I laughed.

"I mean, I'm not saying I'm in love or anything, but I can definitely see myself keeping my promises with her," he replied.

"Good for you, man. I'm happy for you." I said truthfully. Wyatt was a ladies man, and I never thought I'd ever see him in a serious relationship, but it sounds like he might have found something with this girl Vanessa.

"Thanks. Now we just need to find you someone." He replied then he got this mischievous smile on his face.

I pointed a finger at him. "No. If you set me up on a blind date with one of Vanessa's friends, I'll kill you," I threatened jokingly, and he laughed.

"I'll just be your wingman with wings, then!" he shouted and laughed even harder. He made a little flying motion with his hands as he got up from the chair as he walked to the bathroom. Fucking asshole had jokes.

TWENTY-FIVE
Aubrey

The week passed by in almost a blur. The longest day was sitting with the funeral director discussing Nana's burial. Dean had dropped me off at the funeral home while he and Dylan went back to Nana's house to investigate. They found out that he had broken into the basement and was lying in wait for one of us to come home. Some drawers in my old room were open, and clothes were scattered all over the floor. I guessed he was in the middle of searching for clues for my where-abouts when my Nana came home and caught him. At least, that was their working theory anyway. I stopped listening to them after that. It didn't matter to me what their theories were. He still murdered her.

I chose to have a private graveside service for her. We didn't have any family for an elaborate one in the chapel. I wanted something small. My parents were both dead, and they didn't have any siblings. It was only Nana and me... now it was just me. Nana would be put to rest at the same cemetery as my parents, so I was thinking of dropping some flowers off at their site too. I tried to come down at least once a month to visit them, but I hadn't been in a while. Plus, I knew that I was going away to a safe house with Dean, and I wasn't sure how long I would be there.

Dean and I had been getting along better since the

first night we were here. I didn't press him on Wyatt anymore, and he never left me alone again. I was either with him or someone else he trusted to look after me if he had some things to do. If you would have told me a week ago that I would be stuck in a place with Dean for God knows how long, I would have rather gouged my eyes out with a spork. But the thought of staying with him now was comforting in a way I had never expected. Only time would tell if that would be a good thing or a bad thing. Who knew, we might kill each other before Ray would even get the chance.

I was sitting on the bed in a bathrobe when there was a knock at the door. I glanced over at Dean, who had gotten up from the table to walk over to see who it was. I heard familiar voices and jumped off the bed. When I peeked around the corner, I saw my friends. My eyes immediately started watering when Dean stepped aside and let them in.

"Oh my God, Aubrey," Cassie said as she and the other girls brushed past Dean and enveloped me in a hug. I had no idea that they would even be coming down here —it wasn't safe. I shouldn't have been shocked though; we would walk through fire to be there for each other. I looked up and saw Rhett talking to Dean by the door.

"We weren't going to let you do this alone," Sophia whispered, hugging me tighter. The relief I felt having my girls here was indescribable.

Chloe pulled away first and cupped my cheeks. "Sophia is right. We show up for each other."

I led them over to my bed, and we all made ourselves comfortable. I hadn't really talked to them much since I'd been a little bit preoccupied down here.

"What time is the service?" Cassie asked.

"In an hour," I answered. "Although I don't really have anything to wear. I didn't pack for a funeral."

Before anyone could say anything more, Dean walked into sight carrying two large suitcases, and Rhett was just behind him carrying one.

"What's all this?" I sat up a little straighter and realized that they were my suitcases.

"I had called Dylan to have your friends pack your things up for you. We are leaving right after the ceremony to go to the safe house." It was Dean who answered me.

"Don't worry, I packed all your essentials. And no, I didn't forget the camera equipment," Cassie said, and I smiled.

"Rhett and I bought all ten seasons of *Friends* for you too." Chloe smiled, looking over at Rhett.

"Yeah. She dragged me all around town looking for them," Rhett said, coming over a giving me a hug. "All worth it though."

"Thanks, guys. I really appreciate it." I wiped a tear from my eye that had slipped free.

"And I packed you my Kindle. I downloaded some great books by some of my favorite authors," Sophia chimed in. Sophia was an avid reader and always had the best recommendations when it came to romance novels.

Cassie leaned in to whisper, "The books with the half-naked men on the covers aka lady porn."

I chuckled for the first time in a week. "The best kind."

"We'll be next door," Dean's voice cut through. I watched as he picked up his bag, and then his green eyes met mine from across the room. "Let us know if you need anything."

I nodded as he and Rhett left us alone in the room. He was only going right next door to Dylan's room, and I knew that I would be fine with my girls for an hour. The girls were already dressed in black when they arrived, so it was only me who still had to get ready. If they hadn't shown up, I would have been wearing jeans and a sweatshirt to Nana's little service. I knew she wouldn't have cared what I wore, but I didn't want to show up looking like I had just gone to the grocery store.

I opened the suitcase that Cassie told me had my black dress in it. I pulled it out and went into the bathroom to change. Stepping into the dress, I pulled it up over my hips and slipped my hands through the quarter-length sleeves. I glanced at myself in the mirror. I saw bits of my nana and my parents etched into my features. I had my mother's eyes and cheekbones and my nana's nose. I knew that if I were to smile right now, there would be a small dimple in my left cheek that my father had passed down to me. I blinked and saw bruises around my neck, and my right eye was black and blue, as if Ray had just beaten me. I choked on a sob as I blinked once more, and the bruises were gone.

"Aubrey? How are you doing in there?" I heard Cassie's voice through the door.

I sniffed and cleared my throat. "I'm fine."

My voice cracked, and a second later the bathroom door opened, and I caught Cassie's gaze through the mirror.

I sucked in a breath and spun around. "C-can you p-please zip my dress?"

Tears started flowing freely down my cheeks as she nodded and grabbed my hand, pulling me out of the bathroom. As Cassie zipped my dress, I realized that it was feeling a little loose around my waist, and the sleeves were baggier than they used to be. Chloe dabbed my eyes with a tissue while Sophia held a small bag in her hands. They sat me down on the bed. Sophia pulled out a simple pearl necklace and clasped it around my neck as Chloe got to work on my makeup. Cassie ended up brushing my hair and pulling half of it up and out of my face. I clutched onto Sophia's hand as the other girls were still working on me.

"I went light," Chloe said and held up a small mirror. I peeked at myself and then quickly looked away. I couldn't look at myself right now. It only reminded me of what I had lost and was never getting back.

About twenty minutes later, Dean came back with Dylan and Rhett, and they helped carry my things down to Dean's truck. I was thankful when he allowed me to ride with my friends over to the graveyard. It was the last time I would be seeing them for who knew how long, and I wanted to soak up their strength and love.

When we parked along the grass by the gravesite, Sophia gave my hand a reassuring squeeze.

"We're here with you," she told me. We climbed out of Rhett's SUV and I glanced back at Dean's truck. Dylan hopped out and headed over to me, glancing around as he did so.

"Is Dean not coming?" I asked, voice low.

Dylan shook his head. "No, he's staying back to keep watch."

I nodded and looked back at Dean's truck. He was looking down, but then he must have felt me staring at him because he lifted his head. It made sense that he stayed behind, but a part of me didn't believe that was the whole reason. I felt that things had shifted between us the other night when he came back into the room. I'd thought for a split second that he was going to kiss me, but that was a ridiculous notion. He barely tolerated me, and who would want a girl who let her ex beat her up?

I glanced away as Dylan led me up the grass toward the blue tent. The priest was already there, and my heart skipped a beat when I saw Manny and Oliver standing up there. I wasn't sure what to expect, but I didn't expect to see them. I gave them both hugs and thanked them for being here. I knew that my blood family was gone, but family didn't end with blood.

Once the priest was finished talking, I wanted to be alone with Nana for a few moments. After setting a red rose down, I placed my hand on her casket and said a silent prayer. *Goodbye, Nana. I'll always be your little bee.*

A shiver worked its way up my spine as I stood there. I felt a jacket being draped over my shoulders and looked over to see Dylan standing there.

"I'd like to visit my parents if that's okay?" I whispered. Dylan nodded. "Of course."

We walked in silence toward my parents' headstones. Once we reached them, Dylan took a few steps back to give me some space. I knelt and placed the rest of the red roses in the vase. *I miss you guys so much. Please help me get through this. I love you so much.*

I wiped the tears from my cheeks and stood up. I stayed there for a few more minutes, thankful for the peaceful silence. I heard footsteps approaching, and I turned to see Dean walking toward us. He had a grim look on his face, and I knew I had to draw on every single ounce of strength that I had in order to get through this.

You're a survivor, little bee. The breeze blew my hair, and I tugged Dylan's jacket tighter. The news he was about to deliver would be bad, so I sucked in a deep breath and walked back over to Dylan.

You're going to get through this.

TWENTY-SIX

Dean

I reached Dylan at the same time Aubrey did. I needed to get her away from him so I could explain what the call I'd just been on with Sergeant Miller was about. It pissed me off, and I knew it would make Aubrey feel worse than I already knew she was feeling. I'd been in her shoes not that long ago, and I relived that day over and over again in my head daily. She handled herself a lot better than I had, and the fact I couldn't get my shit together long enough to go stand with her was more reason that I didn't deserve her. Her strength was astounding.

"What's going on?" Dylan asked.

I hesitated for a moment. I looked at her and saw that she was wearing Dylan's jacket. A twinge of jealousy flowed through me, and I had to remind myself that Dylan would be the better man for her.

I shook my head. "Nothing. We just have to get going, that's all."

Dylan nodded and started to walk away, but Aubrey remained planted where she was.

"You're lying," she said, once again calling me out on my shit. "I can see it in your eyes."

I studied her. "You're right."

"You can say it, Dean," Aubrey said softly. "Whatever

165

it is, you can tell me. There's nothing you could say that will make this day any worse than it already is."

Damn, was she perceptive. I didn't think I could bury my emotions down in front of her even if I tried. And I had been trying.

"Holden?" Dylan's voice broke through my thoughts, and I cleared my throat.

"Okay. Someone broke into your apartment, and we think it was Ray. It doesn't look like anything was stolen, but your apartment was trashed," I explained.

"Oh no," Aubrey gasped, covering her mouth with her hand.

"Thankfully no one was home, but there was something left behind," I growled. She shouldn't have to see this, but we needed to know what this meant, *if* it meant anything to her.

"What is it?" Aubrey asked. I looked at Dylan, and he knew from the look on my face how bad it was.

"We don't have to do this right now," I told her, hoping that she would wait. I wasn't ready to show her this, and I didn't think she was either.

"Yes, we do." Aubrey inhaled sharply and moved to stand next to me. Her arm brushed up against mine, and her scent of roses and peaches hit my nose. "Show me."

Reluctantly, I pulled up the message on my phone and showed the picture to her. I didn't want to look at it again, so I studied her face. Her brows furrowed as she reached up and zoomed in on the photo of lingerie covered in blood. All of a sudden, her nose scrunched up, and she pushed the phone away.

"I've seen enough," she murmured, grabbing onto my arm to steady herself. I handed it to Dylan, and he cursed under his breath. "Those are mine. It was the bra and panty set Ray gave me on our six-month anniversary. I didn't bring those with me when I moved to River Falls."

Her voice was trembling, and I felt her hand tighten around my arm. I hated what he was doing to her.

I turned her to face me. "We're going to catch this son of a bitch, I promise."

She nodded, and I led her back to my truck. We let her say her goodbyes to her friends, and Dylan told Cassie what was going on back at her place. We had enough reason to believe Ray was still in River Falls because her apartment was broken into at some point this morning. But we needed to get on the road soon in case he was headed back down here to her grandmother's house. Our window was closing fast to get her to the safe house which was also the last place I wanted to be. It was my parents' lake house. The place Wyatt and I had spent a lot of time at. No one knew that this house even existed except for my parents, Wyatt, and myself.

I checked my truck for bugs before hopping back in and waited for Aubrey and Dylan to finish up.

Aubrey climbed in the back seat while Dylan rode shotgun.

"Dean?" Aubrey's voice trembled when she said my name.

I turned my head to look at her. "Yeah?"

"Do you mind if we stop by my Nana's house real quick? There's something I need to grab."

I wanted to tell her no, but I answered, "Yes," instead. I didn't think it was a good idea to go back there, especially since I didn't think that the crime scene cleanup crew had been there yet. But here I was, pulling into her neighborhood and parking my truck in the driveway.

"I'll be right back," Aubrey said, jumping out of my truck.

I opened the door and got out too. "You're not going alone."

I followed her to the door, and she slipped her key in the lock. I knew what she was thinking when she pushed the door open and stepped inside. Fuck, it still felt like I was stuck in a loop walking through my apartment I shared with Wyatt that day after his funeral. The pain was unbearable, especially remembering the little things. Aubrey led the way down to a bedroom that was next to her grandmother's. Dylan and I were in here for a little bit, and I remembered thinking that this was such a neat and tidy room for a teenage girl, minus the drawers being open and clothes scattered everywhere. It was also bare, not something you typically see when investigating teens. White walls, barely any photos, and the bed was neatly made. I mean, I guessed her grandmother kept it clean all these years, but I would have assumed she would have left it as-is for Aubrey.

I stood in the doorway while she walked around the room. She grabbed a small bag and put a tiny jewelry box inside it, then went over to her bed.

"Can you help me slide this over?" she asked, setting the bag down on the bed. I nodded and came over to stand next to her as we pushed her bed across the room. She got down on the floor and lifted a small piece of the floorboard up.

"That's a pretty good hiding place," I told her, impressed that I didn't even think to move the bed.

She glanced up at me and smiled, although it didn't reach her eyes. "You mean, I could have hidden drugs here and you never would have found them?" I lifted a brow, and she chuckled. "I'm kidding. I kept things in here I didn't want Ray to find."

It was refreshing to see her old self come out, even if only for a moment. She pulled out a small box, then put the floorboard back into place. I helped her move the bed back into place, and we walked out of her room. We got back in the truck and took Dylan back to where his truck was parked. He ended up following us up the interstate to the lake house, each of us making sure that we weren't being followed. As we started to get closer to our destination, I knew that I needed to get my emotions under control. I couldn't sink off the deep end, not when Aubrey's life was in danger.

TWENTY-SEVEN
Aubrey

*D*ean pulled into a long driveway that led to a beautiful house that sat near a lake. It had a wraparound porch, which was something I had always dreamed of having when I could finally afford to buy a home. The house was surrounded by trees, but the yard was huge. There was a short pier at the lakeshore and a small boat sitting in the grass. I bet it was peaceful out in the water, and I wondered if I would be allowed out to take photos.

He parked his truck, and I jumped out. I needed to stretch my legs and take in some fresh air because we had been on the road for about five hours. My stomach had been tied in knots since we left Nana's house, and I just needed to breathe. I waved to Dylan as he pulled up behind Dean, who was at his tailgate getting my suitcases out. Moving to stand next to him, I reached for one of my suitcases.

"I got them," Dean murmured when he saw me struggling to pull it toward me. What the hell had Cassie packed?

"Thanks. I can wheel it inside though," I offered, but he didn't say anything. He seemed to get more tense than he had been all week on the drive up here, and I thought it might have something to do with whoever Wyatt was to him and this place. I knew not to press him on that sensitive topic, but if being here made him on edge, then he was a ticking time bomb. We were just starting to get along; I didn't want to revert to hating each other. Not that I ever really hated him to begin with.

I grabbed the handle of my suitcase and clutched the bag I had brought from my nana's house and followed Dean to the door. When we stepped inside, my eyes widened. This place was just as beautiful on the inside as it was on the outside. It had a cabin feel to it, but more elegant. It was the perfect snapshot home to have in a catalog. The living room area had a fireplace, something I'd always dreamed of having too. There was a long hallway that had doors along the way back to what led into what I assumed to be the master suite.

"This is a nice place," Dylan said, stepping into the house behind me, closing the door.

Dean nodded. "Yeah, it's alright, I guess."

I could tell he would rather be anywhere else but here, and I added that to the endless list of things that I should feel guilty about. He had to endure more pain because of me.

"Pick any room," Dean told us, and Dylan and I exchanged glances. I knew that Dylan would be here with us from time to time, but he would mostly be staying back in River Falls. Dean would also be traveling back with him a few times just to keep up appearances. I trusted that they knew what they were doing so Ray wouldn't follow them back here.

I grabbed one of my suitcases and walked toward the first bedroom I saw. I went to go open the door, but a hand covered mine and slammed the door shut.

"Not that one," Dean snarled.

I turned my head to face him, and we were a breath

away from each other. I saw the pain in his eyes when our gazes locked, and I knew that this must have been Wyatt's room. After a beat, he let go of my hand, and I pulled my suitcase down to the next room.

"Not that one either," Dean grumbled, and I rolled my eyes and spun around.

"If you didn't want me in any other room but this one"—I pointed at the largest bedroom in the house— "then why did you say 'pick any room'?" I did a really bad impression of him, and he scowled. He wasn't the only one hurting here, and I could only take so much right now. I saw Dylan watching us from the living room, and I honestly felt bad for him. He was getting caught in our crossfire.

"I'm not doing this." Dean turned on his heel, heading for the front door. I flinched as it slammed shut, then wrapped my arms around my waist. I felt tears threatening to spill over as anger coursed through my veins. I stomped past Dylan and went outside. I saw Dean down on the dock, and I marched down there.

"Hey!" I shouted, and Dean turned around. He looked shocked to see me coming at him like a hot grenade. I stopped right as I got to him. "You don't get to do that. Not anymore." My bottom lip quivered as I spoke, and I felt a tear slide down my cheek. "You can't just check out whenever you feel like it right now. I know you're hurting, but I am too."

I shoved my thumb into my chest for emphasis. "I've experienced loss too, Dean. Don't think I don't know exactly how you feel. One of us has to keep their shit together because Ray is still out there. It's not a matter of *if* he will find me, it's *when*…and I need you." I paused, wiping a tear away. Our eyes connected as I said my next words. "I need you to not check out on me."

Dean's jaw clenched as we stared at one another. When he didn't say anything, I shook my head and whirled around. I walked back up to the house, passing Dylan, who was headed down to the dock.

"Aubrey, are you okay?" Dylan asked as he halted his steps.

"I'm fine," I lied. I was far from fine, but if he wouldn't keep his shit together, then I had to keep mine on lockdown. Which meant that I needed to gather my wits about me. What I really wanted was to talk to my friends, but since I wasn't allowed to do that and had already given them my phone, I decided on soaking in a bubble bath. I saw that they had a tub earlier when I walked past the bathroom. Then I would curl up on the couch and watch TV.

AFTER MY BATH, WHICH TOOK ME LONGER THAN IT should have to figure out how to work the tub, I changed into some comfortable clothes and was on the couch watching *Friends* with Dylan. Dean had spent the entire evening chopping firewood, which was fine by me if that meant he stayed away. He'd come in not too long ago to take a shower, and I guessed now he was sulking in his room.

"Would you ever take a girl on a date to a museum like Ross does with Rachel?" I asked Dylan, who was casually leaning back in the recliner.

He chuckled. "Maybe."

I smiled, and then Dean walked around the corner. He

looked at the two of us, then went into the kitchen. The second I got inside earlier, I felt bad, but I was still fuming. Now that I'd had a chance to calm down and relax a little bit, I decided to be the bigger person. I got up from the couch and went into the kitchen.

Dean was grabbing a beer from the fridge when I walked in. He popped the cap off before he turned around and saw me standing there. His eyes roamed down my body, and I instantly felt hot. *Was he checking me out?*

I tucked my bottom lip between my teeth, not sure how to start my apology. "I just wanted—"

"I've been meaning…"

Dean and I both started speaking at the same time. I let out a nervous chuckle as Dean ran a hand down the back of his neck. He handed me his beer, then grabbed another one from the fridge. I vaguely wondered how long that beer had been sitting in there, but I remembered that Dean's parents had come up here and stocked the place with food and drinks.

"I just wanted to apologize for my outburst earlier," I said, taking a sip of beer. I made a face as the liquid went down my throat. I was more of a rum and cola girl than a beer girl. But after another sip, I got used to the flavor, and it wasn't so bad.

"You were right," Dean finally said, voice deep and rough. "I am hurting, but I have a job to do, and that's to keep you safe." He paused for a moment, as if he were thinking about what he should say next. "I won't let you down again."

My brows furrowed, and I wasn't sure if I heard him correctly. "Again? Dean, you haven't let me down at all."

I stepped up closer to him and placed my hand on his

arm. "I trust you because even though you are going through something, you always come back."

"Yeah, well, I didn't have a choice." He sounded thick with emotion.

I moved my hand to his cheek, and he briefly closed his eyes before opening them. "Yes, you did."

I wasn't sure when it happened, but it happened. I realized in this moment that I cared about Dean. I found his presence comforting and safe. Whether or not that was a good thing remained to be seen, but I cared about this broken man standing in front of me.

TWENTY-EIGHT
Dean

*I*t'd been a few weeks since we first arrived, and Aubrey and I had fallen into a routine. I was the first one up and the last one down. Since I had cut back on my alcohol intake, I felt sharper and less lethargic in the mornings. Of course, I was still getting nightmares, but I wasn't getting them as often as I had been. I was chalking that up to the fact that I had something else to focus on. Back when I was still in the city, I wasn't allowed to work on anything new or anything that required extensive work. One, because my knee was still fucked-up, and two, well, I was binge drinking to the point where there were a few times I had shown up to work more hungover than I should have been. Those were the days Sergeant Price sat me down in his office and lectured the fuck out of me.

I put on a pot of coffee before I went outside to do a perimeter check and to touch base with the patrolmen at the end of the driveway. That was our routine every day. She would wake up about an hour later, drink her coffee, and come outside with me while I chopped wood and she took pictures. Then, we would come inside. At first, we would be in separate rooms, but now we'd share the living room together. I'd work, and she would edit pictures on my laptop. I let her use mine because it was safer. We had our very own safe space here that was protected.

She would make us dinner, and I would clean up while she watched *Friends*. One night though, I'd just sat down to finish up some work but ended up watching a few episodes with her. She gave me shit for never having seen an episode before. Then we argued over whether or not Ross and Rachel were on a break, and at the very end of the night, I ended up agreeing with her.

When I came back inside after checking in with the patrol officer, Aubrey was standing at the counter, dressed in tight blue jeans and a formfitting sweater. I couldn't stop myself from staring at her. We've been getting to know each other lately since we were both cooped up in here. Turns out, we had more in common than I had thought. We shared more than just loss. We had the same music taste, we both liked action movies and we also liked pie.

It wasn't the same as cake.

I found myself waiting for her to break though. She'd handled her loss a helluva lot better than I had. Even if she would have a moment, I would be there for her. The night she told me she cared about me, it struck something in me. I was a total dick to her, and she still saw something in me to care about. She was becoming the reason why I wanted to stay sober. She didn't deserve to be treated the way I was treating her. She deserved the world and more. I was disappointed in myself as a man for who I was when I was drinking. I wanted to be the man who deserved her, but I didn't think I could. Not while I was still craving the numbness. Granted, I didn't crave it as much as I realized I was starting to crave tasting her. But I wouldn't pull her down in the hole with me. I had to pull myself out, and I wasn't sure I was ready.

"Are you coming outside with me today to take

pictures?" I asked Aubrey, and she nodded, taking a sip of her coffee.

"Yes. Would you mind if I went to the lake today?" She set her mug down on the counter and started to rinse the pot out.

"I don't see why not. Just stay in my line of sight," I told her. I didn't like her being out of eyesight when we were outside. Even though I did a sweep of the perimeter, there was still a chance that something could happen. A chance I didn't want to take.

"Of course." She smiled at me. You know the saying "Your smile could change the world?" Yeah, her smile could change the world, because it was slowly starting to change mine. Aubrey grabbed her mug and went back into my parents' room. I waited for her to get ready while I sent a quick text to Dylan. He's been back in River Falls for a while now. Apparently, our arsonist had struck again, and while nothing was really happening here, my dad and Sergeant Miller wanted him back with them. I'd give him credit—he was a natural at being a detective, even though he was newer to the job. He was growing on me.

Me: How's it going with our arsonist?
McCormick: It's not. This guy is smart. We'll catch him. Eventually he'll get cocky.
Me: They always do. And Ray?
McCormick: He's in the wind too.
Me: I wish he'd pop up somewhere. It's driving me crazy not knowing what he's up to.
McCormick: Same. How's Aubrey?

He always asked about her when we chatted. I knew that she and Dylan had formed some sort of bond. That much was obvious when he was here for few nights when we arrived. I thought it was because I was an asshole, and she needed a friendly face. Of course, when I confronted him about it teetering on the line of unprofessional, he said that they were just friends, and that he had a thing for Aubrey's friend Cassie. I could guarantee he would give me give me crap for me starting to teeter on the line now.

Me: She's good. Hanging in there.
McCormick: Good. Let me know if you guys need anything.
Me: I will. Thanks.

Aubrey walked around the corner, holding her camera, and was in a hoodie. "Ready?"

"Yep." I got up from the couch and followed her outside. I grabbed the ax and went around to the back of the house to chop wood while she walked down to the lake. I made sure to face her so I could keep a watchful eye out. The weather channel stated that we could expect snow as early as October, and I wanted to be ready.

I HAD A NICE PILE GOING WHEN I LOOKED UP AND saw Aubrey approaching me.

"I'm going to go inside. I'm a little chilly, and I want to get dinner started," she said, her nose a little rosy in color.

"Okay," I responded. "What are we having?"

She beamed. "I guess you will just have to wait and see."

I felt the corners of my lips tip up, and her mouth gaped open.

179

"Is that a smile?" She lifted a brow.

"No."

"Oh my gosh. Is *the* Dean Holden smiling? Hell must have frozen over." Aubrey chuckled, and I couldn't help but smirk. She lifted her camera and snapped a picture, then glanced down at the screen. She stopped laughing, but her smile stayed as she looked up at me.

"You should smile more often. It suits you." With that, she turned, and I was left just standing there staring after her. I had smiled before, but it didn't feel genuine, not like it did just now. I wasn't sure what version of hell she thought I was in, but mine was beginning to thaw out.

TWENTY-NINE
Aubrey

I walked inside, shutting the door behind me. Staying with Dean hadn't been so bad. I liked his company, and I hadn't felt comfortable in a man's presence for an extended period of time. Rhett and Ford were different because I wasn't dating them. But with Dean, it almost felt…natural. It seemed easy and organic between us, and that scared me because I wasn't used to someone so attentive as he was. He remembered what coffee creamer I liked, and he even told Dylan to grab more of my shampoo that I'd only just mentioned in passing that I needed more of. That was probably just the detective in him, but I wasn't so sure.

I felt myself getting nervous around him. It was a new feeling I'd felt toward him in these last few weeks. I wished that I could talk to my friends to get their advice on what those feelings meant. This was all new territory to me. I was attracted to him physically, but emotionally? I'd turned down every guy that'd ever held any interest in me. I couldn't let myself be vulnerable like that again. I had trouble letting my guard down with any of them, and they seemed like great guys. But something in the back of my brain kept telling me, "Ray was a nice guy too."

I was in the kitchen making dinner for Dean and me. Tonight, I was making my nana's famous chicken cacciatore, and I decided to bake a pie for dessert. It was the first time I'd made dessert for us, and I just felt like making it as a thank-you of sorts. Honestly, I liked making dinner because it made me feel closer to Cassie. I was nowhere near as good a cook as her, but I did my best. I started with the pie first, and then once that was in the oven baking, I started getting everything ready for dinner.

I missed my friends. I put on actual clothes instead of wearing my leggings and T-shirt all day just because I could hear Chloe yelling at me, "You never know when there will be a fire, so dress accordingly." I also started reading more books since Sophia loaned me her Kindle. My favorite so far had been a supernatural trilogy with demigods and wolf shifters. I didn't think I would like those kinds of books, but they were a great escape from reality.

I saw the bottle of wine sitting there and decided to pour a glass. Dylan had brought it back on one of his trips back here. I pulled a wineglass out from one of the cabinets and went over to the mantle in front of the fireplace. I noticed that some pictures were missing. You couldn't tell if you weren't looking for it though. You'd have to see where the dust never settled. There were only pictures of Dean and his parents. I picked up a frame and looked at a seemingly happy family. It was at a Little League baseball game, and Dean was missing his front tooth. I smiled, putting it back on the mantle when the door opened.

I turned and my breath hitched. Dean had discarded his flannel button-down shirt and was only in a white tank top. He was dirty and sweaty, and I let my eyes drop down to his abs that I knew were hidden under that shirt. I mean, it didn't leave much to the imagination. His muscles bulged and flexed as he shut the door and set the ax down.

He spun around, and I've never felt so turned on in my life. His eyes flashed a dark green, and I flushed. I was totally caught checking him out. I knew he knew it because I saw a smirk form on his perfect lips.

"I'm going to take a shower." He took his boots off by the door, then walked past me down the hallway. "Dinner smells good, by the way."

"Please hang up your wet towel!" I shouted after him. I hated when wet towels were left on the floor. They always got a funky smell to them.

"Uh-huh," I heard him say from his room. I rolled my eyes and went to go finish making dinner. I put the pie on the cooling rack and placed the chicken in the oven. It wouldn't be ready for a while, so I grabbed my Kindle, poured my second glass of wine, and sat down on the couch.

I was reading a story about a hot CEO who had a one-night stand in the bathroom of a nightclub only to find out that she was one of his new employees when the timer went off in the kitchen. I got up and pulled the chicken out of the oven and turned it off. I was letting it cool as I set the table when I realized Dean never came out like he normally would. Once I finished setting the table, I went in search of him, but I didn't have to go far. The door to Wyatt's bedroom was open, and I was shocked I didn't hear him go in there. I stood in the doorway when I saw him sitting on the bed, looking down at a picture, and there was a box lying next to him. He was staring so intently at the photo that I thought he was going to burn holes in it.

I knocked softly, and he jumped. "Oh. I'm sorry. I didn't mean to disturb you. Are you okay?"

He scrubbed a hand down his face and placed the photo back in the box. "Yeah. I'm good."

"Was that Wyatt?" I asked, and he turned toward me after setting the box down in the corner. He didn't look angry; it was quite the opposite. His face was pained, and I regretted asking my question. I knew by the hurt and broken expression on his face that it was Wyatt.

"I don't… I mean… I can't…" His voice broke, and then he cleared his throat, steeling his resolve. "We aren't talking about it."

I stepped out of the doorway as he walked out, shutting the door behind him. Dean was always locked up when it came to Wyatt. I could see that being in that room was a step for him, and that seemed like it was progress. I followed him out into the kitchen where I had just been.

"You set this up?" he asked.

I chewed my bottom lip. "Yeah, I just wanted to do something special as a thank-you."

"It looks nice. But you don't have to thank me. It's my job," he answered, taking a seat at the table.

"I know. I still wanted to do this. I also baked a pie for dessert." I sat down opposite Dean and placed a napkin in my lap.

His eyes shot up. "You made a pie?"

I flushed. "Yeah. It's apple."

It turned out we both liked apple pie. I took a sip of my wine, which was now my third glass, and I was starting to feel a little tipsy.

Dean smiled. "Let's eat, then we can dig into that pie."

By the time we finished eating dinner, I was feeling giddy. The wine loosened me up, and I felt like I had let my guard down. I wasn't completely drunk because the meal had soaked up most of the alcohol. It was the most I'd eaten in weeks too. But I was still feeling rather buzzed as I helped Dean clean up. He was doing dishes as I was cutting slices into the pie.

I opened the fridge and pulled out some whipped cream, and without thinking, I removed the cap and sprayed some in my mouth. I smiled when I saw Dean looking at me in amusement.

I held it out to him. "You want some?"

He shook his head, laughing. "No, but you…" He trailed off, motioning his finger to his nose. "You got some right here." He stepped up closer to me and swiped his thumb across my nose. Our gazes were locked, and all humor left my body under his intense stare. The heat radiating from his body set mine ablaze, and I leaned in closer to him. We were face-to-face and chest-to-chest. Was he going to kiss me? Did I want him to kiss me? Could I let myself give in to whatever was happening between us right now?

I felt his breath caress my lips as his forehead brushed against mine. I closed my eyes, and my heart rate accelerated as our bodies inched closer and closer together. We were dangerously close to crossing a line that we wouldn't be able to come back from. Our lips were just a hairsbreadth away, and all it would take for them to meet in a kiss was if one of us shifted our body slightly.

Before anyone could move, Dean's phone rang in his pocket, and we both pulled away. Dean cleared his throat before answering the call. "Holden."

I let out a shaky breath as Dean walked into the living room. Did that almost just happen? Did I almost kiss Dean Holden? Oh my God. I needed room to just breathe. I ran into the room I was staying in.

Could I surrender myself to him? Give him a piece of me that I haven't given anyone else since Ray? Realization stormed in like a hurricane, and I sat down on the bed. I was already letting Dean in. I was already showing him pieces of myself that I hadn't shown anyone.

I'm scared.

THIRTY
Aubrey

I was scared. I was scared of never seeing my friends again. I was scared of being away from home, my safe haven. I was scared of falling in love with someone who had the potential to break my heart. I was scared to let down the people I loved…I was scared of Ray finding me.

I'm scared of dying.

The loud thoughts in my head couldn't be silenced, not even with the alcohol that was running through my veins. I missed my friends, my home, my life. I missed taking pictures for clients and processing them in the darkroom. I missed my nana; I missed my parents, who I barely remembered. My life had been turned upside down and inside out.

Ever since Nana passed, I was a ticking time bomb ready to go off. I tried to be strong. I tried to push the pain away, to force it to be better. I felt like I was suffocating on toxic fumes of guilt. I looked at my reflection in the mirror, something I hadn't done since Nana's burial. I hated seeing glimpses of her and my parents staring back at me. They should be alive.

It's all my fault.

I did this. I killed Nana. Her death was on me. If I'd have just left Ray when he first slapped me across the face, none of this would've happened. Ray might have pulled the trigger, but I was holding the gun, so to speak. I felt nothing yet everything at the same time. I needed to find peace. I needed to be *free*.

My body felt hot from the wine, and I wanted to cool down. Grabbing the box from Nana's house, I stormed out of the room, passing Dean, who was still on the phone.

"Aubrey?" I heard him say, but I ignored him. I opened the door and felt the cool autumn air soothe my heated skin. My feet hit the ground running, and I didn't stop until I got to the dock by the lake. I knew Dean was hot on my heels because I heard him call out from behind me. My tears felt frozen on my cheeks, and I stood on the edge, staring out into the water. The lamp above was illuminating the area around me, and the moon was full above me. I was scared of the dark, but I welcomed it now. I wanted it to take everything in this box and swallow it whole.

"What the fuck are you doing?" Dean shouted as he stepped onto the dock. I didn't turn to face him, but I felt the dock move with every step he took. His tone wasn't angry, he was concerned. It almost sounded like he was nervous and scared.

"Please go," I whispered, hoping that he would leave, although deep down I knew that he wouldn't. If I jumped into this water right now, I knew he would jump in after me. It was in his nature. *It's also his job.*

"I'm not *going* anywhere," he told me, voice steady and even now. "Why don't we go inside. We can talk about it."

I spun around, narrowing my eyes at him. "Why? Like you talk about Wyatt?"

I knew that was a low blow, even for me.

Dean frowned. "Don't do that."

"Why the hell not? You want me to open up to you,

when you can't even open up to the people who give a fuck about you," I shouted. The steely look on his face was back. The one he put on whenever Wyatt came up and he shut people out.

"No one gives a fuck about me," Dean admitted, and I wanted to laugh.

"Are you serious?" I scoffed. "People care about you, Dean. Your parents, Dylan…me."

Dean's features softened at my admission. "What's in the box?"

I flinched back. I almost forgot the reason why I was down here.

"I need to let go," I whispered, then before I could even think twice, I handed the box to Dean. "Open it."

"Aubrey, you don't have to do this." Dean's voice was soft as he stared at me.

"I know I don't have to." I met his stare. "But I want to. I need to not keep this a secret anymore. This is what's holding me back. I need to let it all go, so then I can be free from it all."

His jaw clenched as he opened the lid on the box and pulled out the photos. A range of emotions flashed across his face: anger, disgust, sadness. It was all there. Out in the world. I knew that showing him a glimpse into my past wouldn't change the circumstances of where I was at now. I would still be in danger until Ray was arrested and put away for good. But knowing that I didn't have this reminder waiting for me every time I thought of home was the relief I was looking for.

When Dean glanced down at me, his resolve was broken.

"I took a picture of myself every day throughout my relationship with Ray and in the months following his arrest," I told him. My voice trembled with emotion as I broke free of my own demons. "My first and only love told me this is what love means."

Dean's eyes flashed a dark green as his gaze met mine. "I hate to be the one to break it to you, but someone who does this to you doesn't love you."

"That's all I know," I whispered. "I did this. This whole thing is all my fault. Nana is dead because of me." I started crying, letting out everything I had been holding in for a while now. My body was trembling as I covered my hands over my face. My legs gave out from under me, and I expected to hit the cold wood, but instead, warm arms caught me.

"Listen to me, Aubrey," Dean said, cradling me into his chest. "This isn't your fault, you hear me? You did nothing wrong."

The world came crashing down around us. I was broken, torn apart by the loss of the one person who meant everything to me. Who raised me and taught me what the word "love" meant. I barely remembered my parents, but I remembered Nana. She was everything amazing in this universe.

"What's wrong with me?" I asked out loud between sobs.

Dean placed a hand on my head and held me as I broke. He held me as long as I needed him to. I felt calm and safe in his arms. I believed that everything happened for a reason, and I was meant to know Dean. Our paths crossed for a reason, and I was grateful for it. Our dynamic had shifted into something that we both needed.

I realized then, being here in his embrace, that I could let my walls down and be close to someone again. The thought of being close to anyone else terrified me, but the key to any good relationship is trust. And I had trusted Dean with my life.

He scooped me up and carried me across the lawn and back into the house. He laid me down on the couch in front of the fireplace and put a blanket over me. He knelt in front of me and looked into my eyes.

Dean tucked a lock of hair behind my ear. "You are one strong woman, Aubrey Daniels. Any man would be lucky enough to have you."

When he went to get up, I reached out and grabbed his arm. "Stay with me?"

Dean hesitated for a moment, then sat down on the couch by my feet. He turned on the TV, and I fell asleep watching *Friends* with a man that I was slowly letting into my heart.

THIRTY-ONE
Dean

blinked my eyes open and stretched out. Memories of last night came flooding back, and it took me a moment to figure out that I was still on the couch. I fell asleep out here with Aubrey after she had her panic attack last night. I didn't think it was a good idea after I almost kissed her.

Yeah, I almost kissed her. All I had to do what pull her to me and our lips would have met. I was inches away from tasting her, and I didn't. If Dylan hadn't called me, I wasn't sure if I would have given in or pulled back. She was already on her path of healing. She shared a traumatic experience with me, and she didn't have to. She had been through so much and was willing to share something so personal. I'd admired her strength, and when I was holding her in my arms as she was crying, I vowed to keep her safe. It wasn't just a job to me anymore. The walls I had built around myself were starting to crumble, and I knew, sooner or later, I wanted to tell her about Wyatt. Right now, I couldn't bring myself to do it. I couldn't be weak.

"Good morning," Aubrey said, and I looked over at her. Her hair was damp, and she was working on the laptop. I realized that I had slept through the night peace-fully. I didn't wake up once, and I wanted to chalk that up to a busy day yesterday, but I knew it was Aubrey who kept the nightmares away. I knew that because I had dreamed of her last night. Her laugh rang through my dreams like a siren, and her beauty chased away the demons.

"Morning," I replied, stretching my neck. It hurt like a motherfucker, but it was worth it.

"Coffee is still warm on the pot," she told me, taking a drink from her mug.

"Thanks." I groaned as I got up from the couch. My muscles were a little tight from chopping wood, and my knee was starting to hurt. Walking into the kitchen, I took some ibuprofen and poured myself a cup of coffee. Then I went to take a shower. Once I was feeling more alive, I walked back out into the living room and sat back down on the couch.

"Can I ask you a question?" I said, glancing at Aubrey. She paused what she was doing, then looked over at me. "What made you want to take a picture of yourself during your relationship with Ray?"

I didn't feel like I had any right to ask such a personal question, but the thought had been on my mind since last night. After she had fallen asleep, I had gone back down to the dock and grabbed the box of photos and brought them back up to the house. I wasn't sure why she even took them down to the lake in the first place, but I thought I'd let her decide.

She was thoughtful for a minute. "At the time, I was happy, and I wanted to commemorate those moments. After a while it just became a habit. Then, when our relationship turned south, I don't know." She fiddled with the hem of her oversized sweater. "I just didn't want to go back to feeling like I was weak. I wanted to remind myself that I could overcome even the darkest of times. Once the bruises healed, I shoved those pictures into that box and would only look at them if I needed to. I didn't want to feel stupid for loving a monster again."

Aubrey sniffed, and a tear fell down her cheek. "Am I broken?"

I scooted closer to her, wiping the tear away, then cupping her cheek. "No. You are anything but broken."

Our eyes connected, and I hated seeing her look so sad. If I could take her pain away, I would. I was a monster in my own way, and I deserved all the pain I could get. As much as I wanted to be with her, I couldn't be the man she deserved. How could I love someone when I hated myself?

I removed my hand from her cheek and glanced at the computer. I'd never seen her work before, but the photos of the lake that she was editing were amazing.

"Wow." I tilted the computer toward me a bit so I could get a better look.

"I can't decide if I like color or black and white," she admitted, chewing on her lip. That was starting to become a bit of a turn-on to me, so I needed to change the subject.

"Do you have a version of it in black and white?" I asked, and she nodded. Aubrey clicked the next button, and the same photo appeared before me but in black and white. "Oh yeah. I see why you're conflicted. But if I'm being honest, I love the colored one better. It captures the colors of the changing leaves perfectly. Gives me that autumn feel."

"That's what I was thinking too. Black and white is just so elegant." She smiled. I agreed with her, and she closed that file and opened a new folder. "These are the ones I took back in River Falls."

She was excited when she talked about her pictures.

She was scrolling through them, each one a different shot of the park. I did notice that she avoided people as much as possible, but there was someone that caught my attention who was in almost every single shot.

"Hey, can you go back?" I asked, sitting up straighter.

"Uh, yeah, sure," Aubrey said, clicking the back button.

"Can you zoom in on this person?"

She did what I asked, and the picture came up clear as day. I recognized him immediately, and so did Aubrey.

"Oh my God!" she screamed, jumping up from the couch. I caught the laptop before it hit the ground and set it on the coffee table. I slowly stood up as Aubrey was hyperventilating.

"H-he was t-there! Oh my God!" She started clutching her chest, and her breathing became erratic. "I-I knew s-someone was w-watching me that day. I felt it."

"It's okay." I kept my voice soft as I approached her. I had the urge to pull her close and never let go, but when I reached out to her, she pushed my hand away.

"No! It's not okay." She sobbed. "H-he knows where I live! He knows my friends! He's going to hurt them! Please, you have to protect them!"

Finally, she sunk into my arms, and I held her tight. "Your friends are safe, I promise."

Aubrey was the object of Ray's obsession, and I had to assume he knew she was gone. Her friends were useless to him. He would know that they wouldn't know where she was. It was all a waiting game now, and that was the part that scared me the most. He'd wait until the perfect moment to strike, so I would have to be on guard. If I had been drinking, I never would have noticed him in the pictures right away.

When she pulled away, her blue eyes looked up to meet mine. "I'm sorry I keep crying on you."

I wanted to kiss her. I wanted to make her forget about all of this for a moment. I knew it would be a bad idea, and I wanted it anyway. *She's just a job. Focus, Holden.*

"Don't worry about it," I ended up saying and taking a step away from her when I knew she would be okay. Things were going to start getting more complicated the longer we stayed cooped up here. Aubrey Daniels was the only person who would be capable of chasing the demons away. She was the light that I didn't even know I was looking for, and I wanted to be blinded.

THIRTY-TWO
Aubrey

*I*t was late in September now, and I was beginning to come out of that slump I had been in. Dean and I'd been walking on a tightrope around each other. Tiny moments would pass between us, moments that I found myself wanting to give in to time after time. Sometimes I thought that I was imagining things, but when we would watch TV, I noticed instead of sitting in the chair, he would sit on the couch. They were small changes, but they showed me that it wasn't just me feeling like something was happening between us.

We touched more. It almost felt like our bodies were being pulled toward one another. Whether it was just a casual arm brush or him setting my feet in his lap, we were connecting in ways that I never thought possible. Sometimes I didn't think that he really knew what he was doing, but I did. Dean's touch was gentle, never rough. It was the opposite of Ray, where I was scared whenever he would lay a hand on me.

It was raining outside, which was a good indication that we were in for a rough winter. I was sitting in the bay window, curled up in a blanket, sipping on hot tea as I read about a football player who fell in love with a woman high school football coach. I laughed at the part when they were making out in a classroom and the desk toppled over. They had a hate-love relationship, kind of like Dean and me. *Maybe we do stand a chance.*

I heard something fall and a string of curses that would make a sailor blush come from one of the bedrooms. Getting up, I made my way down the hall but stopped in my tracks at Wyatt's open door. I glanced in and saw Dean on the floor, picking up pictures and putting them back in a box.

Without thinking, I rushed over and started helping him. I didn't think he noticed me, at least not until I picked up a recent photo. It was with Dean, his father, and a man I didn't recognize. When I quickly scanned the other pictures, there were a lot of the man I didn't know. He had short brown hair, brown eyes, and his smile was infectious. I set the picture I was holding in the box, and my hand rested on a piece of paper. I flipped it over and saw the words "In Loving Memory" written on the top, with a picture of the same man in his cop uniform. *This must be Wyatt.*

"What are you doing in here?" I jumped at the sound of Dean's gravelly voice. Did he not know I was helping him? His eyes were glossed over, like he was on the verge of tears but he was holding them back.

"What's that in your hand?" he asked. His voice broke with emotion. Everything in this room reminded Dean of Wyatt.

"Who was he to you, Dean?" I knew I was pushing my luck, but I saw the cracks in him. I saw how bad he needed to say the words aloud. It broke my heart to see him in pain. This wound hadn't started healing for him, and I was under the impression that he wanted it to get better. He just needed a little push.

"I don't want to talk about it." Dean scrubbed a hand

down his face. "Put it back in the box."

I did as I was told, and he put the lid back on then got up. He placed the box back in the corner and brushed past me, but I couldn't let him leave.

"Dean," I said sternly, and I was surprised he stopped walking. He just stood there with his back toward me. "He was clearly important to you. Was he your brother? A partner? Your best friend?"

I saw him shake his head. "Stop."

I took a step toward him. "He was your best friend, wasn't he?"

I knew he didn't have a sibling. His father only so much as said so at the banquet. All he could talk about was Dean.

"Aubrey, *please*." His voice cracked, and I knew I was getting his walls to tumble down.

"He was all of the above. He was your partner, your brother in arms," I whispered as I got closer to him. His body was shaking, but he made no moves to leave or turn around.

"S-stop it." His head fell forward as he murmured those words.

"I'm right, aren't I?" He didn't have to say a word because his body answered for me. Dean's head fell back, and I saw his back tense as he grabbed the back of his neck with both hands.

I reached out, placing my hand on his shoulder. "It's okay, Dean."

"For fuck's sake," Dean growled, spinning around and walking me backward until my back hit the wall. The way he was looking at me wasn't threatening. It felt weird to be pinned up against a wall and not fear for my life. Dean was not Ray; that much I already knew.

"Stop talking," he growled again, his body pressed up against mine, his breath coating my lips like a sweet minty caress. "*Please.*"

That last word was whispered against my lips. My heart raced, and my breathing was erratic. My lips parted on an exhale, and his eyes dropped down. He licked his lips as his pupils dilated, and for a heavy moment, we stood there. It was like a standoff on who was going to break first or walk away. The second his lips crashed into mine, I knew the thin line that we had drawn was now crossed. There would be no coming back from this moment, and part of me didn't care. His tongue swiped across my bottom lip, and I opened my mouth for him. As he pressed his body harder into mine, I felt exactly how this kiss was affecting him.

His kiss was intoxicating, bourbon and mint, my new favorite flavor.

He trailed kisses along the side of my jaw, down my neck, and nipped at the sensitive spot by my ear. I let out a breathy moan when he lifted my leg and pushed his erection onto me. When his lips found mine again, it felt like for a moment it was just us. The demons we both bore were silenced as we got lost in the peace of it all.

Dean suddenly pulled away from me, and I found myself missing his touch.

"Fuck," he hissed, then abruptly left the room. I leaned back against the wall and brought my fingers up, brushing my swollen lips. I was in a daze as I tried to navigate my way around what just exploded between us. Sinking down onto the floor, I came to one realization that rocked me to my core.

I had finally surrendered myself to Dean Holden, and there was no coming back.

THIRTY-THREE
Dean

What the hell was I thinking? I just kissed Aubrey. I wasn't even sure why I did it. She wouldn't stop going on about Wyatt, and I didn't know why I was in his room to begin with. I just walked in and started looking at pictures. It wasn't on my to-do list for the day, that's for damn sure. I had made myself vulnerable, and when she walked in and started asking questions, I knew right then and there I would break.

Kissing Aubrey was like breathing in fresh air after a night of rain. I had forgotten all the pain and the grief as my mouth moved against hers. I gave in to temptation, and I would sell my soul to the devil if it meant getting to taste her just one more time.

But I couldn't subject her to more darkness. She was only supposed to be a job, and here I was, kissing her as if my life depended on it. I wanted to turn my ass around and go back in that room and finish what we started. From the way she kissed me back, it felt like she wanted it just as much as I did. One of us had to stay strong though, and that had to be me. I needed to be able to focus and do what I needed to do. Even if that meant putting space between us. We were getting too close, and I couldn't lose control like that again.

I started to go outside to do my last perimeter check before nightfall when her voice stopped me in my tracks.

"Please don't go." Her voice was soft yet commanding. "We should talk about this."

I had one hand on the doorknob but kept my back toward her. If I turned around, I'd never leave the house. "There's nothing to talk about."

"We *kissed*, Dean."

"I know. I was there." Damn, I was a fucking dick. But this needed to be done. "Stay in here. I'll be right back."

I opened the door and walked out onto the porch, then out into the driveway. I was scanning the area, but I just couldn't focus. I still tasted her on my lips, and it was enough to cause a new addiction.

"Dean!" Aubrey shouted, and I spun around.

"I thought I told you to stay in the house!" I shouted, lifting a brow. Her cheeks were flushed as she ran toward me. Her blue eyes sparkled in the twilight as she caught up to me. "Go back inside, Aubrey."

Aubrey pursed her perfect, lush lips. "Come with me back inside, then."

My cock stirred at the word "come," and I started second-guessing my age. I was thirty-one, for God's sake.

"I have a job to do," I responded, hoping that she would at least understand that and go back inside and drop it.

She crossed her arms over her chest, and that pushed her breasts up. *Get it together, Holden.*

"It can wait," she said crossly.

I rolled my eyes. "No, it really can't. Go back inside."

We stood there, glaring at each other. She looked absolutely stunning standing there, holding her ground, and I had to fight the urge to kiss her again. My will was breaking with every moment that passed by.

I sighed. "Alright. I crossed a line with you, and I'm sorry. It won't happen again."

The disappointed look that crossed her delicate features damn near broke my heart. I wanted to scoop her up in my arms and show her just how much I wanted to keep crossing that line.

I made my face blank so she couldn't read my emotions. "Will you please go back inside now?"

Her lips formed a thin line as she straightened her shoulders. She started walking back to the house, but she stopped and turned back to me. "For the record, Dean. I'm not sorry a line was crossed."

With that, she spun back around on her heel and went inside.

Fuck.

She's ruining you in the best possible way, Holden.

Yeah, but I needed to keep her safe. I wasn't sure I wanted to face judgment day, knowing I was the reason she was dead too.

THIRTY-FOUR
Aubrey

The rain smacked me in my face as I ran from the house down to the lake. I was all alone in darkness as Ray walked down the yard, following my footsteps. But it felt as if I wasn't running fast enough. My lungs burned as I pumped my arms and legs, forcing myself to run faster. Just before I reached the dock, my foot caught on something, and I tripped, falling face-first onto the hard surface. Ray grabbed ahold of my foot and yanked me back down toward him, my back scraping against the rocks and gravel.

"Let go!" I screamed, but nothing came out.

"You belong to me, Bree," Ray said, leaning over me. He held my hands against my chest, pressing all his weight on top of me so I couldn't move. My air was cut off, and struggling proved to be useless, but I would fight until my last breath. I brought my knee up, kicking him in the crotch. I twisted my body and started crawling away until I could get back on my feet.

Ray hollered, "Get back here, you bitch."

He reached forward, grabbing my arm and swinging me over the edge of the dock, straight into the water. The frigid temperature felt like tiny pinpricks all over my body as I kicked up to the surface. I gasped for air, only to feel a hand on my head pushing me back down. I was submerged into the dark abyss of the lake, surrounded by nothing but water. My feet never reached the bottom as one would think being this *close to the shore. I clawed at his fingers that had tangled themselves in my hair. He hoisted me up and brought my face up to his.*

"You are a worthless piece of shit. Say hi to your precious Nana for me."

He dunked me back under the cold water, and I screamed until my lungs started burning. Panic set in, and I knew that this was it. He finally had me right where he wanted me. I thrashed my body, trying with all my might to get Ray to let me go so I could get away. Then my arms felt heavy, as if someone was holding me still in the water.

"Aubrey!"

"Aubrey, wake up!"

"Aubrey!" I was jolted awake by the sound of a male's voice. I sat straight up in bed, gasping for air. I couldn't see, I couldn't breathe, I didn't even recognize where I was. My heart was beating a mile a minute in my chest, my skin felt clammy, and all I wanted to was crawl out of it. I was clutching onto the person holding on to me for dear life. These arms weren't familiar, that much I knew to be true.

"You're okay. You're safe." When I focused in on the voice, I realized it was Dylan I was clinging to.

"W-where's Dean?" I asked once I gathered my wits.

"He left to run some errands. He'll be back later," Dylan answered, studying me. I started to recall the only conversation Dean and I had had in the days following our kiss. He'd told me he would be out for a few hours and that Dylan would be here with me. That was it though. The rest of the time he spent avoiding me, and every time I tried to talk to him about anything, he said he was tired and was going to bed or that he needed to talk to the patrolmen outside.

"Right," I said, pushing the hair out of my face.

"Are you okay?" Dylan's tone was full of concern. "You were screaming in your sleep."

I stared at him for a few moments, debating on whether I should tell him about the dream. But what I really wanted to do was talk to Cassie or any one of my friends. I missed them so much, and it pained me that I couldn't talk to them.

"I wish I could talk to Cassie," I whispered. I felt a tear slip down my cheek, so I swiped it away. "I know that I can't, but it still doesn't make any of this easy."

Dylan sighed. "I know. But I'm here, ready and willing to listen."

I shot him a look. "Thanks, but you definitely don't want to hear what's on my mind."

He smiled. "Sure I do."

"I'm pretty sure you don't."

"Try me," Dylan said. I tucked my bottom lip between my teeth, contemplating if it would be a good idea to spill my guts. Before I could arrive at a conclusion, Dylan spoke up. "How about I whip us some breakfast, then we can take Moose outside so that you can take some pictures of him."

I lifted a brow. "Moose?"

"My dog. He's a husky, who will start throwing a tantrum if I don't feed him soon. I promised him bacon and eggs."

The idea of taking pictures of anything other than nature perked me right up.

I smiled. "Okay."

AFTER BREAKFAST, DYLAN AND I TOOK MOOSE outside. Dylan was right; Moose did throw a tantrum when he didn't get his bacon and eggs on his terms. Moose was just what I needed for today. He was always talking back to Dylan and growling at him when he didn't get his way, and I'd only been with them for a few hours now.

I snapped a picture of Moose leaping high into the air and catching the Frisbee with his teeth. I also snapped a few candid ones of both of them, much to Dylan's dismay. Dylan and I had grown to be good friends since my time here, but he wasn't Dean.

"So, want to talk about it?" Dylan asked, just as I took a picture of Moose running with his tongue out.

I shrugged, although I was feeling more at peace than I was earlier. "It was just a nightmare. You know the ones you can't really wake up from. The ones that feel a little too real."

When Dylan didn't say anything, I continued. "Ray had found me here and chased me down to the lake. I was drowning right before I woke up."

"Damn. Well, I can promise you, we won't let that happen," Dylan reassured me. I believed him, but I also knew Ray. He was unstable, and the more I thought about it, the more I realized how naive I'd been all those years ago. It seemed like a different lifetime ago, but the memories were still fresh.

"Look. I know you miss your friends, and I wish that I could let you use my phone to call them, but it's for their safety and yours that I don't," Dylan said, and I turned to look up at him. "I know what it's like to be far away from the people that you love and not have any way of communicating to them like you normally would."

I frowned. Dylan was young, but his eyes were wise.

They'd experienced more than just loss, and I couldn't even begin to imagine what weight he carried with him on his shoulders day after day.

"If you write a letter, I can make sure it gets to your friends. And I'll be sure to bring their responses with me next time I visit," Dylan offered, and my eyes welled up with unshed tears.

"That would be amazing. I can't even begin to thank you enough," I started to say but saw Dean's truck driving up the driveway. My heart flipped in my chest, and I felt relieved to see him back home in one piece. I was worried about him all day, hoping that nothing would happen to him while he was gone. If Ray knew how much Dean meant to me, he would go after him. Now an unsettling fear gripped my insides, and my stomach churned.

"He's been different, you know," Dylan said, pulling me from my thoughts.

I glanced up at him. "What?"

Dylan nodded toward Dean. "He's been different ever since he brought you up here. He doesn't drink anymore, and he's not half the asshole he used to be. He's changed. So, whatever you two got going on up here, your secret is safe with me."

I felt all the blood drain from my face. "Was I that obvious?"

Dylan smiled. "Let's just say that poker isn't your game."

"How did you figure it out?"

"For starters, you've been checking your watch and looking at the driveway every five minutes," he explained with an easy smirk on his face. I didn't even realize I had been doing that. "Not to mention that since he pulled in, your eyes keep darting in his direction."

I blinked, opened my mouth, then closed it again. "I…I guess there's no denying it now. Although I think it's a one-way street," I admitted softly, and Dylan's hand rested on my shoulder.

"I definitely don't think so. I caught him looking over here at us since he parked," Dylan told me. "Give him time."

I glanced over at Dean's truck, and I saw him looking over at us. I couldn't read his facial expression from this far away, but something inside me told me to not give up on him…to not give up on *us*.

THIRTY-FIVE
Dean

I got out of my truck just as Aubrey and Dylan walked back up to the house. I could have just told Dylan to bring me what I needed, but I wanted to get out of the house. Being around Aubrey made keeping my distance damn near impossible. Every time I thought of Aubrey, I thought of what Wyatt would miss out on. He had his whole life ahead of him, and I let my brother down. How could I be happy when he was dead? I stood out on the porch, looking out at the lake, just as Aubrey went inside with Moose and Dylan.

"YOU'RE ONE LONELY SON OF A BITCH, HOLDEN," WYATT *joked before casting his fishing rod out into the lake.*

I finished baiting my hook. "What makes you say that?"

Wyatt laughed, "Can you even remember the last time you got laid?"

I cast my line, then sat down in the chair. "It was a month ago."

"My point exactly. You're one lonely son of a bitch. What-ever ever happened to what's her name?"

I lifted a brow. "You mean Lisa?"

"If that's her name."

I shook my head. "She was too clingy. We only went out a

couple times, but she started talking about marriage and kids."

"What's so wrong with that?" Wyatt asked. I thought he was joking, but when I glanced over at him, he wasn't laughing. "I mean, someday you want that, right?"

"Yeah, maybe one day, but not after less than a month of dating," I responded. I hadn't given much thought to the whole marriage and kids thing.

"Some people just know," Wyatt said.

"Dude, are you thinking about settling down?" I asked, taken aback. "Is the Wyatt Coleman looking to put his dick back in his pants for one woman? Be a one-pussy man?"

Wyatt scoffed but then smiled. "Maybe. You know that bullshit saying, 'when you meet the one, you just know'? Well, it ain't bullshit, man. I think Vanessa is the one."

I looked out at the water as I pondered his statement. "Good for you, bro. I'm happy for you."

Wyatt laughed. "Thanks. But like I said, you're still one lonely son of a bitch."

A SLAP ON MY SHOULDER JOLTED ME, AND I GLANCED over at Dylan. I checked behind him to see if Aubrey was with him, but she wasn't.

"You good?" Dylan asked as he leaned forward against the railing next to me, looking out at the lake.

"I'm fine," I answered in a clipped tone.

I saw Dylan nod his head from the corner of my eye. "When I was overseas, a buddy of mine was promoted to lieutenant, and on his first day, his unit was in a helicopter when out of nowhere they were shot down. He was the only one to make it out alive."

Fuck. I scrubbed a hand down my face, not knowing what to say.

"He went downhill fast. He started drinking and wouldn't talk to anyone. He took the mandatory counseling, and you know what they called it?" Dylan stood up straight, and I looked at him. "They called it survivors' guilt. He blamed himself for what happened. It was *his* unit. He didn't blame the enemy who shot them down. He blamed himself. That's a heavy burden to bear…for anyone."

I looked back out at the lake. "What happened to him?"

Dylan leaned back down against the railing, and I didn't think he would answer, but then he said, "The weight of that guilt was too much for him to carry on his shoulders."

Dylan didn't need to say the words out loud.

I knew.

I hung my head and said a silent prayer before lifting my head again.

"Dean, I read about what happened to Wyatt," Dylan said, and when I stood up straight, he held his hands up in defense. "Before you get mad, let me just say this. What happened to him was not your fault. You did everything you could, and I was worried about you. I didn't want to see another one of my brothers in arms going down a road they can't turn back from."

I stood still for a moment, feeling suppressed emotions coming to the surface. "What am I supposed to do?"

Dylan let out a long breath. "That's up to you, man. You know I'll always have your six. The question is, are you willing to live your life the way you were meant to?

The way Wyatt would want you to live? Or do you want to be burdened with guilt for the rest of your life?"

Dylan walked away and back inside and left me to my own devices.

The thought of moving on and living my life seemed like a foreign concept to me. I didn't want to drown in my own guilt, but I didn't know if I could live the rest of my life happy knowing that my best friend couldn't experience it with me. All I did know was that whenever I did picture myself happy, it was with Aubrey. And I wished my brother could be here to meet her.

THIRTY-SIX

Dean

I went back inside, and it was like I was the moth and Aubrey was the flame. The first thing I searched for was her, and I found her sitting on the couch with Moose. She was watching *Friends* while the dog was lying on her lap. Aubrey must have sensed me hovering because she turned her head to look at me.

Her eyes met mine, and the silence between us said a thousand words. I longed to touch her, feel her body pressed up against mine, taste her just one more time. But we both knew it couldn't happen again, no matter how much we both wanted it to. I heard Dylan, and while I wanted to move on, something was holding me back. Was it guilt like he said? Maybe. But all he did was read the report, he hadn't lived through it. Sure, it pissed me off that he read it, but it also didn't surprise me that he did. Hell, my father probably told him to, just so he would know what he would be walking into.

Aubrey glanced away first, breaking our eye contact, and fuck did that sting like a bitch. It was for the best, though, because I wasn't ready to move on with my life. I honestly wasn't sure if I'd ever be ready to move on. Turning away from Aubrey, I started walking toward the kitchen when my phone starting ringing.

"Holden," I answered.

"Detective, we have a situation outside," Officer Tudor said.

I stopped dead in my tracks, and my gaze caught Dylan's.

"What is it?" I asked, my body already going on alert. I started scanning out every window in the house and moved to close the curtains. Moose jumped off the couch when Aubrey got up.

"We saw some movement in the woods. We're out checking it now."

"I'll be right out." I hung up the phone, shoving it back in my pocket. I hurried over to my gun safe and pushed in the code. I grabbed my firearm and made sure it was loaded before slamming the safe shut. It was probably nothing— I'd made sure I wasn't followed heading back, and there were hiking trails around here. It was probably just a couple of kids who'd lost their way, but I wasn't taking any chances.

"What's going on?" Dylan asked, body tense as he stepped closer to Aubrey.

"They saw something in the woods. I'm going to help them check it out. You stay in here with Aubrey," I commanded. I glanced over at her, and I was so close to making Dylan go out there to check it out and staying with her myself. She had her hand on her stomach, and her other hand was petting Moose.

I spun around and headed for the door, and I felt a hand on my arm the second I grabbed the knob. I turned my head, and my eyes met Aubrey's.

"Please, stay." She whispered low enough so that only I can hear. I felt my body leaning toward hers, and I shut my eyes for a brief moment. God, I wanted to stay.

I opened my eyes, and damn did I want to kiss her

right then and there. If I stayed here a moment longer, I just might. "I'll be right back. I promise."

Aubrey frowned but then nodded and took a step back. I instantly missed her calming touch as I closed the door behind me on the way out. With my firearm at my side, I jogged through the yard and went into the woods, careful not to make much noise as I weaved through the trees. My heart rate was steady, my breathing even as I looked around. A twig snapped behind me, and I spun around, aiming the gun. Seeing nothing, I kept moving deeper into the woods. I wasn't even sure how long I was searching, but I kept going. I wasn't going to jeopardize Aubrey's safety.

I saw Officers Tudor and Gomez on the path up ahead. I whistled to get their attention, and they turned around. Once they saw me, they made their way over.

"It was just some people who lost their way. None of them fit the description of your suspect," Officer Gomez informed me.

"Alright. Thanks, guys, and nice job." I walked with them back up the path. It led us out toward the road, which was a couple of hundred feet from the driveway. There was a main road that wound up and around the area, but it was a dead-end road. It just led to houses in the secluded area, and each house was spaced apart enough that you still feel like you were all alone.

Off in the distance, we heard tires screeching, and a car gunning it. It flew around the curve, fishtailing just a smidge, before speeding toward us. There was no time to react. I threw my body into the wooded area, hitting the ground hard. I got all sorts of scratches and cuts as I rolled into the fall, my shoulder scraping along a rock.

I got up on my feet, ignoring the stinging pain, and

tried to make out the license plate, but it was too late. The car veered off, and the only thing I was able to get was the color of the two-door sedan.

"You guys okay?" I asked the other two officers, and they nodded, brushing off their uniforms.

"You need us to go after that car?" Officer Tudor asked.

"That car is long gone by now. Just keep your eyes peeled to see if it comes back. Stop all black two doors," I commanded as we made our way back to my driveway. "You two need any first aid?"

"No, sir. We're good," Officer Gomez responded, and I just nodded. My knee started hurting as I walked up the driveway, and I had just passed my truck when the front door burst open, and Aubrey ran out.

"Oh my God! Are you okay?" she asked breathlessly as she approached.

"What are you doing out here?" I lifted my gaze to Dylan, who looked panicked.

"She just took off…" Dylan started to say, but Aubrey's fingers grazed my cheek.

"You're bleeding." Aubrey's eyes searched over my face, her brows furrowed together, and that damn lip was between her teeth again. "What happened?"

"I thought I told you to stay inside," I answered her, ignoring the question.

She narrowed her blue eyes. "No, you didn't. You told Dylan to stay with me, and then you said you'd be back. None of those words told me that I had to stay inside."

This woman and her smart mouth.

"What part of 'they saw something in the woods' made you think it was okay for you to run outside?" I countered. She opened her mouth, then closed it. "That's

217

what I thought. But lucky for you, it was nothing. Except for the speeding car that almost hit us."

"What!" Dylan and Aubrey shouted in unison.

"We're fine, but I couldn't get a plate number. The patrolmen have orders." I moved past Aubrey to make my way into the house. There was a bottle of ibuprofen that was calling my name.

"Speaking of orders," Dylan said as I passed him. "I have to get going. Sergeant Miller wants me back."

"Okay. What for?"

"He didn't say over the phone. I assume it has to do with Aubrey's case," Dylan answered, and I nodded.

"Keep me posted."

Aubrey said goodbye to Dylan, and then he and his dog left. I went into the kitchen to take some meds while Aubrey disappeared, only to return a few moments later with some cotton balls and some rubbing alcohol.

"Sit. Let me clean those cuts," she commanded. I didn't feel like putting up a fight, and to be honest, I wanted to feel her touch again. So, I sat my ass down in the chair. She poured a little bit of rubbing alcohol on a cotton ball and began to dab at the small cuts on my arms. It stung, but I let her work. It wasn't until she got to the ones on my face that I flinched away.

"Sorry," she said softly, then gently blew on the scratch. Her breath caressed my cheek, and I closed my eyes, savoring the moment. Her hand rested gently on my cheek, and when I opened my eyes, my gaze connected with hers. The pull I felt toward this woman was getting harder and harder to resist. If I moved just a fraction of an inch forward, our lips would meet, and I so desperately wanted to feel her lips against mine, to relish the feeling one last time.

So, I moved. My lips pressed against hers in a chaste kiss, and fuck, I wanted to deepen this kiss. Our last kiss. It had to be our last one. I wasn't ready to allow myself any form of happiness.

Pulling away, I clenched my jaw, hating the words that came out of my mouth. "We can't, Aubrey."

I gently pushed her hand away from my cheek and got up. And fuck, did that hurt worse than pouring salt in an open wound.

THIRTY-SEVEN
Aubrey

I. Was. Bored.

I was going out of my mind with boredom. Dean was…well, he was being Dean and avoiding me. For weeks now I would make dinner, and he would take it in his room. He wouldn't sit and watch TV with me; he'd barely speak unless he had to. But I didn't miss the way he looked at me. It was like he was committing me to memory. We would make eye contact, and whether he wanted me to see it or not, I saw the look of regret in his beautiful green eyes.

The fact that I found myself longing for his touch made me realize that I was willing to be patient. Our last kiss was enough for me to know that Dean was pushing me away. It was almost like he didn't want to be happy, like he didn't deserve it. I'd never felt this way about anyone, not even Ray. I'd never wanted to expose the deepest parts of myself to anyone, but when it came to Dean, it was different. It didn't feel like an obligation. Not once had this man made me feel like what I went through was nothing. If anything, he made me feel stronger and braver than ever. I didn't want to cower away from the things that went bump in the night.

I was reading in my room when a song started playing out in the living room. I quietly got out of bed and tiptoed down the hall. I thought it was a CD player, but no, it was live music. I peeked my head around the corner and saw Dean sitting on the couch, strumming away on a guitar. I was pretty sure it was called "The Weight" by the Band.

His eyes were closed as he played, bobbing his head to the rhythm. Then he started to sing, and I had to cover my mouth. I had no idea that he could play the guitar, let alone sing. His voice was smooth like velvet as it carried in the room. I walked around the corner, and he looked up at me. He didn't stop playing as I sat down next to him, leaning back on the couch. I just let him play, and he seemed to be content with my presence. When the song came to an end, we sat there in silence. A heavy weight settled between us, and Dean scrubbed a hand down his face as he set the guitar down.

I took a risk, sitting up and looping my arm through his. I rested my head on his arm, and he leaned his on top of mine. It was the most intimate interaction we'd had since we kissed, and it honestly was the closest in proximity we'd been too. It felt natural, sitting here like this. He grabbed my hand and held on. It was almost like he was looking to me for strength, and if that was what he needed, then he could have it.

"I haven't played in a long time," Dean murmured. I stayed quiet, hoping that if I did, then he would continue to talk. "Not since before Wyatt died. We used to play together, and I guess...I guess I just missed it."

I was afraid to speak because if I did, he might shut down again. Instead, I reached over him and handed him his guitar back. "Will you play another song?"

He gave me a small smile. "What do you want to hear?"

I pondered that for a moment. "Whatever you want."

"Okay." He started playing a song that I immediately recognized as "Free Falling" by Tom Petty. I leaned back on the couch, and Dean shifted his body toward me, his fingers dancing over the cords as he sang one of my favorite songs. It was Nana's and my favorite song. She played it all the time when I was growing up, and I wished that I had the voice to sing with him, but I sucked.

He had shared something with me about Wyatt, and while it might not have been much for anyone else, it was everything to me. We were bonding over our losses but getting closer to the feeling of being free from our grief. I knew Dean had a long road ahead of him, and if he wanted me along for the ride, then I'd be there.

Dean played a little bit longer before he put his guitar back in his room. I started making dinner when Dean said he was taking a shower. I had just put the spaghetti noodles in the pot when Dean came around the corner in nothing but a towel. Water dripped down over his pecs and down his abs before getting soaked up by the towel which, might I add, was sitting really low on his hips.

My mouth went dry, and I felt my face heating up. I'm also certain my panties even dampened. He didn't even notice me staring as he grabbed his phone off the table and checked his messages. Who knew he was hiding that body underneath all those clothes? I mean, I knew the man had some biceps, but holy shit.

"Aubrey?" Dean's voice snapped my attention back up to his face. "You okay?"

I nodded and blinked a few times. "Don't forget to hang your towel up."

Don't forget to hang up your towel—really, Aubrey?

He smirked, knowing damn well how much it irked me. Cassie was the best roommate. She always hung her wet towels up. Dean kept leaving his on the floor, and it drove me insane.

Dean didn't say a word as he about-faced and went straight back to his room. I let out a long sigh and leaned up against the counter. This man knew how to piss me off and turn me on at the same time, and you know what? I loved it.

THIRTY-EIGHT
Aubrey

*D*ean and I fell back into a routine, only this time things were different. The air around us had been thick with tension since he played the guitar. We were sort of dancing around each other, neither one of us ready to make the move to let go and just be. Many intimate moments were shared without any actual intimacy, and I wasn't sure if that was a good thing or a bad thing. He had spoken of Wyatt again last night when the freak October snowstorm started. He said that they'd got snowed in up here once, and they were without power for almost a week. He didn't say much more than that, but I could tell it was a good memory because of the way he smiled.

Dylan had been in touch that he would be up after the storm, and I was excited for that. I had written a letter to all my friends, basically spilling my guts on paper. I was grateful for Dylan for suggesting I write my girls a letter. I missed them, and I couldn't wait to wrap them up in hugs when Ray was caught. Speaking of Ray, he appeared to be in the wind. Ray was smart, and he wouldn't give up trying to get to me. He'd wait forever if he had to, which was what scared me the most. I felt safe in my little bubble with Dean, but I knew he was out there somewhere. Which made every little noise extra frightening.

I was sitting at the kitchen table, flipping through a

magazine, when the lights suddenly went out, and my body froze. Only the light from the fire illuminated the room. If it weren't for the raging snowstorm out there right now, I'd be afraid that Ray was here. It would be the perfect time to strike. During a snowstorm when people's guards were down.

"Stay right here," Dean ordered as he got up from the couch. "I'm going to start the generator and grab some more firewood. It's going to be a long night."

He put on his snow boots and jacket and grabbed his flashlight. He stopped when he got to the door. "You hear anything, you run into my room, lock the door, and don't let anyone in until I come and get you."

I nodded. He'd left me alone in the house before, that was nothing new. But now when the power was out and there was a storm outside, I felt anxious being alone. Part of me knew that I would be fine, but there was that sinking fear that Ray was waiting just outside with a pickax ready to chop me up to bits and dump them in the lake.

A shiver worked its way down my spine at that thought. I couldn't think about that now. I took a deep breath, closing my eyes. I needed to calm my jittery nerves.

I felt hands grab my shoulders, and I opened my eyes.

"I'll be right outside," Dean said softly. He placed his finger under my chin, and his thumb tugged my lip from my teeth. "I'll be back, I promise."

"I know," I whispered. He gave me a small smile, then walked outside. Ever since our kiss and all the little moments we'd shared between us, I found myself needing him in more ways than I expected. I wanted more—I needed more.

A loud bang pulled me from my thoughts, and I jumped out of my chair. My heartbeat accelerated as I stood there, listening to make sure I really heard a noise and it wasn't just a figment of my imagination. The only sounds I could hear were my own heavy breathing. I didn't move a muscle, not even one. *Oh my God, he finally found me.*

I heard another thud and a man's voice that sounded like a string of curse words being said. I didn't even think twice as I threw my snow boots on, not caring about anyone but Dean. If Ray was here, I couldn't leave Dean alone with him. Although I knew I would be no good against him. But maybe my presence could distract Ray long enough so that Dean could get the upper hand. I was closer than the patrolmen at the end of the driveway.

I was putting on my jacket as I ran outside into the bitter cold. Strength was better in numbers, right? And being with Dean made me brave. I rounded the side of the house and saw Dean hunched over.

"Dean?" I called out right before I reached him. His head swung toward me as I got closer. "Are you okay? What happened? Is it Ray?"

He looked puzzled by my question, and then he scowled. "I thought I told you to stay inside?"

"I thought something had happened to you. I thought Ray had found us." He stared at me for a moment. That moment lasted so long I thought he froze before my very eyes.

He lifted a brow. "And you just ran into danger?"

"Yes." My lips parted on a whisper, and his eyes narrowed in on my mouth. A few tense moments passed as we stared at each other. Dean's features were filled with adoration and also confusion. Like he really thought that no one would have his back. "You needed to know that I've got your six."

His lips crashed into mine, and the air around us combusted with electricity. He took my breath away with just a kiss, and I decided I no longer needed to breathe when I was with him.

He pulled away, resting his forehead against mine. "When will you ever just do as you're told?"

"When it comes to you? Never," I admitted, and his lips found mine again in a searing, hungry kiss. My fingers curled into his hair as he pulled me to him. He dipped low, grabbed my legs, and hoisted me up in his arms. I moaned into his mouth as I wrapped my legs around his waist.

If kissing Dean meant giving in to temptation and possibly damnation, then let me be damned.

I didn't care if the patrolmen could see us. As far as I was concerned, it was just us. I heard the door open and then shut behind us. He set me down in front of the fire as we were in a frenzy, unzipping each other's jackets. I pushed his coat over his broad shoulders and let it fall to the floor as he did the same with mine. He lifted my thermal long-sleeved shirt over my head, and then I made quick work of his flannel button-down. At some point we had toed our boots off, and I heard them skid across the floor.

He cupped my cheek as his cold hand scorched the small of my back as he pulled me close. I felt it glide up my back, and with the snap of his fingers, he undid the clasp of my bra. It slipped off my arms and fell to the ground. Dean growled as he pulled away from me. Our breathing was erratic from our heavy kissing. I knew in the back of my mind why he was stopping, but I didn't want him to.

His forest-green eyes searched mine as if they held all the answers he was looking for.

"You are one remarkable woman. I don't deserve this…you," he whispered against my lips.

"How about you let me decide what I deserve," I whispered back, then pressed my lips against his in a jarring kiss. His answer was kissing me back and lifting me up again, only to kneel, then lay me down gently on the carpet in front of the fire. He hovered over me, his hands exploring my body, and I shivered under his touch. But it was a good kind of pain.

"If I ask you to wait here, would you stay?" he asked, running his nose against mine.

"Yes," I breathed, and he quickly got up and left the room only to return a few moments later with a condom.

I glanced down at the bulge in his pants before he stripped down in front of me. His cock sprung free, and my eyes widened. As nervous as I was, I was ready. I had only ever been with Ray, and I wanted to erase those memories and make new ones. Doing this meant that I was giving Dean something special. Something no one else had ever gotten out of me because of fear. I wasn't scared, not with Dean. His touch was a gentle caress, and I knew that he knew what this meant for me.

My panties were damp, and I needed him. I was practically panting as he got on his knees and removed my jeans, taking my panties along with them. His fingers slipped between the apex of my thighs before he inserted a finger inside me. He worked me up, then caught my orgasm with his lips. It wasn't enough—I so desperately needed more.

"*Please*, Dean," I begged, writhing underneath him.

He growled as he removed his hands; then in one swift movement, he inched himself inside me.

He let out a breathy groan against my neck, then started trailing kisses along my jaw, down my collarbone, then back to my lips. He moved slowly in and out of me, and I could tell he was holding himself back. Emotionally and physically. And if he wouldn't let go emotionally, then I was going to let him physically.

"Let go," I moaned. He paused, looking down at me, his face confused by what I meant, but I saw the moment realization kicked in. "Let go, Holden."

My words were his undoing. He started moving faster, and I felt him sink deeper into me. I cried out in pure ecstasy as another orgasm ripped through me. I tugged on his hair as he moved inside me. He hiked my leg higher up on his waist as he kept his rhythm.

"Fuck," he groaned, and less than a second later, he found his release just as I found my own. We were dealing with our own personal hells, but things could only get better now that we'd finally found each other.

THIRTY-NINE
Aubrey

*L*ying naked in Dean's arms by the fire wasn't something I'd thought could happen, but it did. I wanted to soak up this moment for as long it lasted. If this was the first and last time I'd be in his arms, then I'd commit it to memory. I'd rather have this one memory than a thousand other ones that included Ray.

Ray never held me after we had sex. Even when we first started dating, we would have sex, and then when we were finished, we'd get dressed, and that was that. I didn't have anything to compare it to, so I didn't know any better. He was my first and only because I'd been too afraid to let anyone else in. I wasn't sure if I would have given Dean the same treatment if we weren't stuck together. We didn't particularly get along when we first met. But being here and getting to know him, I realized that we both had things we needed to deal with. He wasn't who I thought he was.

Dean was kind, thoughtful, and he cared deeply about people even if he was pushing them away. The thing I'd learned about him was that he opened up about things when he wanted to. I could appreciate that because everyone grieved differently. Dean sometimes just needed a tiny push in the right direction so he didn't turn to numbing his pain in alcohol. I was young when my parents died, and I consider myself lucky for having someone in my life who could teach me the value of living life to the fullest, even after you lose someone close to you.

"What's going on in that pretty little head of yours?" Dean asked, his voice low and husky. His fingers were caressing my arms, and I was content, relaxed.

"I was just thinking about Nana and my parents," I told him, adjusting my head on his smooth chest.

"How do you do it?" he asked, and I sat up on my elbow to look at him. He turned his head as he brought his hand up to tuck my hair behind my ear.

"Do what?"

"Deal with losing people. How are you so strong?"

I bit my lower lip as I pondered his question. I hadn't really thought about my own grieving process.

I shrugged. "I let myself feel what I feel when I feel it. My parents gave me this life, and I'd be doing them a disservice if I didn't live it. If I let myself succumb to the darkness of grief, I'd never be able to do that. I know that Nana would want me to mourn her death, but she would also want me to celebrate her life. The thing that they wanted most out of everything in this world for me was happiness. Above all, they would want me to be happy. And, in an odd way, I am."

That was the truest thing that had ever come out of my mouth. Given the circumstances of my life and everything I'd been through, I was happy. Not many people could say that, but I hoped one day those people found their own peace and happiness in life because they deserved it.

Dean sat up and cupped my cheek. His green eyes looked longingly into mine before he kissed me. He took his time moving his lips against mine. Earlier, we were in such a frenzy, tearing each other's clothes off, getting lost in the moment, that we didn't get to savor the moment. His tongue swiped across my bottom lip, and I opened willingly. He tugged my head closer to his as he deepened the kiss, letting out a moan in the process. My body heated up, but before I could climb onto his lap, he broke the kiss, resting his forehead against mine.

"I just can't fight it anymore, Aubrey," he whispered against my lips. "I don't want to fight it. But I'm not ready."

I brought my hands up to clasp his cheeks. "We can take our time. We are on no one else's timeline but ours."

He kissed me once more, before lying back down and bringing me with him. He just held me until I fell asleep, and I didn't wake until the sun came up.

AFTER MY SHOWER, I GOT DRESSED IN WARM CLOTHES and made my way out into the kitchen for some coffee. The power clicked back on during the night at some point, which I was thankful for when I woke up. Dean was standing by the counter in his jeans and long-sleeved black Henley shirt. His back was to me, and I took a moment to appreciate the view. He had a nice ass, and I remembered running my hands down his bare back last night as we made love.

"You know, if you take a picture, it'll last longer," he said, but I could hear the playful tone in his voice. The last time he said this to me, we were not on great terms.

I smiled. "Don't tempt me with a good time, Holden."

He turned, and my heart skipped over many beats. There was a real, genuine smile on that man's face. I'd seen him smile, but this…this smile was worth a million bucks.

Straight teeth, perfect lips, and there was even a small dimple in his cheek. He handed me a mug, and I took a sip at the same time he did. Although I felt energized today, so coffee really wasn't needed.

I looked out of the window and saw that the sun was shining. I loved taking pictures of the snow, even though ice had caused my parents to lose control of their vehicle which resulted in their death. Nana said that I shouldn't blame Mother Nature for taking life because it gives life. My mother loved the snow, and I remembered we would spend hours outside playing and sledding. Of course, my dad would be inside making us hot cocoa because he would be working from home.

"You want to go outside, don't you?" Dean asked, pulling me from my thoughts.

"So bad," I said, almost pouting.

He grabbed the mug from my hands and placed it on the coffee warmer. "That will keep it warm for when we get back inside."

I grinned, turning and throwing on my snow gear. I grabbed my camera and was ready to go before Dean could finish lacing up his boots. I waited not so patiently as he put his beanie on, and finally, he was ready to venture out into the snow. I wasn't sure where the road would take us after everything that had happened, but if we continued like we were now, I just might end up being the happiest woman in the world.

FORTY
Dean

I watched Aubrey in her element, taking pictures and getting lost in the process. She was breathtakingly beautiful as she walked through the snow. The sunlight glistening off her hair, her cheeks and nose rosy from the cold air. I walked with her down to the lake so she could take pictures of trees covered in snow that surrounded it. You would think things would have been awkward, but they weren't. It felt...natural.

She stood out on the end of the dock, and it was only a few months ago that she stood there crying. Now, she was smiling, and that did something to me. Something inside me snapped last night. She ran out to make sure I was okay, not knowing if there was immediate danger or not. It was dumb, but it also broke me down. I wasn't sure about anything, but I liked how she made me feel like I was worth something.

The talk with Dylan really put things in perspective, and talking with Aubrey only solidified my reasoning for allowing myself a moment of contentment. I wasn't ready to talk about Wyatt's death, but I was ready to not wallow in self-pity. I wanted to tell Aubrey about Wyatt, and I noticed that I had been in a way. Not about his death, but just some of the things that we used to do. She gave me the push I needed, and one day I'd tell her about the day Wyatt died, but that day was not today.

"Have you always wanted to be a photographer?" I asked her as she pulled the camera away from her face.

She looked at me, and damn did her blue eyes really stand out in the snow. "For as long as I can remember. My mother was a photographer, and she brought me with her to photo shoots all the time."

Aubrey walked over to me before she continued. "I feel connected to her when the camera is in my hands. Sometimes I think she guides me to take the perfect shot. I just want to make her proud."

I smiled at her. "I think she would be proud."

She beamed up at me. "I think so too."

She took another picture, then glanced up at me again. "Can I ask you a question?"

I nodded. "Sure."

She hesitated for a moment, but then she asked, "When you played the guitar the other night, did it make you feel connected to Wyatt?"

If it were anyone else, I would have been caught off guard by the question.

"You know what? You don't have to answer that. I'm sorry." She tucked her bottom lip between her teeth, and I caught her arm before she walked away. Wrapping one arm around her waist, I pulled her to me and used my other hand to cup her cheek.

"Don't do that," I told her softly, looking deep into her eyes. "Don't apologize for asking a question. I know I was a dick before, and for that I'm the one who's sorry. I pushed people away, including the people who gave a damn about me. You called me out on all my shit, and that gave me the push I needed."

I knew we were out of sight from the driveway, so I leaned down, brushing my lips against hers.

"You pulled me out of the hole I was sinking in without even realizing you were even doing it. So, please, don't let me shut you out." I kissed her one last time before letting her go and grabbing her hand. I'd never been one for hand holding before, but here I was lacing my fingers with hers as we walked up the yard and back up to the house.

"To answer your question. Yes, it did. Wyatt and I would sit and play for hours, just jamming away. You would have liked him." I felt myself smiling as I talked about my best friend, which was a first for me. I didn't ever think I could talk about him and remember him the way I was now.

"Would I?" Aubrey laid her head on my arm as we walked through the snow.

"Yeah, he probably would have tried to hit on you, until he realized that you were my type."

"Oh, I'm your type?"

"Ohhh yeah. I'm a goner for blonde-haired, blue-eyed babes, especially ones with a smart mouth."

"I didn't think I had a smart mouth." Aubrey chuckled, and the sound was music to my ears. I loved listening to her laugh.

"Are you kidding me? Wyatt would have given me shit for waiting so long to make a move," I admitted, and a sadness crept over me. But Aubrey stepped in front of me, placing her gloved hand on my cheek.

"I'm glad you finally did." She smiled, then stood on her tiptoes to kiss me.

Someone pulled into the driveway, and I turned to see Dylan coming up the driveway. Aubrey and I broke apart, and she waved to him. He put his truck in park, turned the engine off, and jumped out.

"What are you doing up here, McCormick?" I asked, walking over to meet him. He opened the back seat, and Moose jumped out, beelining straight for Aubrey.

"Moose!" she squealed, kneeling to pet the dog. *Maybe we should get a dog.*

"It's been a while since I've been up, so I figured I'd bring you all some groceries and other basic needs," Dylan said, grabbing some bags from his back seat. He handed me a few, then loaded his arm up before shutting the door. We all headed inside, and Aubrey took Moose with her into the living room with her camera. I watched her grab my laptop and pop her SD card in. Then I turned my attention back to Dylan.

"Still no updates?" I asked, helping him put the groceries away.

"Well, the arsonist case went cold. And nothing yet on Ray," Dylan explained, recycling the empty bags.

We had no luck with the black car the other day. Whoever it was got away, and we haven't seen the car since.

"It pisses me off that we don't have any leads. The waiting game is making me impatient." I felt my blood starting to boil. Don't get me wrong, I liked being here with Aubrey. I needed this, but I didn't want this dickhead looming over us any longer.

"Tell me about it. I'm sure it's not easy on her, being away from her friends. Oh, that reminds me." Dylan reached into a bag and pulled out four envelopes with names on the front. "Aubrey, I have the letters from your friends."

"Oh my God!" Aubrey shut the laptop and came running toward Dylan. "Thank you! Thank you! Thank you!"

She gave him a quick hug and ran off back into her room. I made a mental note to move her into my room once Dylan left.

"So." Dylan dragged the word out, crossing his arms over his chest. A mischievous smirk grew as he leaned up against the counter. "Anything you wanna tell me about?"

"I have no idea what you're talking about," I answered, trying to play dumb. Although, I knew it was no good, because out of the corner of my eye, I saw Dylan nod.

"You don't? Because I'm pretty sure I saw you two sucking face when I pulled in."

"Maybe you should get your eyes checked."

"Maybe you should stop being so full of shit."

I looked over at Dylan, who was trying so hard not to laugh.

I clicked my tongue and smirked but said nothing. You know, Dylan wasn't so bad. I felt like my father had brought him over to be my partner because Dylan would be patient enough to put up with my shit.

I opened my mouth to tell him about Aubrey and I but the moment was interrupted by a scream that made my blood run cold. I didn't even blink before I took off toward Aubrey's room.

FORTY-ONE
Dean

I almost broke the fucking door off its hinges trying to get to Aubrey. I immediately ran over to her and looked her over to make sure she wasn't hurt while Dylan did a once-over in the room. Aubrey was trembling in my arms and staring at the floor. She was pale and on the verge of tears, but I tore my eyes away from her and down at the floor.

A letter was sitting on the floor with a picture of her friend Cassie. I bent over, picking it up, and there was a red X over Cassie's face and in the letter, it said:

Come out, come out wherever you are, Bree. You know my favorite game is hide and seek. You hide, and I will always find you. But I might play with her until I do.
Love always, Ray
PS - She has pretty hair.

I opened the envelope, and there was a clump of red hair tied together with a small bow.

"Oh God." Aubrey choked on a sob. Dylan walked over to me, and I knew the moment he saw Cassie's picture and the hair, he would flip his shit. To my surprise, Dylan kept it together, but I could tell from the look on his face he was pissed off.

Dylan pulled out his phone and hit a button, then put

the phone up to his ear. "C'mon, Cassie, pick up. Pick up the phone, Cass."

Aubrey curled up on the floor, covering her face with her hands. Moose lay down beside her and started whining.

"Damn it!" Dylan yelled and tried calling her again. "Pick up the phone, Cass!"

I watched my partner start to lose his cool, but then he sighed in relief. "Cassie, where are you?"

Dylan glanced at me, then put her on speakerphone.

"Dylan?" Cassie asked.

"Yes, it's me. Where are you?" Dylan said.

"I'm at the firehouse having a late lunch with Ford. Why?"

"Cassie?" Aubrey's voice came from next to me, her hand finding mine.

"Aubrey? Are you okay? What's wrong? Did something happen?" Cassie's tone went from confused to concerned in an instant.

"I miss you s-so much, Cass." Aubrey choked out, and I gave her hand a squeeze.

"I miss you too, Aubs. Did you get my letter?" Cassie asked, and it sounded like she had no idea that her letter had been switched out.

"Cassie, listen to me. Can you stay at the firehouse until I get there?" Dylan asked, changing the subject.

"No, I have a shift tonight at the Bistro."

"She can't go to work!" Aubrey said, wiping her cheeks with her hands.

"Can somebody please tell me what the hell is going on?" Cassie demanded through the phone.

"Cass, I need you to call out of work and stay at the firehouse until I get there, okay? I'll call the Bistro and speak to the manager myself," Dylan offered. There was a long pause, and Dylan took her off speaker. "I promise I'll explain everything when I get there, just...*please* stay at the firehouse."

There was a heaviness in his voice as he begged her to stay put.

He closed his eyes for a brief moment and breathed another sigh of relief. "Thank you. I'll see you soon." He hung up the phone and turned to us. "She's going to stay. I know she'll be safe there, but I'm going to call Nash and update him on what's going on. I'm sorry to make this visit short."

"It's okay," I said, following him out. "We need to find out how in the hell that letter got switched. Where did you keep them?"

"In my truck, but I just picked up Cassie's letter last night while she was at work," Dylan answered. "Moose!"

Moose came running out of the room and stopped when he got to Dylan.

"And were there signs of a break-in?"

Dylan shot me a look. "No. I brought them in the house with me, then put them in the bag this morning."

I nodded. "I just had to ask."

"I get it. I'll call you later after I talk to Cassie," Dylan said, then walked out with Moose on his heel. I turned back around and headed back into my parents' room where Aubrey was now sitting on the bed. She was hugging a pillow, staring off into space. I sat down next to her and tucked a lock of hair behind her ear.

Lightly grabbing her chin, I turned her head to me. I wasn't going to ask her if she was okay because I knew that she wasn't.

"He's going to hurt Cassie. Y-you can't let him h-hurt

her." Her voice cracked on a sob, her bottom lip quivering. I hated seeing her so worked up over this guy. I hated how he was finding ways to torment her.

"Shhh. We won't let that happen." I kept my voice soft. "I don't think he would hurt her. He's just trying to get to you. To get under your skin."

"Yeah, well, it's working," she admitted, and I pulled her to me, kissing her head before she rested it on my shoulder.

"I know, but now we might have a lead. I will do whatever it takes to catch this bastard," I told her, holding her close. If someone were to have told me three months or so ago that I would be falling for my neighbor, I would have laughed. Honestly, being told I had to protect her was the best thing that could have happened to me. I was pretty sure it had saved my life. Aubrey had saved my life.

Wyatt saved my life. I felt like I owed it to him to start living the life that he saved. I didn't have the choice to drown in my own guilt when I was first assigned to this case, but now I had a choice. I could lose myself again when this was over, or I could free myself of the burden I carried and choose to live a life worth fighting for. Holding Aubrey in my arms every day for the rest of my life was worth fighting for.

FORTY-TWO
Aubrey

*D*ean set me down on the couch and went into the kitchen to make me some soup while I read the letters from Sophia and Chloe. He made sure there were no more surprises before letting me open them. Even though I was worried about Cassie, there was nothing more I could do about it. I trusted Dylan would keep her safe, being as he was still in love with her. I mean, it was also because he was a good person. I was just glad I wasn't alone and that I had someone here with me I trusted with my life.

Sophia had aced all her finals, which was no surprise. She mentioned she was taking the winter semester off but going back to finish up her degree in the spring. She said she loaded more books on the Kindle that she thought I might like, which was fine because I was going through them like nobody's business. I was excited to see what she sent me.

Chloe was doing wonderful. Her words, not mine. She said that the boutique has been busy, and she'd had more customers turn into regulars. She was even asked to design a wedding gown and the entire bridal party. I didn't have to read that she accepted right away. Chloe's favorite thing to design was dresses; it was her specialty along with lingerie. She also said that Rhett said hi, and it was going well for him in his new position. That, of course, I didn't doubt because Rhett was a great firefighter. I wished I had Cassie's letter, but I was sure Dylan would bring me one from her. Cassie would have insisted that I get a message from her.

I felt the couch dip, and I glanced up at Dean. "How are you feeling?"

I sighed. "I miss them. They're my family, you know? It's hard being away from them and not being able to chat on the phone or even hug them. I get it's for their safety and mine that I stay hidden, but it doesn't change how I feel. Dylan came up with the letter idea, saying that it was the safest route. I just hope he doesn't blame himself."

"He was right. Phones can be traced; it's why we are using disposable ones. The letters were the only option that would be the safest for everyone involved. At least now we know that Ray is still in River Falls, or near there at least," Dean explained.

My brows furrowed together in confusion. "How do you know that?"

"Because the letter had to have been switched by the time Cassie wrote it, to when McCormick picked it up." Dean grabbed my hand. "Don't worry, once he gets back to River Falls and talks to Cassie, then we will be able to narrow it down."

I gave him a small smile, slightly relieved but also terrified that Ray was still near my friends.

AFTER I ATE MY SOUP— OR RATHER, STIRRED IT AND only took a few bites— Dean sat with me while I watched a movie on TV. I honestly couldn't even tell you what it was about because all I kept thinking about was Cassie. I knew that everyone back home would keep my friends safe, but in the back of my mind, I felt like Ray would hurt them. He would hurt them only to get to me, and I would much rather put myself in harm's way than see my friends suffer by his hand.

I jumped at the sound of Dean's phone ringing, and he placed a hand on my leg as he answered the phone. "Holden." I waited in anticipation as he listened to whoever it was on the other end of the phone.

"Do you have video footage?" Dean sat up, placing his laptop on the table, and I leaned in closer to see what he was doing. He clicked a few buttons, and surveillance footage popped up on his screen.

"Yeah, I got it up now." He put the phone on speaker, then set it on the table.

"Fast-forward until the 2005 mark," I heard Dylan say, and I wanted to ask him about Cassie, but I held off.

"What's 2005?" I asked Dean softly.

"Military time, that would be 8:05 p.m. civilian time," Dean answered, concentrating on the screen. It was weird seeing Cassie on a tiny screen, and she was working with Jared. I could see her writing on a piece of paper for a long time and having to come back to it after she helped a customer. Dean stopped it at the exact time Dylan said, and we watched Cassie fold up a letter, put it in an envelope, and set it down on a shelf under the counter. She had finished writing it just in time for the late-Friday-night dinner rush.

"That's where she usually keeps her phone," I remarked. "No one can see that shelf unless they are sitting on the opposite end of the bar."

Cassie waved hi to one of our regulars and went to assist, stepping out of the frame. Then, someone walked into frame, wearing a baseball cap that shielded their face. My body stiffened as I recognized the cap. It was my high school team's cap they gave to the baseball players.

"He always wore that hat," I whispered, staring at Ray on the screen. My stomach churned, and the soup that I had barely eaten threatened to come back up.

"That's Ray? Are you sure?" Dean asked, lifting a brow and pointing at the screen. He paused the video when Ray turned his head to the side. You couldn't see his face, but I knew.

"I'm one hundred percent positive that's him." I stared at the screen. Dean hit the Play button, and you could see Ray reaching under the counter and swapping out the letters.

I felt sick. My skin felt clammy, and my palms started sweating. I stood up from the couch. "I don't want to see any more."

Dean picked the phone back up, but I couldn't make out a word he said. My ears were ringing, and the floor was spinning underneath my feet. He'd been right there by my best friend, and she didn't even know it. Cassie would have recognized him if she'd served him, and Jared had the memory of a goldfish when it came to recognizing faces. Of course, unless it was a female's face.

"He must have used the dinner rush as a distraction," I vaguely heard Dean say to Dylan on the phone. My body felt like it was on fire. I was out of breath, like I had just run up several flights of stairs. My vision started to blur, but then my gaze locked with Dean's.

"Breathe, Aubrey," Dean commanded gently. "You're okay. Just breathe."

I held on to his wrists as he cupped my cheeks. I inhaled with him, then exhaled with him repeatedly until

I felt the world beneath my feet stop caving in. My vision centered on him, and he was all I focused on as I calmed my mind and soul.

"That's it, baby, just breathe," he cooed softly, bringing our faces closer. He kissed me gently, and it calmed the raging storm inside me. Without a shadow of a doubt, I knew that I was in love with Dean Holden. I wasn't falling anymore—this was real. I finally opened myself up to the possibility of love with the one person I never would have thought I would. As his lips moved against mine, I had no regrets even if our relationship would end in tragedy.

FORTY-THREE
Aubrey

*A*nother month had gone and passed, and it was now November. Tomorrow was my birthday, and it would be the first year I'd spent it away from my friends in ten years. Dean had been great, and I was grateful that he was here, but my friends and I had made it a tradition to spend my birthday together, just the four of us. I'd always hated my birthday up until I met my friends. Nana, of course, always tried to make it special, but I could tell that day upset her too. She'd lost her son the same day I lost my dad. And I knew that was hard on her too, but still we made the best out of the day as we could.

I never did like going out on my birthday because in the back of my mind, I was afraid that something bad might happen. Which seemed crazy to think, but my friends didn't mind staying in, drinking wine, and gossiping. They knew how hard my birthdays were, and we'd made some great memories to try and replace the last memory I had of my parents.

"Hey, I was thinking. Since it's your birthday tomorrow, I thought maybe we could take a drive? Get out of the house for a bit," Dean offered, running his fingers up and down my arms as I cuddled up next to him.

"Hmm," I answered, not sure what to say. I didn't like being in cars on my birthday, so much so that I always took off work and made sure I had everything I needed so I wouldn't have to venture out.

"You alright?" Dean asked. He was very intuitive to how I was feeling, as I was with him. We'd grown accustomed to each other's moods and their telltale signs. I knew when he was thinking about Wyatt because he would be quiet and distant. When he was content, he touched me more. It was almost as if touching me grounded him. When he was stressed, he played the guitar until all his stresses disappeared.

"I'd actually like to just stay in tomorrow if that's alright. I don't like being out on the road on my birthday." I hoped he wouldn't take that the wrong way, although I doubt he would.

"Okay." That was all he said, but it sounded like he wanted to know more. He knew that my parents were gone, but I didn't think he knew that they had passed away on my birthday. If he did, he didn't let on that he knew, and he was waiting for me to tell him.

I sat up. "Do you know what happened to my parents?"

He shook his head. "I know that they passed, which I only know because of that night at the restaurant. As far as details of what happened, nothing."

"My parents and I were in a car accident on my fifth birthday," I told him. Dean grabbed my hand and brought the back of it up to his lips. "We were singing and having a good time when my father hit a patch of black ice, causing him to lose control of the car. We rolled several times before hitting a tree."

Dean gave my hand a squeeze as I continued on. "I remember the sound of crunching metal as the fire-fighters used the jaws to cut us all out. I remember lights shining in my eyes and someone putting white sheets over my parents. I kept thinking that they were only covering them up because they must have been sleeping. That the doctors would help wake them up. Then this officer grabbed me and never let me out of his sight. He stayed with me until Nana came to get me from the hospital.

"I saw pictures of the car. Nana didn't know I knew she saved the news article. I have no idea how I survived and they didn't. It honestly didn't even look like a car, more like a huge pile of scrap metal. But I made it out without so much as a few scratches and bruises."

"I'm so sorry," Dean finally said after I finished telling him the story.

I looked at him. "Don't be. I made peace with their death a long time ago. But for every year on my birthday, I made a point to stay home. At first, I was just afraid, but after a while it just stuck. Of course, now, I won't be spending it with my friends, and I won't get my birthday call from Nana."

The thought of not hearing my nana's voice this year on my birthday really hit hard just then. My eyes started to water, and I pulled my hand away from Dean's. "I think I'm going to take a shower."

I got up off the couch and hurried into the bathroom before I broke down again. I turned the shower on, stripped off my clothes, and stepped into the tub. I let the tears fall as I quickly washed my hair and body, and then I sunk down into the tub and sat under the stream. The last thing I wanted to do was shed more tears. I'd cried more in the last few months than I had in the last few years combined, and part of me hated it. I didn't want to cry anymore. I was sick of it. I wanted this whole thing done so I could finally live in peace, but I was stuck in this nightmare.

The shower curtain opened, and the water was turned off. Dean scooped me up in his arms and brought us into his room. He laid me down gently, then got in the bed with me, covering us both up. I turned my face up to his, and I scooted up to kiss him. I deepened our kiss, and with each swipe of our tongues, I got thirsty for more. We hadn't done anything since our first time, and now I was craving his touch. I needed him, and I knew he was holding back from me.

"What's wrong?" I asked, hurt that he was pulling away. "Do you not want to?"

He adjusted his head. "Believe me, I want to. But not while you're upset."

I narrowed my eyes at him. "I *need* you, Dean."

I was practically panting and squirming around so he would understand just how much I wanted him.

"Touch me," I begged.

Dean's green eyes darkened as his pupils dilated. In one swift moment, he was hovering over me, and my arms were pinned above my head. If this were anyone else, I'd be scared, but with Dean, I was so turned on. He kissed me with such a force that I was sure I would be the first woman to ever orgasm just from a kiss. His tongue dipped into my mouth, and I loved the taste.

Keeping my arms above my head, Dean lowered himself down my body, trailing searing kisses in his wake. He took his time with each breast before ducking down lower, nipping the skin on my stomach with his teeth, then continuing down...down...fuck.

I arched my back as his mouth feasted on me, his tongue working magic on my clit. Threading my fingers in his hair, I cried out his name as he slipped a finger inside me. I started moving my hips, and he placed one hand on my pelvic bone, keeping me still. My legs started shaking as I felt the sweet tension build and build as his mouth and fingers worked in tandem.

"Fuck, Dean!" I panted as I climaxed, but he didn't let up. No, he kept going, lapping up my orgasm and working me up for another. My entire body shook as he kept thrusting his fingers in and out of me, his tongue and thumb working together on my sensitive bud. My hips rocked up off the bed, but he didn't care. He went with me, and just as I was about to come again, he moved to kiss me. He was still fingering me as he kissed me, letting me taste myself on his lips. I moaned into his mouth, clutching onto his shoulders, and the orgasm kept ripping through me. It felt like my body was hovering over the bed. I saw stars I was so high from pleasure.

Dean tore off his shirt and reached into his nightstand to pull out a condom. "I'm not finished with you yet, baby."

FORTY-FOUR
Dean

I was more relaxed than ever, contemplating having Aubrey for breakfast, but one look at her beautiful face while she was sleeping peacefully was enough reason for me to let her be. She tasted like tequila sunrise, and I found that it would be my new addiction. I didn't want to wake her though, and ever since she'd been sleeping in here with me, I hadn't had a single nightmare. My phone started vibrating on my nightstand, so I carefully moved Aubrey onto the pillow, threw on a pair of gym shorts, grabbed my phone, and quietly left my room.

"Holden," I answered as I shut my bedroom door.

"Hey, man, I sent over the videos you asked for," Dylan told me. "They're in your email."

I smiled. "Thanks. I really appreciate you doing that."

"Anytime. I'm sure it will make Aubrey really happy."

"I think it will. Especially today." I opened the fridge and pulled out a bottle of water.

"How are things going with you two, by the way?" Dylan asked.

"Are we going to keep having chick flick moments?" I joked, and I heard Dylan laugh.

"There is nothing wrong with chick flicks, okay. Some of them are actually really good."

I rolled my eyes. "Don't tell me you cried at the end of *The Notebook*."

"Dude, everyone cries at the end of that movie. Don't tell me you pretended to fall asleep, then actually fell asleep." Dylan chuckled.

"Alright, then I won't." I took a sip of water before continuing. "Have you gotten anything more on Ray?"

Dylan sighed. "Nah. We've posted flyers up, but no one has come forward. Cassie is staying with Ford, and I've been working overtime with surveillance, making sure she's safe."

"I bet that's not easy," I said truthfully. I felt bad for the guy having to watch the woman he loved be with another man.

"Tell me about it. But her safety is all I care about now. I'll deal with everything else after we catch this guy," Dylan said, and I didn't doubt it.

"What about her other friends?" I asked, taking another swig of water.

"Well, Sophia is staying with her friend Chloe and Lieutenant Hamilton. That way Noah can keep an eye out for them since resources are stretched thin as it is." I nodded. "Anyway, I gotta run, but tell Aubrey happy birthday from me."

"I will. Thanks for the update."

"Later," Dylan said, and I hung up the phone. I wanted to do something special for Aubrey for her birthday, and since I couldn't go anywhere, I thought having her friends record a birthday message so I could show her might cheer her up. I hated that she couldn't see her friends, and I'd been trying to come up with a way we could bring her friends up here to visit without being followed. If I could figure out a way to make it happen, I'd do it. Seeing her smile was what made me want to get up in the morning. It was the first thing I thought about when I woke up and the last thing before I fell asleep.

I heard movement in my room, then moments later, my door opened and Aubrey walked out. She was wearing one of my flannel button-down shirts and panties. My cock twitched as she walked down the hallway toward me.

"Good morning," she said cheerfully, standing up on her tiptoes to kiss me.

"Morning." I kissed her back, dropping my hands low on her hips as her arms went around my neck. "Happy birthday."

She smiled, and damn, it was perfect. "Thank you."

I kissed her again, and then she wiggled out of my arms to start a pot of coffee.

"Dylan said happy birthday," I told her, and she turned to me.

"Well, remind me to thank him the next time he calls." She grabbed a coffee cup from the cabinet. I took it from her, then pointed to the kitchen table.

"I'm making breakfast," I said, and her eyes widened. "Breakfast is actually my specialty. I am the master when it comes to bacon breakfast sandwiches."

She sat down then set her elbow on the table and rested her chin in the cradle of her palm. "Oh really?"

I nodded confidently. "Oh yeah. Just sit back and relax and let the master work."

She giggled, and we eased into easy conversation as I whipped us up some breakfast sandwiches.

Aubrey moaned as she took a bite. "Oh my God."

"I told you." I took a bite, then swallowed it. "You're welcome."

She laughed. "Well, thank you."

I winked. Once we finished eating, we cleaned up.

After that, we did whatever she wanted to do for the rest of the day. Which I soon regretted because she said she wanted to take pictures of me. I hated being in front of the camera, and I wouldn't have minded being her bitch boy and holding all her gear as we took a hike outside and she took pictures of nature. But no, I was the subject she wanted to take photographs of today, and who would I be if I denied that to her on her birthday?

"C'mon, Holden, crack a smile for once in your life," she joked, and I grimaced. "A real smile."

"I am smiling," I said through my teeth, half-amused, half-annoyed.

"No. You look like you have a stick up your ass."

I shot her a look, and I heard the distinct click of her camera going off.

"You know, that was sexy." She looked at the screen at the picture she just took. "Never mind on the smile, babe. Give me more of that!"

My heart skipped a beat at "babe." She'd never called me anything besides my name. To be fair, I loved when my name escaped her lips, but now we were using pet names for each other. I never really gave much thought to where our relationship was at. To me, we were just us. Aubrey and Dean. I realized right then and there that I hadn't surrendered myself fully to her. There was still a part of me that was holding myself back from giving her all of me. I knew what I needed to do, and I finally thought I was ready.

Let it all out so you can let her all in, Holden.

After we came back inside, we took separate showers so that I could get dinner started. I went outside and fired up the grill, which I hadn't used in a long time, and put two steaks on it. I seasoned up some veggies, put that in aluminum foil, and set it on the grill too. Aubrey was sitting on the couch sipping on some white wine. I grabbed a beer from the fridge and went over to her, sitting down in the recliner.

"You know, Wyatt and I would come up here for fishing trips, and I'd always be the one who cooked," I said, taking a swig of my beer. "He couldn't cook for shit. One time he almost burned down our apartment trying to make ramen noodles."

Aubrey chuckled. "Oh no!"

"Yeah. He was never allowed near the stove again."

"Where did you learn to cook?" She leaned her head down on her arm with a smile on her face.

"Trial and error mostly. I followed a couple of recipe books, and my mom taught me a thing or two," I answered truthfully. "I'll be right back."

I got up and set the beer down on the kitchen table, grabbed two plates, and walked outside. I checked to make sure everything was cooked to perfection, loaded up the plates, then brought it inside.

"Dinner is ready!" I said. I prepared Aubrey's plate, then fixed mine up. I was saving her videos for last tonight because I knew she would want some time alone, and I wanted to be a bit selfish with her today. Conversation flowed effortlessly as we ate. Aubrey got up and told me she would clean up since I cooked. I tried to resist, but she insisted that I go sit on the couch. Reluctantly I went, and about fifteen minutes later, Aubrey came over with another beer for me, and her glass of wine was refilled.

She set her glass down on the table, then straddled my lap. "Thank you for making my birthday so special."

Aubrey leaned forward and kissed me, and while I would have loved to take her on the couch, I needed to show her the videos.

"It's not over yet," I reminded her between kisses, and she leaned back, her face flushed.

Aubrey lifted a brow. "No?"

I tapped her leg, and she got off my lap. I grabbed my laptop, opened my email, and clicked on the link. The video player popped up, and her friends all came into view.

"Hi, Aubs! We miss you!" Cassie said, smiling in the video. "Happy birthday, love bug!"

Aubrey gasped, bringing her hand to her mouth.

"Yes! Happy birthday! Oh my gosh, we have so much to tell you!" Chloe said, taking the camera from Cassie. "But first, I just you to know that we love you, and we miss you."

Tears started flowing down Aubrey's cheeks, but from the huge smile on her face, I knew they were happy tears. I rubbed her back and kissed her temple.

"Happy birthday, baby," I whispered. I kissed her again and got up from the couch.

I needed to say goodbye to an old friend.

FORTY-FIVE

Dean

I was sitting on the bed in Wyatt's room. It was supposed to be a guest room, but we'd designated it to be Wyatt's room since he was the only one who would use it. I was holding his memorial service card in my hands with his dress blues picture on the top. Was I really ready for this? Fuck, I wasn't ever going to be ready. Emotion crept up, and I felt my own eyes tearing up as I stared at the picture. The bed dipped, and Aubrey wrapped her arms around me, resting her head on my shoulder.

I scrubbed a hand down my face. "Wyatt and I were driving down Park Avenue when we got the call about a robbery in progress."

"Do you think Momma and Papa Holden would care if Vanessa and I used the lake house this weekend?" Wyatt asked, turning on Park Avenue. We were headed back to the precinct to get everything ready for the officers on the next shift.

I shrugged. "I don't think so. I know my mom likes to drive up there to clean it sometimes, but I never know when. Just call them and ask. I'm sure it wouldn't be a problem though. Why?"

Wyatt beamed. *"Check the glove box."*

I leaned forward, opening the glove box. A small black velvet box was sitting on top of some papers. I grabbed it and opened it, letting out a long whistle.

"You sly son of a bitch," I said as I looked at the engagement ring. *"When did you even get this? And why am I just finding out about it now?"* Wyatt and Vanessa had only been dating for a few months. That was years in Wyatt terms.

"I didn't want to hear your shit, because you'd end up talking me out of it," Wyatt admitted.

I scoffed. *"No, I wouldn't."* Wyatt shot me a look, and I laughed. *"Well, I wouldn't if you were serious about it. You really love this woman, don't you?"*

He smiled. *"Yeah. I never thought I'd even say it. She was a fantasy in a red dress and had the best tight, wet pussy I've ever had the privilege of being in."*

We both started laughing at that, until Wyatt continued. *"It was just time, man. I was bored with all the meaningless sex. I realized that there's more to life, and I want to see what I could get out of it before I go. Did I want to be alone or surrounded by all my kids, grandkids, and great-grandkids?"*

"Wow." Before I could say anything more, I heard dispatch on the scanner.

"Attention, all units, we have an armed robbery in progress at the corner of Park Avenue and Sixty-Third." Wyatt and I looked at each other.

"Didn't we just pass Sixty-First?" I asked him, and he nodded, turning on the lights and sirens.

I grabbed the radio and pressed the button. *"124. 123 and I are passing Sixty-Second now."*

"10-4, 124. Backup is five minutes out."

"10-4." I put the radio back and readied myself for whatever we were about to run into.

Wyatt weaved in and out of traffic, and adrenaline pumped through my veins. We rolled up to the 7-Eleven, the car coming to an abrupt stop. Wyatt and I quickly got out, using our doors as cover.

"Stop!" Wyatt screamed, both of us holding our weapons out. "NYPD. Stop and drop your weapons!"

"Get on the ground now!" I shouted. Three armed suspects stood there, staring out at us. We couldn't identify anything about them because they were covered from head to toe and they were wearing masks. Dread filtered through my veins as one suspect stepped forward, tilting his head. They were the ringleader, and it was then I knew they weren't going down without a fight.

"Put your weapons down! Now!" Wyatt shouted. "Put 'em down!"

The ringleader raised his weapon, pointing it at me.

"Don't do it!" I shouted, hoping that this wouldn't turn into a bloodbath.

A split second passed, and they fired at us. I ducked down as glass shattered, and it was raining gunfire. I waited a moment, and when I had the opportunity, I fired my weapon. Bullets were pinging off the door, and the loud bangs rang out in the night. I needed to neutralize the threat, but it was hard because you didn't know where the bullets were coming from.

A sharp, burning pain seared in my knee, and I went down.

"Holden!" Wyatt hollered through the car as I cried out in pain. I gripped my knee to try and stop the bleeding as bullets whizzed past. I fired my weapon, but my clip was empty. With bloodied hands, I reached back into the car for my other clip. I had to ignore the pain, even though it felt like my leg was pulsating and burning off.

"Hang in there, buddy. I'm coming!" Wyatt ducked low as

I pushed myself closer against the side of the car. I tried to yell at him to stay put, but this fucker didn't listen. He grabbed me, pushing me behind him, switching our places. Not even a second later, a bullet struck him in his side, right under his arm—right where my head was not even seconds ago. Wyatt went down, and a scream so guttural escaped my lungs. I grabbed him, shielding him with my body as gunfire continued to rain down on us, and I held him until I heard more sirens approaching. The deafening sound of guns going off stopped.

I reached back into the car and grabbed the radio. "Officer down! I repeat, we have an officer down!"

I dropped the radio and turned my attention back to Wyatt. "Y-you're gonna be okay, man."

I tore off my dress shirt, bunched it up, and put pressure on his wound. Wyatt coughed, and blood gurgled out of his mouth.

"Fuck, this hurts," he choked out, teeth coated in his blood.

"I told you to stay put." I choked on a sob, trying to keep my shit together. I noticed Wyatt starting to close his eyes, and I gently slapped his face. "Hey, l-look at me, Coleman."

His eyes lazily opened, and he looked up at me. "That's right. Keep your eyes on me. Hey, hey, talk to me about Vanessa."

I checked his pulse, and it was faint. He was losing blood, and he was losing it fast. I looked up, and I didn't see an ambulance anywhere in sight.

I grabbed the CB mic again. "Where's my ambo! Officer down! Please, fuck!"

Dropping it again, I looked back down at Wyatt. The blood on his face was a stark contrast to his pale skin. "Stay with me, buddy." I grabbed his head and held it between my hands.

His eyes were glossed over as he stared up at me. "D-Dean. T-tell Vanessa and m-my parents I l-love them."

Wyatt's breathing was hitched as he struggled to bring in air. My heart sunk, and an unbearable weight settled on my shoulders.

I scoffed. "What? You're going to tell them that yourself. We're going to get you all patched up, okay? You're going to propose to Vanessa and live a happy, long life. You hear me?"

Wyatt grabbed my hand and used whatever strength he had left to give it a squeeze. He smiled, as if he was thanking me for being by his side. His muscles relaxed in my hand, and his arm went limp. His head lolled to the side as his last breath left his body.

And then he was gone.

"I LOST MY BEST FRIEND THAT NIGHT, AUBREY." I clung onto her arm for dear life as I finished telling her what happened. "Everything after that moment was a blur. They did everything they could to try and bring him back."

Aubrey gently rubbed my back, and I was thankful she was here with me. My body trembled with emotion, and tears were falling down my face.

I wiped them away. "We switched places. He didn't fucking listen, and we switched places. That would have been me if it was just a split second sooner."

I lost control, and Aubrey pulled me into her arms. Months' worth of pent-up grief overcame me, and I just lost it. My best friend of twenty-five years was gone.

Unspeakable pain tore through me, then out of me. It was like I was relieved of my demons, and I felt like I could finally see clearly. Everything snapped into place, and I could breathe again. Aubrey held me close. She gently rubbed my head and didn't give a shit that a grown man was breaking down in her arms.

I finally got my shit together and sat up, wiping the tears from my face. "I feel like I failed him. He asked me not to push anyone away, and that's exactly what I did."

"You were grieving." She spoke softly. "Everyone grieves differently."

"That's no excuse."

Aubrey stayed quiet, but she grabbed my hand.

I laced my fingers through hers. "I just don't want to fail anyone again. My biggest fear is failing you."

I shifted my body to face her. "You aren't just a job to me anymore. You haven't been for a while." I reached up and cupped her cheek. "I love you, Aubrey. You're *it* for me, and I'll be damned if I ever let you go."

Aubrey placed a hand on my cheek as she brought her forehead to rest against mine. "I love you too, Dean."

I cracked wide open when she said those words back to me. Love replaced all the guilt in my heart, and I finally knew exactly what Wyatt was talking about. That feeling you get when you know when someone is the one. It's an indescribable feeling that not even the best writers in the world could portray. I loved this woman so fiercely that I promised myself that I would walk through fire to make sure she always stayed safe.

FORTY-SIX
Dean

I pulled Aubrey into my lap, gripping her hips tightly as I deepened the kiss. This woman broke down every single wall I had put up. I truly loved her with every fiber of my being. I wanted to experience the rest of this life with her. I could almost hear Wyatt in my head saying, "It's about damn time, asshole." I didn't believe in fate, but now I was sure we were brought together for a reason. Everything that led up to this very moment had happened for a reason. Where there was death, there would be life. I needed Aubrey like I needed air to breathe, and I planned on breathing her in for the rest of my life as long as she would have me.

Aubrey's hips rocked against me, and I stood up. She wrapped her legs around my waist as I walked us out of Wyatt's room and into mine. I set her down and cupped both of her cheeks. Her bright blue eyes pierced my soul, and I leaned in to brush my lips against hers. I felt like we had all the time in world, and I would take the time to get myself acquainted with her body, because I already knew her mind.

Reaching down, I grabbed the hem of her sweater and lifted it over her head. Her fingers found the bottom of my shirt, and I helped her lift it over my head. Starting at her wrists, I slid my fingers up her arms, then brushed her long hair over her shoulders. Her hands did the same to my body, as if we were just exploring all the dips and curves of each other. I placed my hand on her ass, pulling her to me, just so she could feel just how much her touch affected me.

I undid her bra and let it fall to the floor. I kissed her lips, her jaw, collarbone, and then my mouth found her nipple. A breathy moan escaped her lips as I sucked and nipped at the rosy peak. I held her close to me as I dropped down to my knees in front of her. I trailed kisses down her stomach and then curled my fingers around the seam of her leggings and pulled them down to the floor. Her fingers threaded into my hair as I kissed her pelvic bone, then continued down to each of her thighs. I looked up at her, and she was a beautiful sight to behold.

She placed her hand on my cheek as I stood, and I brought my lips to hers. Our tongues danced slowly around each other, and her hands dropped down to unbutton my jeans. Then she surprised me by kneeling in front of me, pulling my pants and boxers down. Her small hand wrapped around my cock, and then her lips curled around the tip.

An earth-shattering hiss escaped my lips as her tongue swirled around the tip of my cock. She bobbed her head and stroked me at the same time, and fuck, it felt so good. She was unsure of herself, and she flinched when I went to move her hair out of the way. Her first and only experience was with someone who didn't cherish her. He used and abused her. That's not a man. A man knows the real value of a woman—that was why Aubrey would never be "mine." She belonged to no one but herself, and I counted my lucky stars that this woman trusted me enough to allow me to cherish her in all the ways he never did.

She's my partner. My best friend. My equal.

She wasn't a possession and never would be when she chose to be with me.

I pulled her off me because I was nowhere near ready to finish. She stood up, and I kissed her deeply, showing her how much I loved her. I laid her down gently on the bed, wrapping her leg around my waist as I slowly entered her. She was warm, wet, and oh so ready for me. The sensation almost overwhelmed me. Skin to skin.

It was perfect. It felt right.

I rocked my hips slowly as I palmed her breast and sucked on the sensitive spot on her neck. A staggered groan came out of my mouth as I moved inside her. She was the definition of perfection. I craved her more than I desired anything else. Her nails dug into my back, and her hips bucked against mine. I felt her walls constrict as she came over my cock.

"Fuck, baby. This feels so good," I heard myself say out loud. I placed my head in the crook of her neck, and she held me tight. I wanted to stay inside her forever, but I knew I was ready to come.

"Dean!" Aubrey cried out as she came again, soaking my cock. I moved quicker, lacing my fingers through hers and squeezing tight. My balls tightened, and within seconds, I found my release. My dick pulsated inside her, and nothing had ever felt so powerful. I was breathless, emotionally spent, but I peppered kisses all over her face.

Our gazes locked, and a stray tear fell from Aubrey's eye. I kissed it away, then brushed my lips against her. Our bodies were still entwined, and I wouldn't want it any other way.

"You complete me, Aubrey Rose," I told her, nuzzling her nose with mine.

"I'm irrevocably in love with you, Dean," Aubrey whispered. I pulled out of her and brought her closer to me. I covered us up, and we just lay there, relishing in each other's embrace. She fit perfectly in my arms, and it amazed me how far we'd come since we first met. I never want to be the Dean that just moved in and was a dick again. I was a better man now, and I had her to thank for that.

FORTY-SEVEN
Aubrey

*I*t was Thanksgiving Day, and I was freaking out. I wanted to make a nice dinner for the guys, and I was missing potatoes to make the mashed potatoes. It wouldn't be Thanksgiving without the mashed potatoes. I checked on the turkey, which was baking perfectly in the oven, giving the house a very nice aroma. I wanted to wait to make everything else until the turkey was almost done cooking.

"Dylan is on his way with potatoes, right?" I shouted at Dean, who was sitting in the living room watching the game. I'd fussed at him earlier for being in my way. Chloe and Rhett always hosted Thanksgiving dinner with only one condition: Cassie had to cook. She was the chef, and a damn good one at that. She'd only let me help her in the kitchen because I knew how to cook. Sophia was always late, and Chloe almost burnt down her house. Cassie and I made a great team in the kitchen. But without her, I was a nervous wreck.

"Yes, babe," I heard him say.

Good, now I could relax. Well, sort of. I just wanted tonight to be perfect. Not that it wasn't already because I was here with Dean. Who would have thought I'd ever utter the words "I love you" to another man again? I mean, I'd always dreamed of doing so one day, but fear got in the way. Not anymore—I was a new and improved

269

Aubrey Daniels. I was proud of myself for overcoming the fear of loving and being loved. And boy, did Dean love me. He was so gentle yet commanding, and I loved every single moment of it. Feeling my body heat up at thinking about Dean in the bedroom, I decided I could use some cold fresh air. When I went to go open the window, I smiled because Dylan was pulling into the driveway.

"Dylan's here!" I shouted, and Dean got up from the couch to follow me outside so that we could help him. He was quite literally my only connection to the real world, and I knew that he was coming with a gift for me. It was a care package from my friends, and I was super excited to dive into it.

"Hey, guys." Dylan stepped out of his truck, then opened the back door, and Moose jumped out.

"Hi, Dyl. Did you bring the potatoes?" I asked as I reached him. Moose barked at me until I petted him. He was such a good boy, and I loved whenever Dylan brought him up here.

"Yes, ma'am," he said, handing me a bag. I peeked inside and frowned.

"These are instant." I pouted. I suddenly felt my eyes tearing up but blinked them back. "You know what? It's fine."

"Are you okay, Aubrey?" Dylan asked, looking a little nervous.

I nodded. "Yeah, I'm fine. Just overly tired."

I look pointedly at Dean, who had a smug look on his face.

Dylan smiled. "Nice, you two. Real nice."

He handed Dean more bags and pulled out a box. He shut his doors, locked his truck, then followed us into the house.

"Wow. It smells amazing in here." Dylan took his boots off by the door as I set the instant potatoes in the fridge. It was the kind you just popped into the microwave. I would have much rather peeled, cooked, and mashed them myself, but I had to make do with what I had.

I smiled as I took my care package from him. "Thank you. There's beer in the fridge, so help yourself."

Dean had asked the patrolmen if they would stop and pick us up a case of beer and a bottle of wine for me and dropped it off this morning. I'd been so busy that I hadn't had the chance to break it open.

"Thanks," Dylan said, then turned his attention to Dean. "What's the score?"

"The Saints are up ten to three," Dean answered him, keeping his eyes on the TV.

"They're playing the Falcons, right?" Dylan sat in the chair next to the couch, taking a sip of his beer. Moose plopped down on the kitchen floor in his favorite spot. He loved how cool the hardwood floors were.

"Yeah." Dean turned to me, winked, then went back to watching the game. I remembered that he told me the New Orleans Saints and the Atlanta Falcons were playing today. I'd never watched a football game in my life, but I did join Chloe's football parties she'd throw for Rhett and the guys at the firehouse.

Clutching my care package, I went into Dean's room —or should I say our room now?—and sat down on the bed, tucking my legs under me. I ripped open the box and was not surprised to find some sexy lingerie from Chloe's boutique. I picked up the lacy black bra and panty set, and a note fell out.

. . .

Aubs,

These would look great accessorized with handcuffs ;) I just know your detective would love this. Miss and love you babe! Rhett and the guys at the firehouse send their love!

Love, Chloe

I laughed and shook my head. In my video I had recorded the day after my birthday, I told them all about Dean and our relationship. So, it didn't surprise me in the least that Chloe would send up some lingerie. There were spa gifts, magazines, more SD cards, my favorite candy, and of course my favorite shampoo and conditioner. It was a good thing they'd sent this; I was almost out. I chuckled at a scrunchie hidden at the bottom of the box after I pulled out some books.

Aubrey,

Miss you! I packed some paperback books for you just in case you got sick of reading from a kindle. I hope you like them; these are some of my favorites! Can't wait for you to come home! Love you!
　xo Sophia

. . .

A TEAR FELL DOWN MY CHEEK AS I READ THE LITTLE love notes from my friends. I couldn't wait to get home and see them too. A figure stood in the doorway, and I looked up to see Dean leaning up against the frame.

"I'm just checking on you." His eyes flicked toward the bed, and he smirked. "What do we have here?"

He moved before I could grab the lingerie from his grasp. "Oh...oh yeah. I love this."

I flushed, my body starting to overheat again as he picked up the note that went along with it.

Dean leaned down and got close to my face. "You tell Chloe I do love it, and yes, they would look great with handcuffs."

I combusted. I was so turned on, I almost jumped his bones right then and there. Moving forward, I crashed my lips into his, and he growled as I forced him to sit so I could straddle his lap.

"We have company," he said as I bit his lip.

"So?" I kissed his stubbled jawline, then nibbled on his ear. I rocked my hips, desperately needing the friction.

"Baby, I don't know if you're aware of this, but you are *not* quiet." He half laughed, half moaned as I continued my assault. *What has gotten into me?*

"It would be rude, wouldn't it?" I panted in his ear, feeling him hardening underneath me.

Dean groaned, gripping my hips. "Uh-huh."

"We should stop."

"Uh-huh."

We of course didn't stop until we heard Dylan scream, "Touchdown!" in the living room. Dean and I broke apart and tried to catch our breath.

"Later. We will continue this later," Dean promised, then got up. He stood in the middle of the room, trying to compose himself as he adjusted his erection in his pants. He sucked in a few breaths, then left me alone in the room. I licked my lips, then pulled myself together. Looking back in the box, I grabbed the last note and read it.

MY GIRL!

I HOPE THIS LETTER REACHES YOU, UNLIKE THE LAST ONE *eyeroll* The audacity he had, ugh! Anyway, I packed a scrunchie for you, because "when the scrunchy is present, the night will be pleasant." I hope it gives you some semblance of home. Hope to see you sooner rather than later! Enjoy Chloe's gift (I helped her decide, btw). Love you so much love bug.

WITH LOVE, CASS.

I HUGGED ALL MY LETTERS, THEN PLACED THEM BACK inside the box along with my other gifts. I'd sort them out later, but first it was time to carve the turkey.

FORTY-EIGHT
Aubrey

When dinner was finally ready, we all sat down at the table together. Moose sat by Dylan, hoping for some scraps, but Dylan shooed him away. That was when the dog came over and rested his head on my lap. Making sure Dylan wasn't looking, I gave Moose a slice of turkey while we dug in. I was thankful for a lot of different things, but watching Dean and Dylan laugh together and talk about life was amazing. I guessed I sort of had Ray to thank for that. If it weren't for him, I would never have met the man of my dreams and fallen head over heels in love. However, on the flip side, he had killed my nana, and for that, I hoped he'd rot in jail.

I took a sip of my wine and immediately regretted it. I forced a swallow but made a face as I set it back down on the table.

"What's wrong with the wine?" Dylan asked right before he took a bite of his food.

"It just tastes funny." I grabbed the glass of water and washed down the wine. I was disappointed—it was my favorite. "Maybe it was just a bad batch."

Dean took my wineglass, swirled it around, sniffed it, then took a sip. "It tastes fine to me."

I sat back in my chair, suddenly not feeling so hungry anymore. I tried sipping it again, and it still tasted weird, so I gave up. Maybe it was just me and I was overthinking it. Still, I was put off, so I drank my water instead. I nibbled on my food, giving more to Moose as Dean and Dylan were in a heated conversation about...well, something. I honestly stopped paying attention. I quietly got up from the table and cleaned the rest of my plate off into the trash, then started putting the leftovers away in the fridge. But I made up two plates to take out to the patrolmen sitting outside. I felt bad that they couldn't be with their families today, so the least I could do was make up a warm plate of food for them.

Dean kissed my cheek as he came up behind me to put his plate in the sink. "You alright, babe? You've been oddly quiet."

I nodded. "Yeah. I'm fine. Would you mind taking these to the officers outside?"

Dean smiled. "Sure. I'll be right back."

He put on his jacket and boots, then grabbed the plates and headed outside.

"I take it things are going well?" Dylan asked, setting his plate in the sink to wash it.

I smiled, thankful for the subject change. "Yes, things are going very well."

"Good, I'm happy to hear it." Dylan put his dish on the drying rack. "I'm sorry we haven't found Ray yet."

"He's not going to be easy to track down. But if everyone I love and care about are safe, then that's all that matters," I said honestly. "Thank you for being the middleman between my friends and me. It means so much to me."

Dylan smiled, "I know it does, and I'm happy to do it. Also, if there's anything you need me to pick up for them as Christmas gifts, let me know."

My eyes widened. "Holy crap. I can't believe we're

almost a month away from Christmas. Man, has time really flown by?" We made our way over to the living room, and he sat back down in the chair while I curled up on the couch. Moose had decided he wanted to lie on the couch and rest his head on my lap. His nose nudged my stomach, and I took that as a sign he wanted attention.

"Yeah, I know. This year has passed by quickly," Dylan said, leaning back in his chair. He looked tired, and I felt bad that he was putting in a lot of work trying to catch Ray and making sure everyone was safe. He had dark circles under his eyes, and they started to grow heavy as he relaxed in the chair.

"I might actually take you up on that offer. I can order off Amazon for the girls because I can ship directly to their houses, but I will need your help with Dean's," I said, feeling excited. I had this idea, but I needed to come up with the perfect way to execute it.

"Sounds good." Dylan yawned just as Dean walked back inside.

"It's colder than a witch's tit outside!" Dean joked as he took off his jacket and boots. Moose jumped down from the couch and went over to his spot on the floor while Dean grabbed a blanket and sat on the couch. I snuggled up to him, and he covered us up.

"Aww, don't you two look cozy," Dylan joked and Dean flipped him off. I started laughing along with them as we continued to watch the game. I had no idea what was going on, and I gave them credit for trying to explain it all to me. After a while, I just grabbed my Kindle and started reading a book. About twenty minutes into the story, I was suddenly so tired I could hardly keep my eyes open.

I felt Dean nudge me. "Why don't you go to bed. I'll be there in a little bit."

Nodding, I got up off the couch and gave him a quick kiss before heading to bed.

I shut my eyes, and before I knew it, I was fast asleep.

FORTY-NINE
Dean

We were two weeks away from Christmas, and Dylan was coming up to sit with Aubrey while I ran out to the store. I had some personal things to grab, and then I wanted to pick up the gift I'd had made for Aubrey. I made sure I placed my custom order before the cutoff, and they were able to get it done quickly.

Aubrey walked out of my room, looking a little pale. She'd complained of a stomachache last night and had been lying in bed all morning until she got up and took a shower.

"How are you feeling?" I asked as she walked into the kitchen. I felt her forehead, and she didn't feel warm, but I made a mental note to pick up a thermometer to check it when I got back.

"I just feel sick. Honestly, I just wish I would throw up already. This waiting in limbo thing really sucks," she admitted, sitting down at the table. I opened the fridge and handed her a bottle of water. She scrunched her nose and pushed it away.

"Babe, you have to drink something," I said, worried about her. I wondered if it was something that she ate that wasn't agreeing with her, but we'd been eating the same thing. She did eat some leftover pie she'd made the other

279

night, so maybe it went bad. She took the water bottle and tentatively took a tiny sip.

"You know what, I'm just going to stay here—" I started to say, but Aubrey cut me off.

"No, go. I'll be okay. It's just a bug—I'll be fine. Go do what you need to do," she murmured, laying her head down on the table.

"Do you need me to pick you up anything?" I asked, sitting down in a chair and scooting closer to her. I tucked a lock of hair behind her ear. It killed me seeing her like this and not being able to help. "Ginger ale? Soup? Crackers?"

She nodded, and a tear rolled down her nose.

"Why are you crying?" I asked, wiping the tear away with my thumb.

"I don't know!" She sniffed, picking her head up and covering her face with her hands.

"How are you on your lady stash?" I called her drawer in the bathroom full of tampons her lady stash. That was her drawer that I had cleaned out for her when we first got here.

Aubrey lowered her hands and started counting her fingers. Her eyes widened as she looked at me, and then she quickly got up and ran to the bathroom. I was right behind her as she opened the drawer and pulled out an almost full box of tampons.

"Oh no," she whispered as I just stared at her. "No, no, no, no, no."

Aubrey covered her mouth, dropping the box of tampons on the floor, and turned to the toilet. I went over to her and held her hair back as she threw up. I filled up a tiny rinse cup up with water, then sat down on the edge of the tub, rubbing small circles on her back. She flushed the toilet and set the seat down, shifting her body to sit on the lid. I handed her the cup of water, but she batted it away.

"How could I not have noticed?" she murmured.

"Noticed what? Aubrey, talk to me," I said, grabbing her hands.

Our gazes locked.

"I'm late." Her voice was barely above a whisper.

I blinked. Then realization punched me right in the nuts.

"Oh shit." My eyes grew wide as everything continued to click into place.

"Oh my God!" Aubrey quickly got up from the toilet and left the bathroom. "How could this have happened? I mean, I know how it could have happened but…oh God!"

Aubrey started breathing erratically, and I walked over to her. She tried pushing me away, but I held on to her, cradling her head to my chest. Only one of us could freak out at a time right now, and I was still processing her words. She could very well be pregnant…with my child.

"Listen, everything is going to be okay," I said, holding her close. "I'll pick up a pregnancy test from the store, and we'll do this together."

She pulled away and looked up at me. "Y-you're not mad? Or upset?"

I was taken aback by the question. "I'm feeling a lot of emotions right now, but angry and upset are not any of them." I cupped her cheeks and kissed her, not caring that she'd just puked. "I love you, and we will take this one step at a time. First things first is taking a test, and we will figure the rest out as we go."

Aubrey just nodded, and I pressed a kiss to her forehead.

I didn't care what the test said. I was all in with her,

that much was certain. The timing sucked because we still didn't know where Ray was, and if she was pregnant, then we would have to take extra precautions. But I'd cross that bridge if we came to it. I led Aubrey to the couch and laid a blanket over her. I turned on *Friends* for her, then sat down on the couch, bringing her feet onto my lap.

I didn't want to leave her here after the realization, but I also didn't want Dylan to know. At least not yet anyway. Not until we knew for sure. He finally showed up about twenty minutes later, and I left him with Aubrey. I knew she was in good hands with him, and he'd help take her mind off things.

I got in my truck and drove down the road. I hadn't given a whole lot of thought into our future together. I was just taking it all one step at a time. I was feeling like my old self again and felt on top of the world. Did I want *more* with Aubrey? You're damn right I did. I planned on forever with her. I wanted the marriage, a house…kids…I wanted it all with her. I came to the conclusion as I was driving that regardless of what the test said, I was going to spend my entire life cherishing Aubrey.

My first stop was picking up her Christmas present, and then I went to the local Walmart. I grabbed the things I needed, while also picking up some ginger ale, saltines, and soup for Aubrey. If she wasn't pregnant, then she was just sick. Of course, then I went down and picked up some Pepto-Bismol, thinking it would help with the nausea and upset stomach. But I wondered if she could even take that if she was pregnant. I tossed it in my basket and headed down the aisle with the pregnancy tests.

I had no idea what the fuck I was even looking at. Which one did I even buy? Fuck. I picked out two different brands and put them in my basket, then headed for the checkout. I didn't want to be away from Aubrey for too long. I quickly got back in my truck and went back to the lake house, carefully scanning the road to make sure I wasn't being followed.

I pulled into the driveway as Dylan was walking out with Moose. "Hey, welcome back! That was quick."

I smiled, although it felt a little forced. "Yeah. Aubrey isn't feeling well, so I wanted to get this back to her."

He nodded. "Yeah, she got sick while you were gone. She's lying on the couch now, sipping on some water."

"Good. Are you heading out?" I asked. It was such a long drive from here to River Falls that I felt bad for making him come all the way out here for less than two hours. It wasn't an easy drive, but he'd repeated multiple times he doesn't mind the drive.

"Yeah. Cassie has a shift at the Bistro tonight, and Ford is working the night shift. So, I told her I'd follow her back to Ford's and keep watch until he got off," Dylan explained.

"Alright, cool. You best be getting back, then. Don't want you to hit rush-hour traffic." I waved him off as he walked toward his truck.

Dylan opened his back door, and Moose jumped inside. "You and me both. Hopefully I'll have enough time for a catnap. Later."

I watched as Dylan drove off, and I went inside. My palms started sweating as I set the bags on the table and toed off my boots. Was I ready to be a father?

One look at Aubrey as she walked over to me was all the answer I needed.

Even if I wasn't ready, I'd get ready for us.

FIFTY
Aubrey

I was a huge bundle of nerves as I walked over to Dean. I couldn't turn my brain off while he was gone. What if it was negative? Would I feel relieved, or would I feel saddened? On the flip side, what if it was positive? Would I make a good mother? What if Ray found out? I didn't want to keep my entire pregnancy a secret from my friends, but if Ray found out... I didn't want to even think about that.

Dean ran a hand down his face as I got to him. "I wasn't sure which ones to get, so I got two different brands."

I gave him credit for at least trying to act calm and collected. But by the way he was rubbing the back of his neck, I knew he was just as nervous as I was. He'd seemed so sure before he left, and now I was wondering if maybe he was having second thoughts. I mean, he had only just told me about Wyatt and that he loved me. Neither one of us was thinking of having kids, especially this early in our relationship. We'd never even talked about marriage and kids, at least not thoroughly anyway. I knew there was a risk having sex without protection, so I was just as much at fault in this as he was. Of course, I wasn't blaming this on anyone. I loved Dean with all of my heart and trusted him in ways I'd never trusted anyone before. Regardless of anything, if there was a baby inside me, it wouldn't be a mistake. Not to me.

I glanced down at the bag and pulled out the First Response box.

He reached forward, tugging my lip out from under my teeth. "Whatever you're thinking, stop."

"I can't help it," I admittedly softly. He took the box from my hands, opened it, and pulled out a test stick.

"First things first," he said, leaning down to kiss me before continuing. "We take the test. Then, whatever it says, we talk about it."

I sucked in a deep, calming breath and took the stick from him. "Okay."

I'd made sure to drink as much water as I could before he got here without feeling like I was going to vomit again. I was able to drink enough because I really had to pee. I closed the bathroom door and took the test. I set it on the counter, washed my hands, then sat down on the edge of the tub. I felt like I was going to be sick again, but I chalked that up to the nerves. My palms were sweaty, and my heart started racing. Was I even ready for a baby? Were we? I didn't know the first thing about babies except what I'd learned in health class.

There was a knock on the door, and then it opened. Dean walked in, and I lost it. I rushed to him, gripping him tight as I cried into his chest.

"Why the fuck can't I stop crying?!" I sobbed into his shirt. I felt him kiss the top of my head, and I guessed he was smart not to say anything. Was it normal to be this hormonal this early on? What if it was negative—then what could I blame my tears on? Stress? We stood in the bathroom holding each other until the timer I had set went off. But I needed to hold on to him a little longer.

I let out a shaky breath when I finally pulled away from him.

My eyes locked with his.

"We'll look together," he whispered, grabbing my hand.

Keeping our gazes on each other, I reached over and grabbed the test and brought it in between us. Staring into his forest-green eyes, I knew right then and there that whatever this said, everything would be okay. He told me with his eyes that he would be all in no matter what, and that was all that I needed to gather the strength to look down.

He gave my hand a squeeze, and then we both glanced down. My breath hitched in my lungs as I stared at the word written on the tiny screen.

Pregnant.

FIFTY-ONE
Dean

*P*regnant.

Holy fuck, I was going to be a dad.

I had all but given up on my future when Wyatt died, and yet here I was standing in the bathroom with the woman I was head over heels in love with, staring down a pregnancy test that told me I was going to be a father. I didn't think I deserved anything but darkness, but Aubrey taught me that when life gives you a second chance, you must make it something worthwhile.

I couldn't help but smile because all I felt was joy. Time meant nothing when you were with the one; Wyatt was proof of that. I was one lonely son of a bitch until Aubrey knocked on my door, welcoming me into the apartment building.

MY HEAD STARTED POUNDING AS I LAY ON THE COUCH. I cracked an eye open, and the sun was shining through the curtains. I passed out again after a night of drinking myself into a stupor. It was how I blocked out the pain of losing Wyatt and moving back home to River Falls. I refused to live with my parents and ended up moving into this apartment building. I had only been here a few days, and the only time I'd left was to go to work.

It took me a moment to realize that my head throbbed with every knock on the door. My muscles ached as I got up from the couch to take some ibuprofen for this fucking headache. Then I made my way to the door to tell whoever it was to fuck off. I opened it, and I thought I was hallucinating for a moment.

A beautiful woman with the bluest eyes I'd ever seen. Long, wavy, honey-blonde hair fell just past her shoulders, and she had the most perfect smile. For a moment, I thought I had died and gone to heaven, but I knew better than to think I'd make it past those pearly white gates with the sins I had perched on my back.

"Hi," she said, her voice soft and tender. "My name is Aubrey. I live in the apartment next door."

"Uh-huh," I grunted out. If I thought I deserved a woman as breathtaking as her, I'd put on the charm.

She frowned, and I hated seeing that pretty smile wiped from her face.

"Uhm, anyway, I just wanted to introduce myself and…"
She went to hand me a plastic container, and I lifted a brow. "I baked some cookies and thought I'd give you some to welcome you into the building."

Of course, she just had to be sweet and thoughtful too.

"Thanks," I said, voice husky from being hungover and sleepy. "But no thanks."

I shut the door, and I knew if Wyatt were here, he'd kick me right in the nuts for shutting the door on the woman of my dreams. But he wasn't here, and she didn't deserve a man like me. There was a heavier knocking on the door, and without thinking, I turned and opened it again.

Aubrey's face was flushed, and she narrowed her eyes at me. "Usually when someone does something nice for someone else, that person doesn't slam the door in people's faces."

She shoved the plastic container into my arms. "You're welcome."

Then, she shut the door on me. I could hear Wyatt's laughter ring out through my empty apartment, and I heard him say, "Game. Set. Match, Holden. That girl's a keeper."

I took the test from Aubrey's grasp and cupped her cheeks. "I'm all in. I want this. I want all of this with you. Even if that test said negative, I'd still be all in. I've never given love, kids, marriage…any of it a second thought until you came into my life. I know you'll be the most caring, loving, selfless mother for our baby. Whatever doubts you have swirling in that mind of yours can be put to rest."

"I don't know anything about babies," she whispered, and I couldn't help but chuckle.

"I don't either, but we'll figure this out together." I tipped her chin up so I could kiss her. Slow and steady, I moved my lips against hers.

"I'm scared." Aubrey's voice cracked as she admitted her truth.

I grabbed her hand, leading her out of the bathroom and into the living room. I sat down on the couch, and she lay down with her head in my lap. I covered her up with a blanket as she wiggled around to get comfortable.

Brushing her hair back from her face, I asked, "What are you scared of?"

Aubrey sighed. "I'm scared of a lot of things, but the thing I'm most afraid of is Ray finding out."

If I were being honest with myself, I had to admit that was what I was afraid of too. Which was even more reason to find him and arrest him before he even got near Aubrey.

"We will just have to be careful, then." Now I had to come up with a way to get her to and from the doctors without detection. Unless they made house calls, so we'd have to figure that out too. "Let's not worry about that because I won't let him get to you."

It was a promise I intended to keep.

FIFTY-TWO
Aubrey

Christmas this year felt bittersweet. Once I had gotten over the complete shock of my pregnancy, I'd been feeling better about all of it. Dean and I were figuring things out as we went. We had our first doctor's appointment just to confirm that we were, in fact, pregnant. They gave us some pamphlets, and we came back to the lake house. Dean was on edge the whole time and didn't relax until we got back home. I couldn't blame him though, because I was worried about Ray finding out about us, too. But I needed to stay positive for my own sake.

I lifted my shirt and looked at my flat belly in the mirror. I stood to the side and tried to picture it getting bigger, but the only things that had gotten bigger were my boobs. I was only six weeks or so along, and that's when Dean and I figured out this was a birthday sex baby. I'd found myself crying over the dumbest commercials now, and I wouldn't let Dean anywhere near my boobs. One, because they were tender, and every time he rubbed them to make them feel better, it would lead to non-issue number two. We'd always end up having sex. He'd come up and gently caress my breasts from behind me, then before I knew it, I was sitting on the counter and Dean was moving inside me.

Pull it together, Aubrey. You just had shower sex, and before that it was morning sex.

"You won't show for a while, babe," Dean said from the doorway of his parent's room. They had a full-length mirror standing by the window.

I let out a long sigh. "I know. I was just trying to picture it in my head."

Dean walked over to me and I turned to wrap my arms around his neck, while he grabbed my waist.

I stood on my tiptoes to kiss him, then pulled away smiling. "You'd take pregnancy photos with me, right?"

"The answer to anything you ask for the next nine months will always be 'yes,'" he answered.

A mischievous grin played on my lips. "Anything?"

"Within reason." Dean rolled his eyes playfully, and I chuckled. "But yes, I'd do it for you."

"Good." I kissed him once more, and then we went out to the living room to sit by the fire. We were keeping our pregnancy between us for now. We just wanted to celebrate it with just us, and then after our twelve-week checkup, when we got to see our little one, we would tell people. Not many people knew about our relationship either, so I was sure it would come off as a surprise.

Since my nausea happened at all hours of the day, I ate when I felt like I could. I felt so bad for Dean because even just the sight of red meat made me vomit, let alone the smell. So, he'd been stuck eating various chicken dinners. Our Christmas dinner was chicken and dumplings, which was what I was craving at the moment. We came up with a few meals to choose from for today because my cravings changed on the daily. Yesterday, all I wanted was Cheerios with extra honey. Today, it was chicken and dumplings.

Dean had set up the floor with blankets and pillows around the tree, and we ate dinner there. He cleaned up, then came over to me carrying a small gift in his hands. I smiled when he handed it to me, but I couldn't wait any longer. I grabbed his present from under the tree, which was also in a small box.

I handed it to him, giddy with excitement. "You first! Open it!"

He laughed, then carefully ripped the paper. His smile when he lifted the lid off the box lit up the room. He pulled out the key chain that had "Protect and serve to the highest degree but promise to always come home to me" engraved with a hole in the shape of a police badge. Then he pulled out the matching necklace shaped like the badge that could fit perfectly in the spot on the key chain with his badge number, 124, engraved in it.

"I know it seems a little cheesy. But I will always carry your heart around with me wherever I go, and you know that when you come home to me, your heart will be complete," I explained, and of course I started to cry. "Gosh, that sounded so much better in my head."

Dean chuckled, then leaned over to kiss me gently. "No. It's perfect. I love it. Thank you, baby."

I sniffed, and then Dean told me to open the gift from him. I tore the paper open, and here came the waterworks full force. It was a heart-shaped pendant with my parents' birthstones and Nana's on one side of the loop and diamonds on the other.

"It feels a little weird, giving you another necklace to wear." Dean ran a hand down the back of his neck nervously. An idea sprung to mind, and I picked up the necklace with his badge number and removed it from its chain. Then I carefully threaded it onto the chain of the necklace he got me.

I held it out to him. "Would you do me the honor?"

He took the ends of the necklace as I twisted around and moved my hair to the side. He brought it around me, then clasped it together. I closed my eyes as I felt his lips press against the nape of my neck. I straightened the pendants out as I turned to face him again.

"There, now I can have everyone that I love most near my heart," I said, climbing into his lap. "I love you, Dean. I feel more alive than I've ever felt when I'm with you."

He gripped my hips as I leaned my head down to kiss him. His tongue swiped across my bottom lip, demanding entry. It was slow, sensual, and everlasting. A kiss that sent my body into orbit with every tender brush of his lips against mine. We showed how much we loved each other by the way we touched.

We broke apart, breathless, and my body felt like it was on fire.

"I want to play a song for you," he breathed as our bodies were still rocking together. "It's the other half of your present."

I wanted to tell him it could wait, but he and I both knew he would never get to play it for me if we didn't put this heavy make-out session on pause. I got off his lap, and he grabbed his guitar. I caught on to what the song was in the first few chords.

"Oh my God!" I squealed as he played my favorite Christmas song, "'Have Yourself a Merry Little Christmas.'"

He smiled, then started to sing. I didn't think I could love this man any more than I did now, but here I was falling deeper in love with him. The summer had ended in tragedy, but the New Year was bringing me so much joy and life. I let myself forget about the fact that Ray was still out there. I wouldn't let him ruin this or taint it with his foul play. Just for tonight, I'd live my life as if he didn't even exist. Tomorrow, I'd pick back up the anxiety I felt every day knowing he was still out there.

FIFTY-THREE
Dean

I was just finished getting ready to head back to River Falls. It was February, and since we hadn't had any more leads on Ray, we needed to come up with a plan to draw him out. I hated the fact that I had to leave her here alone without myself or Dylan to keep watch, but the officers outside were trained to handle threats. I had no choice but to trust them, and Aubrey was safest here. Dylan was on his way up here to pick me up because he was headed up this way anyway to drop some things off for Aubrey.

"Why? Why can't you just hang the wet towel up? It's not hard!" Aubrey shouted in frustration, coming out of the bathroom. I still hadn't told her that I was doing it on purpose, because it turned me on when she yelled at me. Apparently, Aubrey bossing me around was my kink. But I was certain that me controlling her in the bedroom was her kink. I was taking it slow with her because of her past; I would let her tell me what she needed. Lately, with the raging hormones, she'd become surer of herself, and the confidence in her was sexy as fuck.

Her mouth snapped shut, and I saw her pupils dilate when she took me in, standing there. I was dressed in business casual, and apparently, she loved what she saw. I let my eyes drift down her body, and they stopped at the tiny baby bump. God, she was perfect. She was carrying my child, and that was the hottest thing in the world. My cock was getting harder with every second that passed as my gaze drifted over her.

Her shirt was tighter across her breasts, and her chest was heaving as if her breathing was erratic. I could practically smell her arousal from here, and fuck. *How much time do I have before Dylan gets here?*

I unbuttoned my shirt and tossed that to the floor. I distinctly heard her sharp intake of breath from halfway across the room. I continued my path of destruction toward her until her back was pressed against the wall, my body flush with hers, my cock hard against her leg but itching to be inside her. I brought my face close to hers, brushing my nose along her jaw and breathing in her scent. *Roses and peach.*

I could feel her body trembling with need, but I hadn't touched her. "Do you want me to touch you, Aubrey?"

"Yes," she whispered, her hot breath hitting my ear and sending all the blood racing to my dick.

"Do you want me to pick up my towels or touch you?" I asked, hovering over her skin. I desperately wanted to dart my tongue out to nip and suck my favorite part of her neck that always made her squirm.

Her reply was arching her hips forward.

I smirked. "What do you want, baby girl?"

My eyes looked deep into hers.

They darkened to a stormy blue, and she lifted her chin. "You."

The moment those words left her perfect lips, my mouth was on hers, demanding entrance to taste her. She reached up to wrap her arms around my neck, but a deep, guttural sound emitted from me, and I spun her around. I was rock fucking solid as I pressed her carefully up against the wall, her ass grinding into my crotch. I forced her arms up, making her place her palms on the wall.

Gripping her hips, I pulled her back to where she was bent over in front of me. I wrapped my arms around her, one hand skimming down her belly, then diving down into her sleep shorts. The other went under her T-shirt. I groaned when both hands met bare flesh. She wasn't wearing a bra or panties. *Fuck me.*

My left hand squeezed her nipple, while my right hand played with her clit. A moan escaped her lips, but I needed more. I wanted to hear her scream my name. I slipped a finger inside her, then another, working her to an orgasm.

"Ride my hand, baby," I commanded. Her hips were starting to move in tandem with my fingers. She was so responsive, and I was loving every minute.

"Fuck," she hissed through clenched teeth. "Dean!"

Hearing my name come out of her mouth was something I would never grow tired of. She stood up straighter, removing her hands off the wall. I stopped, and she whined. She was panting, and her hips were still moving against my dick.

I pressed a kiss on her neck and gently forced her hands back on the wall. "I didn't tell you to remove your hands. Keep them on the wall, Aubrey."

We trusted each other explicitly in the bedroom, and I never forced her to do anything she wasn't ready for, but she loved this. Aubrey did as she was told, and I slipped my hand back into her shorts. I started to work her back up again, and it wasn't long till I felt her pussy walls constrict around my fingers. She cried out, and I used my hand that was just on her breast to turn her face so I could catch her orgasm with my mouth.

I physically couldn't wait any longer. I removed my hands long enough to undo my pants, and she pulled down her shorts. I bent her back over, putting her hands back on the wall. With one quick thrust, I was buried deep inside her. With one hand holding her shoulder and one gripping her hip, I continued to push myself in and out of her. I threaded my fingers through her hair and pulled gently.

You know how I knew when she liked what I did to her? She moaned, loudly and that sound was always music to my ears. She apparently *really* liked her hair being pulled because her moans were echoing through the house. Who knew my partner in crime liked it a little rough? Although Aubrey was anything but breakable.

"Fuck," I growled, wrapping my hand around her neck and tilting her face toward me so I could taste her. "You feel so fucking good, baby."

"I'm so close," she breathed, and didn't I know it. I was in so deep, and fuck…if this was what heaven felt like, then I didn't ever want to leave. I felt her pussy constrict around my cock, and I knew that the second she came, I'd be coming right along with her.

"That's it, Aubrey, lose control. Surrender yourself to me." I groaned, and just like that, my words were our undoing.

I HAD AN UNEASY FEELING IN THE PIT OF MY STOMACH as we were driving down the highway. Since Wyatt's death, I always liked to drive because being in the passenger seat always brought up bad memories of that day. Now here I was, sitting in Dylan's passenger seat, staring out the window and contemplating telling him to turn around. Something just felt wrong about leaving her there, and it wasn't that I didn't trust Officers Tudor and Gomez, I just wanted to make sure she was safe. My dad wanted us back, though it went against my better judgment to leave.

"Penny for your thoughts?" Dylan asked.

I adjusted myself in the seat. "I just don't feel right about leaving her."

"Do you want me to turn around?" he offered. Dylan cared about Aubrey, and he was scared for her safety as well.

"No," I answered, shaking my head. "She'll be safe there. It's just…"

I trailed off. Aubrey and I had our twelve-week doctor's appointment in the morning, and I guessed I was getting all up in my head. We told each other we'd tell everyone together, but I needed to open up to the person I trusted with my life, other than Aubrey.

"Aubrey's pregnant," I told him, and his head whipped toward me.

"What?" His voice cracked, and I almost asked if he had hit puberty yet. "That's great, man. Congrats!"

I was a little bit taken aback by his reaction. "You're not going to give me shit?"

Dylan scoffed. "For what? Having a baby? Hell no. Life's too short for all that. You've got to do what makes you happy."

I shot him a look. "What about Cassie?"

"What do you mean?"

"When are you going to make your move?" I asked. Dylan got quiet for a moment, and I thought he wasn't going to answer, so I dropped it.

"She's with Ford, and she seems happy. She's the one

that got away, and that was on me." His mouth formed a thin line as he stared out at the road in front of him.

"I don't know. I still think you have a shot," I told him truthfully. "Second chances start by coming home."

I knew his time in the military had something to do with their breakup, but he was tight-lipped when it came to her. Dylan went quiet after that, and we sat in a comfortable silence until we arrived back in River Falls.

FIFTY-FOUR
Aubrey

Officer Tudor was sitting inside with me, while Officer Gomez was sitting out in the car. Dean would only be gone for a few hours, but I was still a little worried. I had only talked to these men a few times, but Dean seemed to trust them. I learned that Officer Tudor's name was Theodore, but everyone called him Teddy. He did kind of remind me of a teddy bear. He was a little fluffy and had a mustache that was peppered with silver to match his hair. He was quiet for the most part and very respectful.

I made sure to change into a baggy sweater and leggings before Dean left. I wanted to hide my baby bump as long as I could. Not that it was a big bump, but it looked bigger than a food baby. I was comfortable sitting on the couch watching TV when Teddy's radio beeped.

"Officer Tudor, could you come out here, please?" I heard Officer Gomez say through the speaker. He didn't elaborate on why he needed Teddy to come out, but I didn't think more of it when he got up from the kitchen chair.

"Wait here, Ms. Daniels. I need to go see what he needs. I'll be right back," Teddy said, then went outside.

I turned my attention back to the TV and got immersed in the show I was watching. It was a reality show where people marry someone they just met, then go on a honeymoon. Then at the very end, they choose to stay together or get divorced. It was such a bizarre show, but I couldn't stop watching it. I was about halfway through the episode when I had to pee. I got up to use the restroom, and when I came back out, I noticed that Teddy had not come back inside yet. I checked the time on the oven, and it said it was almost 10:00 p.m. Dean should be on his way home now.

I slipped on my boots, opening the front door and peering down the driveway. Although, I could hardly see anything past Dean's truck. Without thinking, I stepped outside, shutting the door behind me and making my way down the driveway. The closer I got to the end, there was a little voice in the back of my mind that told me to turn back around and lock myself in Dean's room. Something felt…off…in the air around me. Turning around would be the logical thing to do, but the moment I saw Teddy lying on the ground, my feet were moving toward him.

Once I reached him, I had to cover my mouth to stifle my scream.

His neck was slashed open, and blood was still draining from his neck. I reached down, grabbing his wrist to try and feel for a pulse, but he was dead. I swallowed down the bile that was rising in my throat and glanced inside the cop car. Gomez was dead too. His throat had been slit as well.

He's here. Oh God, he's here.

My flight-or-fight instincts kicked in, and I knelt and searched Teddy's body for a phone. When I couldn't find one, I pulled open the driver's-side door and immediately froze. Lying on Gomez's lap was a bouquet of yellow roses. Panic filtered through my veins, and with shaky hands, I slowly picked them up and pulled out the card.

. . .

FOUND YOU, BREE.

I TOSSED THE BOUQUET ON THE GROUND AND immediately went for the radio, but it was busted. Tears filled my eyes, but I had to blink them back. I couldn't break down—I needed to be strong. *You're a survivor, Aubrey.*

My heart raced through my chest as I searched the car for a cell phone. My hands wouldn't stop trembling as I fumbled around, getting Gomez's blood over myself. I kept apologizing to him as I searched his body and found a phone in his pocket. I pulled it out and dialed Dean's number. He'd made me memorize it in case of an emergency.

"Holden." He answered on the first ring, and a sob escaped my lips. My entire body relaxed for just a fraction of a second until I heard a branch snapping in the woods. I dared not say a word as I stood frozen in fear. "Gomez?"

"D-Dean." I kept my voice barely above a whisper and tried to keep my voice even as I spoke.

"Aubrey? Aubrey, is that you?" His voice was pure panic now. "What's wrong? Talk to me, baby."

"He-he's here," I said as I felt that feeling that I hadn't felt since I was back in River Falls. I turned my head slowly and came face-to-face with my nightmare.

"Hey, Bree." Ray smirked, and it was pure evil.

"Aubrey! Get inside the house now!" I vaguely heard Dean through the ringing in my ears.

I took a step back as Ray stalked forward.

"I've waited such a long time for this. I didn't ever

think that prick would leave." Ray's face turned angry, and I knew that look all too well. His eyes were pitch black, and I knew he came here to kill me.

"Baby, don't hang up the phone. I'm coming for you. You hear me? I'm almost home. Just keep him talking." To anyone else, Dean's voice would have sounded calm and void of any emotion. But I knew his voice better than anyone. He was pissed off and scared to death.

"How did you find me?" I asked, doing what Dean told me to do. I vaguely heard Dylan in the background talking to dispatch. I just needed to hold off until someone got here. I could do that; I could be brave.

Ray laughed humorlessly. "I knew I should have swerved a little bit more to the left when I sped out of here."

My eyes widened as I remembered that day. That was the day Dean went in search because they saw kids in the woods.

"Ahh, she remembers." He bowed slightly. "I paid those kids twenty bucks each to walk through the woods to distract whoever was inside keeping you away from me."

Dean went quiet on the phone, and I knew that he was blaming himself.

"Don't," I said directly to Dean. "Don't blame yourself."

"Talking to your boy toy, are we?" Ray's eyes were pitch-black as my foot hit the first step of the porch. "Don't listen to this bitch. It was *your* fault. Ask him how he feels knowing I had you first."

Anger boiled in my blood.

"Fuck. You," I spat.

"Been there, done that. Now you're just a slut with a

dirty cunt." Ray's nostrils flared, and I knew it was time for me to run. I turned and ran up the steps with Ray hot on my heels. I screamed until my lungs burned as I tried to slam the door on him. The phone fell out of my hands as Ray pushed the door open, making it break off the hinges. I tried to grab the cell phone as it slid across the floor. But I couldn't catch it in time. My lifeline was gone.

Just keep him talking, Aubrey. You need to be brave. You need to survive.

I would not let Dean lose any more people he cared about.

I tried to curl up, but Ray grabbed a handful of my hair and lifted me up. He slammed me back against the wall, knocking the air out of my lungs. His body was pressed up against mine, and his hand came up and wrapped around my throat.

His breath reeked of booze, cigarettes, and weed, and I closed my eyes tightly, turning my head away from him.

Ray leaned in and took a big whiff of my hair, nuzzling my neck. My skin crawled as he continued to violate my personal space. His cock was hard against my leg, and bile rose up my throat again, but I couldn't take a breath to heave, so I swallowed it down.

"I thought about you all the time while I was in jail," he whispered against my cheek. He squeezed my neck a little harder as he continued to speak. "I thought about all the ways I could hurt you."

He ran his nose along the side of my jaw, breathing heavily as he thrust his hips forward.

"I thought about all the ways I could hate fuck you." He tightened his grip around my neck and lifted me up slightly. I struggled to breathe, but I kept squirming in his grasp. "I've thought about your sweet cunt for ten years, and now it's tainted."

His fingers cut off all circulation, and his jaw clenched tightly. Ray's face turned red as his lips pursed. He slammed me hard against the wall, and my head bounced off the plaster. My vision blurred, and I blinked, trying to focus on anything that I could to keep me from going under. *Stay alive for Dean and the baby.*

"You. Are. Mine," he shouted; his voice sounded demonic as he repeated the words. "You belong to me!"

I was gasping for air. *Fight, Aubrey.* I saw an opening, and I took it. I brought my knee up with all the strength I had and slammed it into his balls. He went down to the ground, and I made a beeline for the front door. I just needed to get out of the house. I would be alright as long as I got out.

"Don't."

It wasn't the sound of Ray's voice that made me stop dead in my tracks. My hands instinctively raised, and I slowly turned around. My pulse raced, and my mind went blank as I stared down the barrel of his gun.

FIFTY-FIVE
Dean

I heard the gun click, and my world froze over. My hands were shaking as rage ripped through my body. I knew I shouldn't have fucking left. I should have trusted my instinct and stayed put. Have them come to me.

"How far are we out?" I asked Dylan, trying to pay attention. It made me sick thinking of what he was doing to Aubrey as he said those vile things to her. I needed to keep myself in check because Aubrey needed me too.

You had one job, Holden.

"Five minutes out, but I can get there in three," Dylan said, speeding down the road. We had the lights and sirens on. Dylan was focused on getting me home to her. I gripped her key chain in my hand as I listened in.

"We can talk about this," I heard Aubrey say. "J-just put the g-gun down."

"Fuck talking. You had ten years to apologize to me, Bree. You betrayed me." Ray sounded unhinged. I checked the clock, and it didn't change. Three minutes wasn't that long in the grand scheme of things, but it felt like an eternity. Seconds were taking hours to tick by.

One fucking job.

"I-I'm s-sorry, Ray. I should have— "

"Fuck your apology now, you dumb bitch," Ray cut

308

Aubrey off. "Quit looking at the phone! He doesn't want you!"

I couldn't listen to this and keep an even mind, so I put it on speaker.

You blew it.

There was silence, and I could hear footfalls getting closer to the phone. There was a scuffling sound, and then Ray's voice was loud as he spoke directly into the phone.

"You must be the scumbag who's been fucking my girl." He let out a humorless chuckle. "Hey, how did you like my sloppy seconds? She's prettier now, really grown into herself. I hope you don't mind if I help myself to some pussy, Detective."

"Do. Not. Touch. Her," I gritted out, anger coursing through my veins, but I managed to keep my voice even. "This is your only warning. Consider it a courtesy call."

Ray went quiet on the other end of the phone, and Dylan and I exchanged glances.

"Consider me warned, Detective." His voice was dead as he spoke those words.

"No! Dean!" Aubrey shouted as a shot was fired, and then the phone went dead.

"No, no, no, no, no," I whispered, then my anger flared, hot and heavy. "Damn it!"

I chucked the phone, causing it to shatter as it hit the dashboard. Dylan cut the corner and stepped on the gas up the road to the lake house. I unbuckled my seat belt, grabbing my handgun and cocking it to put a bullet in the barrel. Dylan was in the driveway, and we both hopped out before he barely put the truck in park. I led point into the house, looking left and right for a threat.

"Clear," I said, then glanced down.

Aubrey lay motionless on the ground and was

bleeding from a gunshot wound on her shoulder by her collarbone. I couldn't think straight. But I followed Dylan down the hallway, checking to make sure the coast was clear.

"All clear," Dylan shouted from my parents' bedroom. "I'm going to check the perimeter. You check on Aubrey."

I didn't even think. I ran straight to her, falling to my knees beside her.

I checked for a pulse and almost collapsed with relief. It was faint, but her heart was beating; however, she wasn't breathing. God, I felt like I was just here. I was reliving my worst nightmare, but instead of it being Wyatt, it was the woman I wanted to spend the rest of my life with. I placed the heel of my palm on her breastbone and started doing chest compressions.

"Please don't leave me," I gritted out, counting out to thirty. "I need you, Aubrey…*baby*."

My voice cracked as I leaned down to breathe life into her.

"You cannot leave me too."

One. Two. Three. Four. Five.

"Please, baby. Breathe."

Nine. Ten. Eleven. Twelve.

"I won't lose you. You are not dying today."

Seventeen. Eighteen. Nineteen. Twenty.

"Breathe, Aubrey. Take a breath. *Please* take a breath."

My vision blurred as I kept up the pace of thirty chest compressions and two rescue breaths. I felt like the world was ripped out from under my feet, and then I heard the most miraculous sound I ever wanted to hear.

Aubrey gasped, then started coughing as she sucked in air.

"That's it, Aubrey. Slow breaths. I've got you, I'm here.

Everything is going to be okay; an ambulance is coming," I told her, then pressed a chaste kiss on her lips.

"D-Dean." She tried to speak, but I placed my finger gently on her lips.

"Shh. Don't speak. It's okay. You're going to be just fine."

Her eyes fluttered closed again, and I checked her breathing and pulse.

"Can you look at me with those beautiful blue eyes of yours? I need to see them," I choked out and wanted to smile when she looked up at me. "That's it, let me look at you."

I heard the sirens off in the distance, and I smiled down at her.

"They're coming. Just stay with me, okay?"

Aubrey just kept her eyes locked with mine. Everything around me melted away, and I felt like I was giving her every single ounce of strength that I had. I was cradling her in my arms when I heard the distinct sound of a gun clicking right by my head.

My eyes drifted up to meet his menacing gaze.

"Do it," I told him, starting to feel numb inside. "If she dies, then I have nothing to live for."

I felt her go limp in my arms again, and there was nothing I could do.

One job Holden, and you blew it. You couldn't protect her.

Ray didn't say a fucking word as he pressed the gun into my forehead.

"Do it!" I shouted. "Let's get this show on the road."

Ray and I stared at each other. If he was going to shoot me, then I would make sure I looked him dead in the eyes as he pulled the trigger.

One shot sounded off into the house.

Ray fell to the floor with a hard thud. Blood was leaking from the bullet wound in his head.

I let out a breath, then blinked a few times.

"Dean." Dylan's voice called out to me, but I was still in shock. I heard his footsteps behind me as he came over and kicked Ray's gun out of the way. He checked his pulse, but we both knew there was none.

Ray was dead.

FIFTY-SIX
Dean

I paced in the waiting room while Aubrey was rushed off into surgery. They had told me that they would do everything they could for Aubrey and our baby. Of course, the odds were slim that the baby would be okay, but I was hoping. The paramedics worked on her in the ambulance on the way over here, and Aubrey even opened her eyes a few times. She was a warrior, and I could tell by the look in her eyes that she was fighting with everything she had.

My dad and Sergeant Miller rounded the corner.

"Any news?" Sergeant Miller asked.

I shook my head. "None. She's still in surgery. No one has come out to give me any updates."

"Okay, I'm going to see if I can get anything out of them." Sergeant Miller excused himself, and I was left standing alone with my dad. He'd only just learned of my relationship with Aubrey tonight, and while he scolded me for it being unprofessional, he was happy for me.

"She's going to be fine, son," my dad said sympathetically.

I felt my eyes tearing up as I looked my father in the eye for the first time since Wyatt's death. "I can't lose her too, Pop." My chest felt like it was on fire as I struggled to breathe. My world was lying on a hospital bed while doctors worked on her to save her life. I felt hopeless.

"Walk with me." I followed my father down the hall and into the hospital chapel. We sat down in one of the pews, and I wondered how being in here would make me feel better. If anything, it felt like she was dead.

"Whenever one of my officers is in surgery, I always come sit in the chapel. I couldn't even tell you why I started doing it. I'm not one for praying, but I found it to be peaceful in here. It's quiet, and less chatter about all that medical talk. It's here where I found that I do my best thinking.

"I know you, Dean. You're blaming yourself for what happened to Ms. Daniels, and I'm here to remind you that you did nothing wrong. The only thing you are guilty of is falling in love. Ray Owens was a sick man, and he was going to turn up sooner or later regardless if you were there or not. I entrusted you with this because I knew you were the only man for the job. I believed in you, Dean. And now it's high time you stop wallowing in self-doubt and believe in yourself too."

I scrubbed a hand down my face as my dad patted my shoulder and got up to leave.

"Hey, Pop," I called after him, and he turned to face me. "Thanks."

He gave me a curt nod. "Always."

He left the chapel, and I sat there in the pew. I wasn't sure if I could believe him since Ray had followed me back up to the house. I didn't think I was that distracted to not notice a car following me. Aubrey had to live because I needed her to help me see the light. I knew that if she didn't make it out of surgery, I would never forgive myself. As we discussed earlier in our meeting, it turned out Ray had been stalking the restaurant where Aubrey worked, trying to get some intel, and he just happened to hear

Cassie talking about writing her friend a letter. That wasn't Cassie's fault. She never said any names, but Ray knew who she was, and that was the only reason why Cassie was targeted.

Someone sat down in the pew next to me, and I was surprised to see it was Cassie. Dylan must have called her and told her what happened.

"Is it Aubrey?" I asked, starting to get up. I started to panic, but Cassie shook her head.

"No. She's still in surgery," she reassured me. Her eyes were red rimmed as if she'd been crying. Aubrey was her best friend, too. I saw she was holding on to an envelope. "I'm sorry, your dad said that I could find you in here."

"Oh, okay." I wasn't really sure what to say.

She cleared her throat. "Can I ask you a question?"

"Sure." I leaned back in the pew and slipped my hand into my pocket to grip the key chain Aubrey had gotten me for Christmas.

"How do you feel about Aubrey?"

I was pretty sure she knew the status of our relationship, but I humored her. "I love her. I'm head over heels in love with her."

"And you'd spend the rest of your life with her?"

"I'd spend eternity with her."

Cassie smiled, and I thought that was such an odd thing for her to do until she opened the envelope and emptied its contents into the palm of her hand.

"When Aubrey's Nana passed away, apparently she had adjusted her will to give me Aubrey's mother's wedding ring. It came to me with a note that told me to give this to the man I was sure would give my best friend the happiest and most loving life she deserved. I already knew how she felt about you; I just needed to hear *you* say the words."

Cassie grabbed my hand and placed the ring in my palm. "Promise me I won't regret giving you this and that you'll take good care of her."

"I promise." I meant it. Cassie gave my hand a squeeze, and I was happy that Aubrey had such amazing people in her life who loved and cared about her just as much as I did.

Before I could say anything more, the door opened, and my father walked in. "She's out of surgery."

I'D BEEN SITTING BY HER BEDSIDE FOR HOURS, MY body becoming stiff in the chair, but I didn't care. I wanted to be here when she finally woke up because I wanted to tell her the good news. The doctors told me that it was a through and through, and they were able to repair the damage. But the best news I'd heard was that our baby was okay. They wanted to monitor Aubrey and the baby closely, but they said the baby had a strong heartbeat.

I was holding her hand, falling asleep, when I felt her fingers moving. I jolted awake, and my gaze locked with hers. I'd never felt so relieved in my life. She was alive, and by all accounts, healthy. I got up to kiss her forehead, then her lips before I sat down on the bed next to her.

"Hi," she squeaked out. "W-water."

I grabbed the cup of water I was drinking out of and brought the straw up to her lips. She took a few small sips, and then I set the cup back down on the tray beside her.

"What happened?" she asked, and I told her I would tell her everything once the doctors came and checked on her.

"And our baby?" Her eyes filled with tears, and I wiped them away as they fell down her cheeks.

"Do you want to see?" I asked, and she looked at me curiously. I told her to wait while I grabbed the nurse, who was happy to do an ultrasound for us. I told them I wanted to wait to see our baby when Aubrey was awake. Kelly, the nurse, came in and adjusted Aubrey's blankets to reveal her tiny bump.

"This might be a little cold, okay?" Kelly said, squirting jelly onto Aubrey's stomach. "You ready?"

Aubrey's face lit up, and she was more awake now. I grabbed her hand. Kelly smiled brightly, turning the ultrasound machine around and flicking a button on the side.

"Is that…?" I asked, eyes growing wide as I listened to the tiny thumping sound.

"Your baby's heartbeat? Yes, sir," she said enthusiastically. She pointed to the little dot on the screen. "And that is your baby."

I was overwhelmed with joy as I stared at the screen and held Aubrey's hand. I kissed her hand, then leaned over to press my lips against hers. Hearing from the doctors that Aubrey was okay and that our baby was too was one thing. But seeing it, listening to the heartbeat, experiencing it all with the woman I loved was more than I could have imagined. It was everything. I was ecstatic and beyond grateful.

"Our little miracle baby," Aubrey whispered tearfully, never taking her eyes off the screen.

"Yep, someone was looking out for that little one," Kelly said, hitting a few buttons on the machine and printing out our sonogram picture. She tore it off and handed it to us. "I'll be back in soon to check your vitals."

Kelly left the room, and I was stuck staring at the tiny little peanut on the sonogram.

My world was flipped on its axis less than twenty-four hours ago, but staring down at this picture, with the love of my life lying awake next to me, my world was flipped right side again. I never believed in a higher power, but I knew without a shadow of a doubt, my best friend was watching over us. And that...that finally brought me peace.

EPILOGUE

6 Months Later

"I'm so damn proud of you," Dean said, leaning in to kiss my forehead. Seventeen hours of labor —he'd better be proud of me. It was the most painful experience of my life, but I wouldn't trade it for the world. Getting shot seemed like a distant memory now, and I guess I had one thing to thank Ray for. If it weren't for him, I probably wouldn't have gotten to know Dean, and I would never have brought this sweet girl into the world.

I looked down at our little miracle baby in my arms and smiled. She'd only been in this world for a few days, and she was already making an impression. Chloe had already started a baby clothing line, Sophia had already bought her tons of baby books, and Cassie had been learning all kid-friendly recipes. I tried to tell her she had plenty of time because the baby would only be drinking breast milk for a while. This sweet girl was already loved by so many people, especially her daddy. He had zero experience with babies, but from the moment she was born, he'd been so attentive and so gentle. He'd been so good to us, making sure we were comfortable and had everything we needed. And we hadn't left the hospital yet.

"How are Momma and little Savannah doing?"

Margaret, the nurse, asked as she came in to check on us. I looked down at my daughter, her tiny hand grasping my finger, and smiled. I'd always loved the name Savannah, and it was the first name I suggested to Dean when we found out we were having a baby girl. It was also the day he proposed to me, and it was one of the happiest moments of my life.

"I'm in so much trouble," Dean joked as we cuddled on the couch. I was too busy staring at our newest sonogram. The words "it's a girl" were written in the corner. I was over-the-moon happy. But nothing compared to the joy I felt when I heard her little heartbeat in the hospital after I was shot. I didn't remember much after the gun went off, but I did remember feeling an overwhelming sense of peace wash over me. I just knew we were all going to be okay.

"Okay, setting the ground rules now." Dean shifted us on the couch so he was talking to my belly. "You aren't allowed to date until you're thirty. No exceptions. Your daddy is a cop, and I'll tell you right now everyone will be getting a background check. Nobody will harm my little girl, not on Daddy's watch."

I laughed, and she moved around inside me. "Oh wow."

"What?" Dean asked, brows furrowed together. His face was full of concern. I smiled, grabbing his hand and placing it on my belly. He beamed, then pressed a kiss on my stomach. He sat up and gave me a kiss too. "I love you."

I smiled against his lips and rubbed our noses together. "I love you too."

He kissed me again, and I placed my hand on his chest. "I picked out a name."

He pulled back slightly, "Oh, you did? Okay, let's hear it." His tone was teasing.

"What do you think of Savannah Wyatt Holden?" I asked, locking my gaze with his. "I wanted to honor the man that meant so much to you. He means the world to me too."

Dean's lips came crashing down on mine in a searing kiss. His hand came up to cup my cheek as he deepened the kiss. He pulled away, resting his forehead against mine, and swiped his thumb across my bottom lip.

"It's perfect," he whispered. "Who am I to be loved by you?"

I closed my eyes as tears fell down my cheeks. My heart and soul loved this man.

"I pushed you away, yet you still stuck by my side. You love who I really am, and that brought a grown man down to his knees. You've seen the worst of me and grew to love me in spite of my demons. No one should have ever loved me the way you did. You loved me through it all, and I plan on cherishing you for the rest of my life." Dean's voice was soft and tender as I opened my eyes and stared deep into his. "Marry me?"

Pressing my lips against his, I whispered the answer without a second thought. "Yes."

He smiled, then got up from the couch only to come back a few moments later carrying a ring in his hand.

I gasped when I recognized the ring. It was my mother's, and the tears were now flowing freely down my cheeks. "H-how did you get this?"

Dean smirked and winked. "I had a little help."

"WE'RE DOING ALRIGHT," I TOLD MARGARET. SHE checked all my vitals while she chatted with us.

"Well, you have two visitors out in the waiting room. Would you like me to send them back now?" she asked, and I glanced at Dean. We beamed at each other. We told Dylan and Cassie an earlier time to come visit so we could ask them a very important question. We wanted them to see her first.

"Yes, that would be great," Dean responded to her, and he came back over to sit next to me on the bed. We couldn't take our eyes off our daughter until there was a knock at the door.

Cassie peeked her head in first, and then she got the biggest smile on her face. "Oh my gosh! Hi!"

Her voice was filled with excitement as she came over to us. Dean got up and greeted Dylan at the door.

"Congrats, Dad," Dylan said, shaking Dean's hand, then pulling him into a hug.

Dean laughed. "Thanks, man."

Cassie sat down on the bed next to me and leaned her head against mine. "She's beautiful. May I?"

"Of course." I smiled at her, then handed Savannah to her. Dean looked a little nervous, but he went into protective dad mode with everyone who was not him or me who held her.

Cassie bounced her gently and went over to Dylan to show him. He stood close to her, and I wished I had my camera to capture this moment. It was almost like a glimpse into their future, or at least, that's what I wanted it to be. Who knew what their future was going to look like? Ford was a great man, but he didn't have Cassie's heart. She didn't have to tell me with words. Her body language and the way she looked at Dylan, I could tell she was still in love with him. They both lit up around each other.

Dean moved back over to me and grabbed my hand. "Aubrey and I were talking, and we have something we would like to ask the both of you."

"Sure, what's up?" Dylan said, shoving his hands into his pockets.

"You can ask anything you want just as long as I can hold this precious little girl," Cassie spoke in a sweet baby voice as she looked down at Savannah.

"We want you to be Savannah's godparents." I smiled at them.

Dylan's eyes grew wide, but then he smirked. "Absolutely. I would love to have that honor."

"You didn't even have to ask me. You knew my answer would be yes, of course. I can't wait to spoil her." Cassie cooed as she swayed back and forth. Then she glanced up at Dylan. "Would you like to hold her?"

Dylan looked a little nervous, but he nodded. Cassie carefully handed Savannah to him, and I felt Dean's body tense sitting next to me. I leaned my head on his arm and watched as Dylan and Cassie bonded over their shared love of our daughter. As much as I loved the other girls, Cassie was the first friend I'd made since moving to River Falls. We'd been roommates for ten years, and it just felt right for her to be Savannah's godmother. Dean was the first to bring up the godparent discussion. He wanted Dylan to be an important person in our daughter's life. He trusted Dylan with his own life, and that was good enough for our daughter.

I had lost a lot in my life. But I had also gained so

much more. I had a fiancé who I loved unconditionally, a beautiful daughter, and the best of friends, who were like an extended family. Everything happens for a reason, and you can't let the bad take away from all the amazing things life has to give. I was loved, *and* I loved, and I wouldn't have it any other way.

EPILOGUE
Dean

I parked my truck in the parking garage of the Hyatt hotel. We were attending the retirement party for my old sergeant. Mark Price was my mentor, and I was pissed at myself for not reaching out to him sooner. He'd trained Wyatt and me, and we'd given him all sorts of hell. We were troublemakers, but Sergeant Price was the reason why I was so good at what I did. Without his guidance, I wouldn't be the man I was today.

Of course, there was something else about him that I didn't know until recently. Or shall I say, I didn't put it together until recently. When Aubrey told me about the cop who'd sat with her after the accident, it hadn't crossed my mind to check to see who it was. Then when I talked to Sergeant Price over the phone and he told me that story for probably the millionth time, he let something else slip that he'd never let slip before—the name of the little girl, and when he said Aubrey's name, I about fell to the floor. What were the chances that I'd be marrying the woman he'd saved all those years ago? I knew right then that I would surprise him at his retirement party.

Aubrey was stunning in her royal blue cocktail dress. Her eyes really popped, and I couldn't wait to get her out of that dress. She had dressed Savannah in this cute little

325

sweater outfit that Chloe had made with a matching bow. I grabbed Savannah from the back seat of the truck and laced my fingers in Aubrey's as I led them inside to the ballroom where the party was being held. I'd come back out later and grab our suitcases since we would be spending the night in the city.

We grabbed our table places and made our way through the crowd. I had introduced Aubrey to all my old colleagues, and everyone loved her, which I knew they would. She handled herself gracefully, and I was a proud man having her by my side. I spotted Sergeant Price talking to my old captain and his wife.

"I want to introduce you to someone important to me," I told Aubrey.

"Okay," she said cheerfully. I think she loved seeing into my old life. No matter what, these men and women in uniform would be family forever. Aubrey grabbed Savannah and cradled her into her chest, and I led them over to Sergeant Price.

"Well, look who it is! The man who turned my hair gray prematurely," Sergeant Price joked as he saw me walk up. The people he was talking to excused themselves before they saw me coming.

"What hair? You've been bald since I've known you!" I joked back, giving the man a hug. "How are you holding up?"

He grinned, holding up a glass of whiskey neat. It was the only thing he would drink. "I'm great. You know Donna is taking me on a cruise through the Bahamas? I've never stepped foot out of the state of New York."

I put my arm around him. "Ah, you'll be fine, old man. Enjoy it."

Sergeant Price laughed and pushed me off him. "I see

you still think you're funny, Holden." He turned his attention to Aubrey, who was amused by our exchange. "And who is this lovely young woman."

I turned and held out my arm as Aubrey stepped into my embrace. "This is my fiancée, Aubrey Daniels."

Sergeant Price smiled, and then his face turned to shock. His eyes widened as he stared at Aubrey in disbelief. "I always wondered what happened to you."

Aubrey looked at me, a little confused. I kissed her temple, "This is the man that took care of you after the accident with your parents. He's the one who stayed with you."

I heard her gasp, and I didn't have to look at her to know she was starting to cry.

"I-I remember you," she whispered. "You never let me out of your sight that night."

"That was my first shift on the job out of the academy. You were so tiny and scared. I'll never forget that night." He reached out to place his hand on her shoulder with tears in his eyes. "I am so glad you are well."

She beamed at him, then turned slightly. "This is our daughter, Savannah Wyatt Holden."

Hearing Wyatt's name made him turn his attention to me. "He would be so proud and happy for you."

"I know he would." I felt myself getting emotional. There was another reason why we were staying the night. Tomorrow, Aubrey and I would visit Wyatt's grave, then surprise his parents. I'd spoken to them over the phone, but I wanted to see them and introduce them to the loves of my life. Aubrey and I wanted them to be a part of Savannah's life too since she was carrying Wyatt's name. Almost like she would carry on his legacy, whatever that may be.

WE LEFT THE PARTY EARLY AND WENT UP TO OUR room. I set the portable crib up as Aubrey fed Savannah. She was perfect sitting there, rocking our baby girl as she hummed a lullaby.

I lifted a brow, recognizing the song, which wasn't exactly a lullaby. "Are you humming 'Sweet Child O' Mine'?"

Aubrey looked up at me. "Maybe."

I beamed at her with pride. "Thatta girl."

Aubrey laughed as she adjusted Savannah to burp her. Once she was finished, she handed Savannah off to me so she could get ready for bed. I changed her diaper and put her in my favorite onesie. I had to thank Sophia for this one. It said, "I wear bows, and my daddy wears a badge." It was the cutest damned thing.

Savannah looked up at me and smiled. "Well hello, baby girl. You ready for some cuddle time with Daddy? Just promise me you won't poop on me like you did the other night."

She cooed and gurgled as she wiggled her arms and legs. Her pretty blue eyes were staring right up at me, and she smiled.

"Is that your final answer?" I asked, tickling her belly. Savannah giggled and started to put her fingers in her mouth. "I'll take that as a yes, then."

I scooped her up in my arms and lay back on the bed. Aubrey came out of the bathroom and crawled into the bed next to me. I could tell she was exhausted. She'd been such an amazing mother to Savannah, which I never doubted she wouldn't be. I pulled Aubrey into my right side while I held Savannah on my left. I was literally holding my entire world in my arms. Life was messy and hard. But with this woman by my side, I knew I could take on whatever life had to throw at me next. I'd save the world…for them.

THE END

Also by Amanda

The Awakened Trilogy

The Awakened

Rising Moon

The Gift

Rising Sun

Heroes of River Falls

An Interconnected Romantic Suspense Series!

Guarded Souls

Saving Grace

Cassie and Dylan- Friends-to-lovers, second chance - Goodreads link: http://bit.ly/SavingGraceGR

Ignited Flames

Sophia and Bodhi- A (sort of) workplace romance - Goodreads Link: https://bit.ly/IgnitedFlamesGR

Stolen Memories

Chloe and Rhett- Amnesia-second chance - Goodreads Link: https://bit.ly/StolenMemoriesGR

Acknowledgements

As is tradition, I'd like to thank my readers for continuing to shower me with all the love and support. I know this book didn't come out as soon as expected but thank you so much for sticking by my side and allowing me to give you the best story possible. Aubrey and Dean took me on an amazing journey of emotions. From loss to love, grief and acceptance. I really hope that you enjoyed their journey to a HEA.

To Stefanie – Girl, where would I even be without you? Crying in the corner that's where. You helped me brainstorm so many ideas and put up with all my shenanigans. This book would not be what it is today without your brilliant mind! You helped me solve the unsolvable. And bring tears to many a reader. You'll forever be the Jared to my Jensen, the other half of my brain. Love you lots, babe.

To Katey – Thank you for not letting me set this book on fire. You talked me off many cliffs and I don't think there are enough words in the English language that could express my gratitude. You helped push me to give this book my all and to not let my doubts get in the way. This book would not have been released if it weren't for you soothing all my doubts. So, thank you Moose, for never allowing me to give up on my dreams. Love, Squirrel.

To Sedrick – The biggest person I have to thank, is you. I wanted to make this story as believable as possible, to give my readers a rounded experience. And with your help, I did just that. Thank you for answering ALL of my questions about dispatch calls, and how police badges worked. You even gave those dispatch calls a quick once over and gave your seal of approval. You were so incredibly kind and helpful, and I couldn't thank you enough.

To Vixen Designs, Lindee Robinson and cover models Julie Piraino and Logan Shephard – Thank you for bringing Aubrey and Dean to life! I came to Lindee with my muses in mind and she delivered! She knew right away which models would work for me and she did not miss! And Danielle at Vixen Designs breathed new life into those photos, and we had a cover! Logan and Julie captured the essence of Aubrey and Dean, and I could not be any happier with the outcome.

To Sandra, my editor – I loved working with you. This was our first time working together and I couldn't be anymore thankful for you. You guided me to help spice up this book in the best possible way. I'm excited to work more with you in the future!

To Clara, my formatter – You slayed it girl! Although, who am I kidding? You always rock it! We've worked together on all my books, that now we just have an easy flow. I enjoy collaborating with you and can't wait until the next project!

About Amanda

Amanda Carol lives in Westminster, Maryland, but has plans to move to Texas. She is a dog mom of one sassy little Yorkie named Raven (yes, after the Baltimore Ravens). She loves to travel and spend time at the beach. She enjoys writing about different worlds and bringing to life new characters. When she's not writing, you can find her binge-watching shows on Netflix, reading, or taking unexpected family trips to Target. If you would like to follow her and get updates on future works, you can click on the links below.

Website: https://authoramanda27.wixsite.com/website
Between the Covers FB Reader Group: https://www.facebook.com/groups/ACBetweenTheCovers/
Author Facebook Page: https://www.facebook.com/amandacarol27/
Instagram: https://www.instagram.com/authoramandacarol

Printed in Great Britain
by Amazon